# KINGSTON NOIR

# KINGSTON NOIR

## GUIDO EEKHAUT

ISBN: 979-8-3372-0261-7

This edition published in 2026 by Open Road Integrated Media, Inc.
180 Maiden Lane
New York, NY 10038
www.openroadmedia.com

# KINGSTON
# NOIR

The living are the dead on vacation.

—Ian Thomson,
*A Grave Undertaking*

*1*

With screeching tires, the large, dark-blue BMW came to a full stop near the luggage conveyer, which was feeding suitcases into the red and white SwissAir aircraft. The vehicle left a trail of dust and gravel.

Four men. M4 rifles at the ready. Short barrel, suitable for close combat.

"Stop that fucking thing!"

The conveyer came to a stop. Suitcases balanced dangerously on their center of gravity.

"You: hands up!"

"On the ground! ON THE GROUND!"

The loading crew hugged the tarmac.

A Mercedes van, its windows darkened, stopped behind the BMW.

Four more men. Dark gray overalls and tactical vests, balaclavas, and rifles. All looked exactly like members of a police intervention unit. They had been acting appropriately, evading notice until it was too late.

No one from the loading crew had any heroics in mind. That would be above their pay grade, and anyway, the stuff that was going to be stolen wasn't theirs. It probably was insured as well.

Nobody around was going to intervene, nor were other people in danger. The transit bus had already left; the crew was inside the plane with the passengers, no security guards around. Cabin door already closed. This was not the busiest part of the airport. Before someone at the control tower noticed what was going on, the whole affair would probably be over.

Three of the assailants climbed into the cargo hold of the plane, heavy boots clanking on the metal. Behind the windows of the plane, faces watched the proceedings with eyes wide.

The robbers had known there would be no resistance. The plan had been perfect and was executed perfectly.

The three men in the hold had no trouble finding what they had come for. Three small identical bags, canvas the color of Sahara sand, each just large enough for a day trip.

They threw the bags down on the ground.

The bags went into the van.

Two of the men climbed back out.

The third stayed in the hold for a moment—a big, burly man, probably the leader. He wasn't ready. He was looking for something else. And found it.

A small, slightly dented metal briefcase. Aluminum and sturdy.

Without any markings on it, just like the three bags.

He grabbed the briefcase and jumped out of the plane.

The robbers at once drove off in the two vehicles, leaving the loading crew behind. The whole operation had happened fast, almost in the blink of an eye. There had been no shots fired, and no one was injured.

The crew called for help.

Far too late, of course.

It would later emerge that the robbers had cut a hole in the fence surrounding the airport. They had stolen cars that could pass as anonymous police vehicles. They had prepared their operation well. Had received help from an insider, so much was evident. With information about the aircraft and the precious cargo.

They left the BMW burned out thirty kilometers from the airport.

The Mercedes van was never found.

Fifty million worth of uncut diamonds in those bags. Easy to trade, uncut diamonds. No markings, no description, no special features. Diamonds could be used as currency for drugs, and criminal organizations in at least a dozen nations accepted them as a universal means of financing drug trade, arms deals, and human trafficking. Or local wars.

The seven men then disappeared. They were professionals. They would never be found. This type of job paid them well. After this, each of them would have enough money to retire, at least for a couple of years.

The eighth man, however, had other plans. He was not going to retire, not even for a short while. He had been on a special assignment.

He hadn't come for the diamonds, but for the briefcase.

And for what was in it.


Anna Weiss felt her heart pounding in her chest.

As if she had never done this before! Stolen something and calmly walked by the cash register and the alarm, as if nothing was out of the ordinary.

As if she'd just walked into the store merely for a glance around and hadn't found anything she liked.

Calm.

Stay calm, girl. You've done worse things in your life. This is gonna work, as it did before.

But still, her heart pounded in her chest.

Lucy, who was walking next to her, seemed calmer than her mother.

Lucy was twelve and perhaps not fully aware of the consequences of being caught shoplifting. When called, the police officers would discover that Anna had no identity documents on her and would not want to reveal where she lived. All of which would have grave consequences for her and Lucy.

So it came down to not getting caught.

Just keep walking, girl. Actually, they can't do anything to you. They can't stop you. Shop owners or even detectives are not allowed to deprive you of your liberty. If someone grabs you, you just scream. Fall down on the floor. Make as much fuss as possible. Lucy would certainly add to the racket. Regardless, who would want to resort to violence against a young woman and her daughter?

Just a few more steps.

The bottle of perfume burned in the pocket of her jacket.

Damn small bottle of perfume, but worth eighty-five euros. And they would call her a thief?

Three more steps.

Just three simple steps.

Anna didn't dare look around. That would give her game away. Just step through the alarm and walk out. No big deal. And if the alarm should go off . . .

Lucy, well trained in urban guerrilla, started walking faster and passed the alarm first. She glanced back at her mother, searching for the store detective.

Lucy winked at Anna.

No store detective had given chase yet.

Anna took the final step.

The alarm raised its shrill cry for help.

Move on!

Into the street. Turn steeply to the left. Lucy behind her. Ignoring everyone around them.

Hardly anyone noticed. It happened too often: a saleswoman who forgets to neutralize the alarm on a purchased item. Sloppiness.

Once you're in the street, it's over. You can breathe freely.

Home Free.

She didn't look back. Just walked on, slowly. Together with Lucy, Anna disappeared in the crowd of passersby.

Bottle of perfume in her jacket pocket. Her trophy. Her booty.

Managed to get her heart rate under control.

She would have to stop doing this when she'd be sixty. She'd get a heart attack. The tension would be too much for her.

Then, on the terrace of a fast food shop, each with a Coke to calm the nerves.

"We did well, girl."

"You turned all white, mom. Really!" With an amused grin. "White as a sheet!"

"No, I was pretty calm."

Lucy, medium dark-skinned because of her father, and with a head full of frizzy hair, held her cardboard cup in both hands. "You weren't calm. Gyal! You are never calm!"

Anna would give her a piece of her mind, but not here. People watched. They saw the beautiful girl and the young woman. Both looking very innocent.

Especially the beautiful half-dark girl.

Tonight she would scold Lucy about how she addressed her mother. Gyal! She would tell her: speak your mother's language, not your father's.

But tonight Alexei would come around. Then Lucy would have to go to bed early. Alexei wanted the space for themselves.

He especially wanted Anna's body. He loved Lucy too, but most of all he wanted Anna for himself. That's just how he was.

And she needed a man for safety. Not for the rest of her life, she realized, because Alexei would soon be gone from their lives again.

But for now, she needed him.

The heavyset robber watched the last two of his men leave. He took off his gloves and stuffed them into the pocket of his jacket. "Alexei, are you going back to Brussels?" one of the men had asked him, the Serbian prick who would probably one day stand trial for murder and rape, when and if Europol got to him. That would happen soon enough, but preferably—as Alexei hoped—not here, where he could reveal all he knew about their recent collaboration.

In fact, he hoped the man would be shot dead, preferably somewhere in an anonymous part of the world. A war, perhaps. Where he wouldn't get as much of a grave. Dead lips don't speak.

"Maybe," Alexei said. He didn't like the fact that the man had revealed his name. However, that might not really be a problem. A lot of people were called Alexei, but even then he preferred to move through life without leaving traces. Like a ghost.

Furthermore, he had no influence over the team's composition. He would never have vetted the Serb or his buddy, the sort of men who usually dealt in women, weapons, and drugs and could not be trusted with a sensitive operation like this one. They both even looked like idiots. He had men like them executed under different circumstances. This would not be possible now.

But if you needed professionals, you had to get them wherever you could. Mercenaries, usually former soldiers with blood on their hands. You would congratulate yourself on having avoided the real psychopaths, but some of these men lacked the necessary self-control and discipline. But they would be willing to kill if needed.

Even then, there were plenty of suitable candidates for sensitive missions like the one he had organized. There had been more than enough local wars, militias, and failed states, while official armies had reduced in size or ceased to exist at all. But not all of these candidates were suitable.

"Whatever," the Serb said, "it's your problem, mate."

The two men had gotten into a gray Mercedes saloon car, which had been parked in an almost empty lot, and drove off. They would drive all night long. By morning they would be somewhere in central Europe, in a country with no need for too many laws. Dealing with the police and government would be simpler there than in most Western countries.

Very good idea, these open European borders.

By then the diamonds would end up with the financial people, somewhere in Berlin or Prague, where they would be repacked, shipped, and perhaps even cut in the meantime.

The seven men had been paid. Paid quite handsomely.

There would be no complaints.

Alexei, only half awake (he had a long day and night behind him, kept low, moved from place to place, and closed the operation), glanced at his phone.

He had just sent a message. To the man who wanted the briefcase. Wanted it very urgently.

The message itself would look completely innocent, as far as prying eyes were concerned. But the recipient knew what it was about.

And now Alexei waited for an answer.

Meanwhile, and through the night, he had been mulling over the assignment.

The seven men had been paid. The financiers had their diamonds. He himself had received a lot of money, but a fraction of what the diamonds were worth.

And then there was the briefcase.

He was not stupid; he knew the real objective of the raid had always been the briefcase. Those diamonds had only been a means of financing the whole thing. Financing criminal operations was always a matter of hard bargains with unsavory people. And then there was the practical side: finding the right operatives, weapons, documents, fake passports, safe houses, and travel arrangements.

Nevertheless, in this case, the financiers would end up with a considerable profit margin.

But the briefcase?

More diamonds? A giant diamond?

Opening the briefcase would be no problem. He could do it right away before delivering it to the client, or more precisely, the middleman, because the real recipient would not show himself. That much was already clear.

The recipient of the briefcase was someone else than the financiers.

Alexei could not help but find that strange.

He found that very strange.

So what was in the suitcase should be very special. And perhaps worth a peek.

Agent Amos had grown weary of Brussels for quite some time. Really fed up.

The city had nothing to offer him. The so-called capital of Europe was unfriendly, boring, and narrow-minded. A city with excesses of all sorts. Eurocrats enjoying the high life in their overpriced flats; dusty and poorly maintained terraced houses in what remained of the historic center; the even uglier offices and banks; the chaotic traffic. Young thugs with muscle cars. Way too expensive bars and brasseries. North African prostitutes. Not many people he could bond with, even if he wanted to. Even the Jewish community wanted nothing to do with him because he was an outspoken secular Jew.

He never visited the local synagogue, so much was true. Hardly believed in God. But he had looked death in the eye all too often, so he knew what God was capable of.

Wife and children in Tel Aviv, which he visited three times a year, each time for a month. Been in Brussels for thirty months now as Mossad bureau chief. A job without glamour, which the people at home didn't know about. A simple, underrated katsa, a field agent. As far as the family was concerned, he did something unimportant at the embassy.

His work was not exciting; he was often bored out of his mind. Gathering information, drinking coffee, or having lunch with European Community officials or members of Western security agencies, all of them better paid than he. Eavesdropping on telephone calls between Russians. Reading other people's emails. Reading foreign newspapers in any of the languages he was fluent in. Analyzing and forwarding news to Tel Aviv.

Office work.

Bloody desk jockey.

After this assignment, he would receive his promotion. And then what? Another but completely similar appointment in another Western country? Or somewhere in the Third World?

Mossad's ways were inscrutable. He had never been able to understand its politics, even though everything the organization did was aimed at protecting the nation. At all costs. This was its only objective.

He would take his wife and children with him wherever he went next time. He had told his director that much. He would not even want to live outside the borders of Israel. And if possible, something approximating a normal life with his family.

He had applied for a family reunion here in the Belgian capital but had been told off. Did he know how expensive that would have been? Did he assume Israel was going to pay for his luxury?

He wanted to move to London, but again he would be sent there on his own, and for the same reason. They argued that his family would be safer in the old country but could not be guaranteed such safety elsewhere.

They might give him an undercover job in a hostile country, just to teach him a lesson in humility if he made a fuss.

So, for the time being, he was still in Brussels.

His phone beeped, with the sound reserved for the service and only for urgent messages. He rarely received private phone calls. He recognized David's call sign.

"David? What's the matter?"

"Could you come into the office right away?" It didn't sound like a question.

"Right now?"

"It's a priority. Where are you? Sure, you're not with a whore, I hope?"

"Drop dead, David," Amos said. "I'll be there at once. What's the problem?"

But the line was dead. Amos knew the rules, as well as David. No details over the phone.

He glanced at his watch. Half past seven in the evening. A Mossad agent, however dull the assignment, was not supposed to keep office hours. Always on duty.

In Brussels as well as everywhere else.

What was the urgency?

A terrorist threat?

There had been no recent in- or outbound digital traffic between suspected organizations and their fellow believers in Brussels in recent weeks. The current threat level in Western Europe was low for some time already. Most Muslim agents and terrorists were occupied elsewhere, more specifically in connection with Syria. Anyone who could handle a gun or make a bomb would be there. Mostly on the side of the rebels.

Rebels. As if those were one big group of friends. On the contrary. All these so-called revolutionaries were as much at war with each other as they were with the government troops. Syria was heading the same way as Iraq. And the West was incapable of doing anything serious about the problem.

As far as Israel was concerned, this situation, as of now in 2013, was problematic. Assad was a vicious dictator, but at least he kept his country under control, even if it was Israel's enemy. There had been stability. For years. Just like in Iraq under Saddam.

Israel needed stability from its neighbors. Even hostile regimes could provide it.

If Assad were to fall, chaos would ensue. Anarchy. Dozens of groups of well-armed fighters who would not sit quietly. They would look around for new enemies. Each other, first and foremost. But at some point Iran would step in if it hadn't already. And Iran was the most dangerous of neighbors for Israel.

For the time being, however, things were quiet, certainly in Europe. Al Qaeda had ceased to exist, although the Americans insisted the remnants of the organization still posed a threat. But of course the Americans would say that, wouldn't they? Other groups had already taken its place, each more radical than the previous one.

Nevertheless, things were quiet in the West. Yet David called urgently.

Amos closed the door of his apartment and rode the subway to the office, which was located at the rear of a small brick office building belonging to a few bona fide finance companies. Small-scale offices occupied it, mostly Lebanese who had been in Belgium for years and therefore above suspicion. These people had no idea of the proximity of the Israelis.

Their own office was virtually invisible. No more large antenna arrays were needed to communicate with the homeland. The internet had replaced all that. You could set up an office for whatever purpose almost anywhere, once you had safe internet access.

Amos was tall and muscular, but David was a typical Yiddish intellectual: spindly, nearsighted, short, with too much hair but no beard. And extremely intelligent. David was a neviot, a surveillance specialist. He had a significant future ahead of him in the Mossad. He didn't know that yet, but Amos realized it all too well.

Amos was ex-military, IDF, Lebanon, Golan, elsewhere. He was too old to hope for a career in the highest echelons. But he could still hope to work on his pay grade.

David, that was a different matter.

David would probably help shape Mossad's policy during the next few years. Decades even, if he played his cards right.

The office, where two other officers worked or were at least occasionally present, was untidy. It was utilitarian but nothing else.

It had a decent expresso machine, the most important piece of equipment as far as Amos was concerned. The rest of the room was taken in by a number of computers no shop in the city would sell and which serious gamers would like to get their hands on. But these machines were not for gaming. There was some other electronic stuff and several steel cabinets. The windows were not ordinary windows, just like their glass was not ordinary glass. Vibration-free to prevent eavesdropping. The door didn't just open with a handle and a key. It had a keypad and a fingerprint recognition system.

"What is going on?" Amos inquired at once.

The door closed behind him with a hiss, as if it were reprimanding him for his intrusion.

"Encrypted transmission." David didn't look up. His attention was with the screen of his computer.

Amos had a younger brother who had the same relationship with machines as David.

"Is there something I need to be summoned for?" he said.

"As it turns out . . ."

Amos waited three seconds. "Are you done? Can you tell me what this is about?"

"Just a sec."

Yes, Amos thought, exactly like my brother. But the brother had been killed on the Golan Heights in an incident that had not even been part of an official war. It had merely been an incident.

On another screen, Amos noticed the evening local newscast. Robbery on a plane ready to depart, Zaventem, here in Belgium. Diamonds. Important loot. SwissAir. Ah, the Swiss. They would be panicking now. One of their planes. Bad for their reputation.

But a robbery was still not as bad as a crash.

The Mossad emblem appeared on David's screen.

Then the head of a man. A man they both knew.

Division Head Yalom.

It would be nighttime in Tel Aviv. Even Division Head Yalom would be spending the evening with his family. He would not show up on this screen if it weren't important. Too high on the Mossad pecking order for that. Had coffee with the Prime Minister at very regular intervals.

Something very serious was going on.

"Amos, David," said Yalom. His face was unreadable, as always. "Can I have your attention?"

"Sir," said Amos. He already had their attention.

The division head was known for always getting straight to the point.

"Have you seen the news? The robbery on the Swiss plane?"

"Here in Zaventem?"

"Yes," said David.

"It's not one of us," said Amos.

"No, it's Swiss, obviously. But it did transport something that belongs to us."

Anna served Alexei and her daughter a Flemish stew with fries, something they all enjoyed. Her mother had taught her how to make a good stew by simmering the meat for a long time so it became stringy and almost fell apart. And then a thick, dark brown sauce, made with some gingerbread and a dollop of mustard. An old recipe, handed down through the generations.

She noticed that Alexei was not in his usual mood. She knew his mouth formed a hard, thin line whenever he was worried, even though he tried to joke with her and Lucy.

She had never had any illusions about their relationship, and she didn't even know what he did for a living. But she was certain he didn't work in an office, not even had a regular job.

Alexei was not the sort of man to hold a regular job of any kind.

Nevertheless, he brought in money on a regular basis, and as such, he stood a step (or several) above other men Anna had known and had lived with. The sort of men who wanted her to do the work at home all while holding a regular job herself. And getting in her panties every night.

That wasn't Alexei. He wasn't a pushover, but at least he respected her.

She could not ask for more.

She wasn't looking for a new daddy for Lucy. Luce was all hers.

But she needed a man around the place, someone who was respected in the neighborhood, in the streets. That's how things worked in this part of Brussels. Otherwise, without a man living with her, she would be seen as a whore, especially with a black kid. Almost black.

With Alexei around, no one would dare disrespect her.

Not that all the men here were like that. She lived in a very diverse neighborhood, very multicultural. Jordanian restaurants, Egyptian corner shops, Middle Eastern extended families, and Moroccan households. A few shady Russian and Bulgarian car repair shops as a front for drug traffic.

This area of the capital housed a diverse range of cultures, all of which coexisted harmoniously. Europe seemed very distant, with these typical smells, colors, and the vendor's calls in the streets. She stood out due to her white face, her white hands, and the Flemish language, which almost no one spoke.

Alexei too was the exception, but everyone knew he was the man to go to in case of troubles, in case of disputes, all of which he managed to solve peacefully. He made an impressive figure, which helped.

But today, something was wrong. She knew she'd better not inquire about his day.

"I have to meet someone later tonight," he said. Matter-of-factly.

Lucy curled up on the sofa on her own, watching television. She did not expect Alexei, whom she liked quite a bit, would play daddy with her. At least not tonight. Alexei helped clear the table. He had big hands, a big body, he was strong. Clearing the table seemed like an insult to that big body.

"Are you going to be out for long?" Anna inquired.

"No, just for a moment."

"You're staying the night?"

"Yes," said Alexei. "I'll stay the night."

He would like to take a shower after he got back, she knew. He would stay for breakfast. Maybe he stayed all day after that. But he wouldn't take her and Lucy out or anything. They were almost never seen together in public. Had always seemed strange to her, but then again it was one of his quirks.

"See you later," he said, and left.

"So," Division Head Yalom said, "you understand we want that briefcase back. And fast too."

He hadn't actually told the two officers anything of interest, only that the briefcase had been on the SwissAir flight and that it was now gone.

"But, sir," said Amos. "Just like those diamonds, that suitcase is probably already halfway to Moscow." Or anywhere else, eventually.

"No," said Yalom. "It is still in Brussels. We intercepted communications from an organization that appears to be interested in what's in the briefcase and wants to pick it up this evening. They explicitly mention Brussels."

*Communication*, Amos thought. What did that entail?

"We don't know who is responsible?" he asked.

Yalom ignored the question. "We have the location of the briefcase, which carries a tracer. But if the contents are removed from the briefcase, we lose the trail."

"Understood." Amos understood it all too well. They were looking for a briefcase but did not know whether it would be empty.

A damn briefcase.

"We need backup," David said.

Yalom said nothing. Perhaps there was a break in communication between Brussels and Tel Aviv. But it didn't look like Yalom was going to respond.

"Those robbers," David clarified, "there were eight of them and all heavily armed."

"This whole operation must remain top secret," Yalom said. "I don't want any interference from external parties. And most of these robbers have already left the country."

"So we recover the bloody thing, but we have to do it as discreetly as possible," said Amos.

Finally, he thought, I'm going to see some action. He was going to show what he was made of.

"First of all, you will observe the situation as it develops, and you will take action only at the appropriate moment," Yalom ordered. "You will go in armed, of course."

"Backup?"

"None available. Not at the moment. Things are happening too fast."

This didn't feel at all right as far as Amos was concerned. No backup? He would see action, but he was not a trained special agent and no longer a soldier. Had the Division Head misunderstood his request?

His enthusiasm made a nosedive. Some ITO would be involved. An Islamist Terrorist Organization. The generic name could refer to any of a few hundred organizations of any size and inclination towards senseless violence, as long as the West or Israel was the target. Or both. These organizations sprouted like flowers in a desert after a rain shower, only to dry up at once. They had names, often obscure ones, but mostly called themselves martyrs for some cause or other. And they would go to extremes to hurt their enemy.

Amos inspected the screen in front of him, showing the coordinates of the target, which was not situated in the center of Brussels but in one of its suburbs.

Of course it was.

"This operation is of the uttermost importance," Yalom continued. "The object in question is of supreme concern to us."

*Concern*, Amos thought. Whatever that meant.

"And what is it?" David asked.

Ames knew this was a foolish question.

"There's no need for you to know," Yalom said. "It is something that belongs to us, and we want it back."

"But if it is no longer in the briefcase," David insisted, "how will we be able to recognize it?"

"It is commonly referred to as a data card," Yalom said. "I assume you know what a data card looks like? You have seen them before; you actually have them in your office."

David glanced at Amos. "Understood," he said. A bloody data card, Amos thought. With whatever information Tel Aviv deemed of uttermost importance. He didn't want to know who had owned and lost it. Not his business. It would probably belong to some part of the Israeli security forces that officially did not exist. Maybe an arm of the IDF. Or Mossad itself.

Anyway, it would contain sensitive information. Someone has stolen secret and sensitive information from the Israeli government.

Or the plans of a new secret weapon.

Or the data on every Mossad agent abroad.

Could be anything.

He didn't need to know.

"We could send a team from London or whatever," Yalom

continued, "but we don't have the time. That's why I am counting on you. You're on the ground, and you know your way around Brussels. Move now."

Oh, but what a fine team we make, Amos thought. A desk chief on his way out, accompanied by an ungainly intellectual who likely lacked weapons training. That's whom Yalom was counting on in this battle against international terrorism. On the both of them.

But he understood Yalom's predicament. There was no Mossad intervention team anywhere near, not at this time. These teams were expensive to organize and maintain. London had one, as did Paris. But not the capital of Europe.

But if that data card was so extremely important, why had it needed to fly on a commercial flight—a Swiss flight at that?

He knew why.

For the same reason the diamonds were transported on those same commercial flights as ordinary luggage. And not with heavily guarded transport. Just a sturdy brown paper envelope filled with millions worth of diamonds, among thousands of similar and worthless envelopes.

If it's important or expensive, and you're going to transport it from one place to another, you don't want to stand out. So it goes along as an ordinary, inconspicuous piece of cargo.

Until someone ratted you out. Sold your secret. Whatever had happened here.


"What is it, love?" Anna inquired as Lucy, full of energy, rushed into the kitchen.

"Look what Alexei gave me, Mom!" Lucy, happy with any sort of attention from Alexei. Her occasional pseudo-father, who would never be able to replace her real father. She still had a photo of her and Terrence in her scrapbook. However, she had stopped talking about him. But as far as she was concerned, he was never far away. Always somewhere in the back of her mind. Nevertheless, she liked Alexei.

Anna inspected the locket Lucy showed her. It opened on an image of Jesus and one of Mary, face-to-face. The round locket seemed old and made of silver. Maybe an heirloom. The pictures themselves were made of cardboard and adhered to the interior.

This surprised Anna. Alexei never struck her as sentimental or religious. But she wasn't going to spoil Lucy's fun.

It crossed her mind, however, that the locker might have been stolen.

But Lucy was pleased with it. Better not spoil the kid's enthusiasm. She got that sort of emotion from her father. Terence could be equally happy with a mere trinket. He had come to Europe thirteen years ago, assuming the world owed him something. Assuming that the world would soon be at his feet. Or at least Brussels. Because he was Jamaican, wore dreadlocks and could sing well enough.

Had he traveled to the United States, he might have ended up in the music industry there. Or in crime. Alternatively, he could have become a Yardie in either New York or New Orleans.

But now he came to Brussels. He met Anna in a bar six months later.

She at once knew why she was crazy about him.

His skin. His voice. The shine of his eyes. The promise that an uncomplicated life on a warm island lay ahead for her. Something she would gladly trade for cold and miserable Brussels.

She was immediately sold to the whole idea of Terence.

Not much later, she was pregnant.

And then came Lucy. Her little, chubby, milk chocolate brown baby that she also adored. And so she stayed with Terence.

Who still occasionally sang in a bar but earned his living in the kitchen of a hotel. Not as a chef.

It was the kind of bar you went to, to avoid being seen. Where everyone smoked, in defiance of the law. Where beer and vodka were drunk mixed in the same glass. Slender young women with a special kind of hunger in their eyes roamed the place, like looking out for prey.

Muslims did not come there.

Unless they pretended not to be Muslim.

The courier was already there. Alexei suspected he was a Muslim. He was sitting in a corner, nursing a cup of coffee. But Alexei didn't care about religion, nor of any affiliation the man might have.

A young man with shiny black hair. Neatly shaved. Dark brown cotton trousers, black T-shirt, cheap ocher shirt tucked in.

Alexei, beer in hand, joined him at the table.

The courier looked up. Eyes full of melancholy. He regretted being far from home. But here he was supposed to do his duty. That much saw Alexei in him. He had known this sort of young men before, elsewhere. They could easily be convinced to tie a nail bomb around their waist and explode it in some crowded place, having been promised eternal life after that. They would even be grateful to anybody for allowing them to become martyrs.

However, this one was only a courier, not a would-be martyr. A mere errand boy. For such an important assignment? An errand boy? Perhaps the same principle as the transport of diamonds applied here: you send your youngest errand boy because the security services do not keep an eye on the likes of him. Not high enough on the pecking order.

"Did you bring it?" the young man whispered.

"No," Alexei said.

The courier said nothing. He just looked sternly at Alexei.

The melancholy had disappeared from his look. He was confused and clearly had no scenario ready for this situation.

"Then where is it?"

"Safe."

"Why didn't you bring it?"

"It's worth a lot."

The courier said nothing. His gaze darted about the room. Nervous.

"It's certainly worth more than those diamonds, to the right people," said Alexei.

"Are you not paid enough?" The courier hated him because he himself would not get any sort of money for his troubles.

But Alexei was not afraid of hatred. The hatred of others strengthened him.

"No," he said. "Not enough. After this, I won't be able to work for a long time. I'm the man with the briefcase. I'm the guy who ran this whole operation. I have to disappear. Long time."

"You got money."

"Besides," said Alexei, "I know too much. I know who will get their hands on the briefcase. They will be in the news tomorrow or next month with what's in that suitcase. Then I am a threat to them, to your employers, because I know too much. I need a lot of money to disappear forever."

"That's not how it works. You don't know anything about us. You just want more money. You're greedy."

"A lot more. Those diamonds will earn you quite a bit. I want ten percent. That seems fair to me."

The courier said nothing. He looked at Alexei with hatred and calculation.

As if he had to cough up the money himself. Alexei wondered if the young man was more than just the in-between.

"It seems like a fair proposal. In exchange for the briefcase," said Alexei.

"I didn't come alone," said the courier. "The people who send me will not be pleased with this situation."

"Plenty of money," Alexei repeated. "With so many diamonds."

"I'm just the courier. But I don't like to go back empty-handed."

"Tough luck, kid."

"This is a very unfortunate situation."

"It's the only situation you are dealt with." Alexei rose to his feet. "And my position is clear enough. An answer by tomorrow afternoon? Same place?"

"Alexei," said the courier. "I'm warning you because I like you."

"I do not like you. Bugger off. Bring good news tomorrow."

He walked out into the damp street.

A car passed by, radio blaring.

He reached for the gun on his hip. Prepared for everything, first of all for the fact that his demand would have certain conse-quences. But the car drove on. Kids!

He knew who he was dealing with.

Dangerous people. He had known them in the Balkans.

People without imagination.

And what was worse: without scruples.


Amos and David sat in the Volvo parked at the end of the street. A quiet street. No young people hanging around, no blaring radios or offensive TVs with football matches on. As if this were a decent middle-class neighborhood where people kept to themselves. It was, actually, a decent middle-class neighborhood, but one with a majority of people with foreign backgrounds. And as such, it was not much different from most of Brussels.

He wondered if they had things like milk floats here in the mornings.

For a moment, Amos's thoughts drifted back to Jerusalem, to the neighborhood where he had grown up and where his mother had taught English at the local high school. She had taught him and his brother English as well.

Each had a room at the back of the house, with a view of a wall and the roof of a factory, where Palestinians worked and where they prayed to Allah at the regular hours. Even on the street, Mother forbade Amos and his brother from talking to Palestinians unless they had business in their stores. Only then, out of necessity, were they allowed to have contact with Palestinians. And why wasn't one allowed to talk to these people? What was wrong with that? Because they worship a different God, Mother had said. A false God. You can't trust people who pray to false gods and false prophets.

"And now what?" David wanted to know, interrupting Amos' thoughts. For obvious reasons, he left the operational decisions to Amos.

They had found the house where the briefcase was located. Thanks to the GPS tracker, they knew where the suitcase was down to the meter.

But that did not settle the matter.

They couldn't just knock on the front door and politely request the briefcase back.

They could not even present themselves as Israeli agents, as they obviously had no jurisdiction here. Could not risk an open confrontation with whomever was in possession of the briefcase.

Amos glanced at his watch. Half ten. It had finished raining. The night would rather be chilly. Brussels buzzed and groaned in the distance. A plane flew overhead, almost silently, navigation lights blinking.

They would have to wait until after midnight. Then they would take action. Everybody asleep. Streets empty.

Amos would enter the house. He knew the tricks, had the skillset. He would leave David in the car. Lookout. But the young man lacked the experience for this sort of business. Amos didn't want him along.

He knew he was improvising. He didn't like it one bit, although he didn't have a choice. Improvisation always was messy, and it came with extra risks. It was not the way the Mossad worked.

But he had no choice.

He looked at the screen of his small laptop. The tracker hadn't moved. Everything turned out all right, for the moment.

But inside the house, perhaps eight heavily armed men were waiting for him. With automatic weapons.

No, he assumed they were not. Most of them would already have left. Have left the country, even. He knew how these people operated. But the briefcase was still here. What did that mean? And how many men would be around?

Two, Amos guessed.

He expected two men in the house. Armed.

They kept the briefcase nearby because they were going to hand it over to a third party.

Tonight. A sort of exchange.

Or, at the latest, early tomorrow.

Then the operation would be over. Then the suitcase and contents would be in the wrong hands. And Amos would have failed.

He cursed the stupidity of officials in Tel Aviv.

He cursed Mossad's operational laxity.

The two other katsa from the Brussels office were in Paris for training. Just when he needed them.

Crap. Always problems in this organization. But they wouldn't forgive him if he messed this up.

David nudged him.

A large, powerfully built man walked down the street, passed on the other side, and entered the house.

"Was there a description of the robbers?"

Amos shook his head. "Only in a general sense."

"Could be one of them," David insisted.

"Let's wait just a bit longer," said Amos.

Saleh ibn Khalid al-Fuhan was a short man, broad in the shoulders and hips, but mobile as if he had been allowed by Allah to defy and overcome gravity. His followers (he had no friends, not alive anyway) never asked him about his family or about personal matters. He kept them on the straight path, that of Allah. That sufficed for them.

The courier spoke to him over the phone because al-Fuhan rarely left his hometown. They had met there a couple of months earlier. The courier had been impressed by the intensity of al-Fuhan, of whom he had immediately become a follower. A follower, almost in the religious sense.

Al-Fuhan had not spoken to the courier about martyrdom. Not about bombs. Not about suicide missions or confronting the blasphemous Westerners and killing as many as possible.

He had only mentioned assignments, infiltration, and spoken of couriers and their importance to the organization. Communication and contact were the main arteries through which the lifeblood of the organization flowed.

"You have the necessary resources at your disposal," al-Fuhan told him now, in Farsi. He gave no names, no details. They assumed their communication could be overheard. That's what they always assumed. Here in Brussels, on this side of the conversation, the courier was sure his phone was tapped. No proof, but that was the way the security agencies of the West operated.

"Do I use those resources?" the courier inquired.

"He wants more money?"

"To be able to disappear completely, master. Is what he said."

"A commendable initiative. Rightly so. He needs to disappear. We ourselves intend not to let him live after the transfer of the object. He's not stupid, so he will expect us to terminate the contract."

"No, he is not stupid. And he is suspicious. Evidently."

"So he wants to disappear," al-Fuhan said. "We can use that idea to our advantage."

"But he still has the goods," the courier said.

"Do you know where he keeps it? In his home?"

"Probably. Some loyal friends of mine observed him. He didn't go anywhere else."

For a moment there was silence on the other end of the line, as if al-Fuhan saw through the lie. The courier had neglected to gather friends to shadow Alexei. He only guessed that the briefcase was still in the Russian's house.

That was a dangerous gamble, trying to fool his master.

However, the courier did not expect this gamble to go wrong. He assumed Alexei would want to keep things simple. But the courier had neglected to round up the needed means to finish his own part of the deal with al-Fuhan. He had no backup. Too late for that now.

So he had really messed things up. He was going to have to solve his problems all by himself.

"We want the goods as soon as possible," al-Fuhan continued. "The way in which those goods are obtained is irrelevant. You have a free hand."

"I will do what is necessary."

"And quickly, too."

At once, after ending this conversation, the courier found himself in the street. He had no plan. No real plan, anyway. He knew where Alexei lived. He had a gun. He would improvise. Bad idea, he knew, but the only option he had.

"She's already sleeping," Anna said. "Nice of you to give her that locket."

Alexei glanced up at her. "Where is it?" He had just taken off his jacket but was still standing at the window, next to the curtain, looking outside while trying to conceal himself, something Anna tried to ignore.

"The medallion? In her room."

A break. Then: "I have to go away for a while, Anna."

She had anticipated this. Sometimes she could just read it on his face, his body language.

"For how long?"

"I do not know yet."

He was a bear of a man and capable of extreme violence, but not with her around. She wasn't afraid of him.

And he did not owe her an explanation.

"I truly cannot answer, Anna," he insisted. "But I'll leave you money. Enough money for a year. Maybe more. I do not know yet how long I'll be gone. You won't run out of money. You don't have to worry, and certainly not about Lucy."

While Alexei was around, there had always been enough money, but not plenty. It turned out that he could disappear for a year and still afford to take care of her. All of a sudden, he seemed to have reserves.

But she didn't want to ask him about details.

"A year," said Anna.

"It'll be over soon enough."

A year didn't pass that easily. Not here. Not in this neighborhood. If people didn't see Alexei around regularly, they would jump to conclusions. Which Anna wanted to prevent. She wouldn't get any respect anymore. Or worse. And what about Lucy?

Alexei knew this. And yet he left.

Something significant had occurred in his life.

He was nervous. That's why he was on the lookout. Things were happening that he didn't like.

Anna was not happy. If Alexei was nervous, then she and Lucy were probably as much in danger as he was. They would be in danger as long as Alexei was around.

Police. Or the mafia. Or old enemies of his.

Either way, she didn't want any trouble with Lucy around. Her daughter came first under all circumstances.

"I need that locket," he said.

"Don't you want her to keep it? She is happy with it. Because it's you who gave it to her."

"Just for a moment," he said. "I just need to have it for a moment."

"She asleep."

"Mmm. Later then." He looked out the window again.

Worried.

Prepared for something that was to come.


The courier did not like to take any risks, although he would however gladly sacrifice his life for the cause. He had already in a sense sacrificed his life for Allah. For the Brotherhood. For his master. He had left his earlier life behind for their sake. But being in the strive of Allah did not mean taking unnecessary risks. He saw no reason why he would put his life on the line.

No need for that. At least not yet. He would only do that if he could be a martyr.

First problem: he didn't know if Alexei was alone.

He might have friends in that flat of his. Armed to the teeth.

The courier realized that he knew very little about Alexei.

That was not his fault: the organization had made the contacts, made the agreements, and the preparations. Three men from Lebanon had been concerned, whose names he did not know.

Now they were in Berlin. Where the diamonds passed hands. That part of the deal was their responsibility. Actually it was some sort of decoy operation to draw unwanted attention to the wrong exchange of goods.

He was the courier who had to collect the really important stuff from Alexei. Under the radar of possible enemies. An anonymous low-level pawn.

It didn't make sense, he thought, to be left alone during the most crucial part of the entire operation. No sense at all. Why did al-Fuhan leave that to him? Just so no attention would be drawn?

Why did this all have to be so amateurish? Because some security agency was watching the others, those in Berlin?

What sort of people did he work for?

When he was recruited in Iraq he had been convinced he was going to join a major organization. Ties with Al-Quada. Revenge for Osama's death. Fighting those hated Christians and Jews. Those kinds of things. An organization with hundreds of members. Training camps in Syria before the war, in Libya before the revolution, and perhaps even in Saudi Arabia. Him becoming a real warrior.

He had been convinced of all that.

And that's what the men who recruited him had made him believe.

He hadn't seen any of that happening.

No training. Just a lot of talk about the cruelty of capitalism, about the sins of the West, about the message in the Koran, the Sharia. The will of Allah.

The same sort of things he had learned in the Koran school.

Even as a child.

He had seen four or five men belonging to the organization in the past six months. One of them was al-Fuhan, who at least seemed like a real leader. In his eyes, a charismatic figure. Those eyes. That voice.

And now for this assignment. First time in Europe. A real operation. Responsibility.

He believed in the cause. He prayed to Allah daily. He regularly called al-Fuhan.

But this all seemed so . . .

He stood concealed in a muddy porch.

The house where Alexei lived was fifty meters away.

He had briefly seen the man at the window, one floor up. No mistake possible.

But he didn't come for the man. He came for the briefcase.

The briefcase. He knew what the thing looked like. A small suitcase of tarnished metal with a handle. What was inside was of no importance to the courier. He had to get his hands on it. That's all he had to do.

But here he was, cold, with nothing but an old pistol and six rounds.

He shook his head.

If he stayed here, nothing would happen.

So he started moving.

* * *

"Street brat," said David. "Keep an eye on him."

Amos looked at the figure crossing the street. A young man, judging by the clothes and the way he moved. Just showed up out of the blue.

"Where does he come from?"

"From one of those houses across the street, I guess. Have no clue, really."

"Was he here the whole time?"

"I don't know," said David, now annoyed. "I didn't see anything."

David was useless under the circumstances, Amos knew. Good with computers. Worthless on the street.

Future cadre of the organization. Having coffee with the Prime Minister. Reminiscing about his time in Brussels. Brag about operations in the field. Amos hopefully retired by then.

"He's moving toward Alexei's house," Amos said.

"Doesn't have to mean anything. Other people live there or visit."

"I do not trust this."

David said nothing.

"Screw it," said Amos. "Shitty job."

"Isn't it though."

"What?"

"A shitty job. All of this?"

"Yes, probably." Amos remembered other operations. Not here in Brussels. In conflict areas. He had killed then because it had been necessary. How many times? Twice? Three or four times maybe? He didn't want to remember. It had never been fun to kill.

But then he remembered his brother.

The shifty young man had reached the other side of the street and stopped at a door. The house where Alexei lived.

"We are not properly prepared," said David. There was only concern in his voice.

The young man did something with the door, and then he stepped inside.

"I don't trust this," Amos said. "That guy surely doesn't live there." He pushed open the car door and got out. Looked around at an empty street.

David wanted to follow him.

"You stay here," Amos said.

David looked at him, said nothing, and got back in the car. Behind the wheel.

Amos ran after the young man who had disappeared inside the house. The door stood slightly ajar. Escape route. He gently pushed it fully open. Inside, the hallway was almost dark. Some pale light came in through a rear window, which was no great help. Amos' eyes had not yet adjusted to the darkness.

He stood and listened.

Sounds of families. Noises from TV sets and children. Everything muffled by the walls.

An old house, but solid walls. Better than modern flats.

Worn out, however. Decrepit. Greasy, matted dust, and dirt. Basement smell.

He knew the young man was waiting somewhere above him.

What was he waiting for?

Until Alexei fell asleep?

That boy wasn't just breaking in. He had specific plans.


David, outside in the car, called Yalom on the secure line.

"He is alone?" asked the Division Head. "Amos went in alone? Where is the rest of the team?"

"On a training course in Paris," said David. As if Yalom wasn't supposed to know that. Shouldn't a Division Head know all the details about his local outfits?

"Should I have gone along?" David asked when Yalom didn't respond.

"You're not a field agent," Yalom said. David wondered if the Division Head ever slept. Maybe he had to constantly correct problems. Here. And in Paris. And throughout Europe. No sleep for Division Heads. "You're not going in there. You are to ensure the police stay away. After the robbery on the plane, we can do without further attention from the local authorities."

As if, David thought, I can help it if someone calls the cops. "What about Amos? What if things go wrong?"

"Then get away from the scene at once."

"I can't leave him behind."

There was a short pause in the dialogue. A few satellites and all kinds of equipment might have obscured the message. "It's an order," Yalom said. "You drive away as soon as a problem arises, and when you are safe again, you report back to me. And to me alone. I will send a team to you right now."

That team wouldn't arrive until the morning at the earliest, David suspected. Too little and much too late.

By then Amos would be dead and the package far away.

However, he wasn't going to disobey an order.

Not an order from the Division Head.

"Understood, chief," he said, and disconnected.

He knew it was rude to disconnect the Division Head. He kept an eye out on the house where Alexei lived. It was dark and quiet.

Alexei stood by the kitchen door with his gun in his hand. From there, he could see the entire living room and keep an eye on the front door in the small hallway of the apartment. In the back, Lucy and Anna were hidden in the girl's bedroom, from where they could get away via the fire escape if necessary.

He waited patiently.

He had seen the man crossing the street.

He had seen the car with two other men in it.

This was very strange.

But not unexpected.

Three men targeting the house, waiting for the best moment to act.

That's how he would do it himself, if this were his operation.

The courier had reported his unwillingness to cooperate, and now the clients wanted to recover the briefcase without paying for it. By brute force, if necessary. Which probably meant people would get killed. He, and maybe Anna and Lucy.

No, they would avoid violence if possible, not wanting to alert the police. They would want to find him asleep. Overpower him and get the briefcase.

He had pushed Anna into Lucy's room. Safe, for the time being.

"If shots are fired, you'll run away via the back," he told her. "You don't wait for me. You get away from this place, and you don't come back."

"What do I tell the police?"

"You weren't home when this happened. You don't know what happened. I'll be gone by then. You don't know anything."

He was sure she would do just that. She was a big girl. And her daughter, too. They would do just fine.

He didn't want anything to happen to either of them. Not on account of him being unwilling to play along with the client. Not because he had been greedy. He knew all human failings centered around greed, which made the world turn. He had seen greed with bankers, politicians, and religious leaders. All they wanted was money and power—preferably both. And ordinary people, like himself, acted no differently. You grabbed what you could. Or more, if possible. Life didn't hand out presents. And he had known the risks involved, but these had to be his risks alone.

The gun felt heavy in his hand.

Eleven rounds in the magazine and one in the chamber, ready to use. Three men at the most.

He knew he would use the gun without hesitation on any intruder.

He had switched off all lights in the flat. The darkness would be to his advantage.

The man who had just crossed the street would now enter a dark apartment. An apartment the layout of which he was unfamiliar with. He would be silhouetted in the doorway. The man's eyes would not yet be accustomed to the dark.

But for now, nothing was happening. For now, everyone held their breath and waited for the right moment to act.

If the man was good at what he did, he would throw open the door and roll inside, immediately seeking shelter behind whatever was available.

Worked fine in movies, but not in real life. In reality, almost everybody messes up those kinds of stunts. Anyway, not even a couch would protect him from the bullet of a high-calibre pistol.

Alexei listened.

He heard noises coming from neighbors. But silence in the hallway.

Too quiet.

Not good.


Amos stepped carefully onto the first step of the stairs.

And looked up.

A stairwell, leading up three floors. Smells of Brussels sprouts and grilled bacon. Clothes not often washed. Paint thinner or some other chemical stuff.

The smells of poverty.

Wooden stairs, covered with a thick but worn stuff that looked like sisal. But cheaper. It would keep the stairs from creaking.

He stood there, his gun pointing upward, trying to find a figure in the gloom or hear the man's breathing. None of that. The man may have known he was there and held his breath.

Stalemate situation.

The man couldn't hold his breath forever.

But here they are now. Somehow something had to be done.

Upstairs, something moved. A cat, a mouse, a man with a gun. Shuffling. Searching for the right position on account of stiffening muscles.

Amos slowly climbed three steps and then waited again.

The situation had hardly changed. He could see a little more in the darkness on the first floor landing, but no details yet. Just a dark spot at the top of the stairs.

But he was sure the intruder had gone no higher than the first floor. And was now waiting for him to move again. Stick his head out.

He held his gun in front of him, right index finger extended. Safety off. A round in the chamber. Just like he had been trained to do during his time with the army.

Another sound.

Unmistakably, someone moved cautiously.

On the landing, in the darkness.

Could the man see him on the stairs? Or was his attention elsewhere?

The courier, with his almost ancient Russian pistol and its six rounds, knew he didn't have the advantage. He understood that his strategy left him vulnerable and potentially exposed.

Unless he could surprise the Russian in the apartment. But that wouldn't happen. He knew Alexei was a tough guy and experienced in the art of deceit. A formidable opponent. He would not be taken by surprise.

Why was he here? In a situation as this one, he was worthless. He was a fighter for Allah, but if he had to become a martyr in battle, he wanted his death to have some meaning.

Not here in a rundown building in Brussels. Shot dead by a Russian mercenary. He had envisioned a hero's death. A martyr's death. Something grandiose and honorable.

Still, he couldn't leave here without the briefcase.

He didn't want to betray his master's trust. And he knew his career, even his life, would be over when he didn't succeed tonight.

There was only one door on the landing. One door, and therefore one apartment. The apartment where the Russian lived. And where he perhaps waited with accomplices for an unwelcome visit.

The messenger switched off the gun's safety with his thumb.

He leaned against the door and listened.

It was quiet in the apartment.

That wasn't a good sign.

Not at all.

Amos waited below the landing level. He could just make out the figure of the young man in the darkness. The man hadn't noticed him, or so it seemed. Which was weird because they were no more than three or four meters apart.

But the young man's attention was elsewhere. He was keeping an eye on the door of the apartment. With a gun in his hand.

Soon the young man would make a decision. He would kick down the door. Then there would be no way back. For nobody involved.

Not for the young man, nor for Amos.

His gun, a Glock, felt unusually heavy. He was not used to holding a gun.

It was unpleasant, actually.

As if the weapon didn't belong to him.

He had recently neglected to practice with a weapon. Practicing was not obvious here in Belgium, as he could not use a civilian shooting range. He hadn't shot the gun in a year.

The young man moved.

He stepped back and kicked the apartment door hard with his right foot.

The door creaked but did not give way.

Alexei kept the gun pointed toward the middle of the wooden panel, about five feet from the floor. He was sure to hit the target at that height.

A second kick.

The lock came loose from the door, which swung inward and hit the wall.

A man stood in the opening with a gun. The outline of a figure, at most, but clearly an armed man.

Alexei pulled the trigger.

The man in the doorway did the same.

David, outside in the car, heard two shots. They sounded muffled, and maybe no one around would notice, but he knew there was a problem.

Two shots, one too many.

He got out of the car but then hesitated. He didn't know what to do. Not trained for such operations. Amos told him to wait by the car. Amos was a trained field officer. Or so David had been told.

But now there had been two shots. From two different weapons. David may not have been a soldier, but he knew what guns sounded like.

Then came a third shot.

From a Glock, this time. Unmistakably a Glock.

Amos's choice of weapons.

David looked around left and right. The street remained silent. No lights went on; nobody appeared at a window. Even the house the Russian lived in remained silent. Perhaps the neighborhood was becoming accustomed to gunfire.

Then Amos came running out of the house, gun still in his right hand.

He had a briefcase with him.

"Get in the car!" he shouted at David.

David quickly got behind the wheel and pressed the start button.

Amos crawled next to him and closed the door.

"Drive!"

"What happened?" David steered the car down the street. Only at the corner did he turn on the headlights.

"They're both dead," Amos said.

"The Russian?"

"Yes. And that young man we saw earlier. An Arab, I assume."

"That's crazy, man!"

"It's a mess, David. Complete fuck-up! But at least I have the briefcase. The rest does not concern us, does it?"

He had the briefcase on his lap now. His gun was back in its holster.

"Slow down," he instructed.

David slowed the car down. "What now?"

"Back to the office. I urgently need to talk to Yalom. Maybe we will be ordered to get out of Brussels."

"Nobody is going to connect us to . . ."

"They will find my bullets and the casings. I wasn't able to retrieve the casings. I must get rid of the weapon. But I can't; it's an official weapon."

"We will be talking to Yalom," David reassured him. "But the assignment was a success. We have that, at least."


Anna kneeled down next to Alexei. Right after the third shot, she had walked out into the hallway despite what he had told her. She had closed the bedroom door behind her. Lucy was still there. Maybe Lucy was in danger, and so was she, but she needed to know what happened to Alexei.

He lay in a pool of blood.

A pool that grew larger.

Life was being drained from him. She knew there was nothing she could do. Even an ambulance would be too late.

By the door lay a young man in jeans and a hooded woolen jacket. He looked up at the ceiling with dead eyes. She had no idea who he was. But he was dead, so she didn't care.

Someone left the house in a hurry.

She held Alexei's head in her hands. He blinked. Tried to move his hands. Tried to say something.

"Do not talk. I'm calling for an ambulance."

"Don't," he whispered. "Too late for doctors."

She knew it was indeed too late. There was already too much blood on the floor.

"I am with you, Alexei."

A car drove away outside.

"Get out of here," he urged her. "They'll be back. Soon enough."

"Who?"

"Arabs. And the Israeli." There was pain in his eyes. The inevitability of death.

"Why? What do they want?"

"Go now. Now. Grab some stuff. Get as far away as possible. Away from Belgium."

"Why?"

"They want something you have," he said.

"Something I have? What do I have? Alexei? What are you talking about?"

"Worth a lot of money. For all parties involved. Lots of money. The medallion. That I gave Lucy. But now: get out!"

"Alexei? What are you talking about?"

But Alexei was no longer alive.

She got up. She needed to flee. Arabs. Israel. What was worth a lot of money? Something that both the Arabs and the Israelis wanted? What then?

Lucy stood watching her and Alexei. Big eyes, hands over the mouth.

She grabbed the girl. "Oh, girl," she said. "I'm sorry. About all this."

Where could she escape to?

She looked around and quickly stepped into the bedroom, pulling Lucy with her. She grabbed a large travel bag and stuffed some clothes for the two of them in it. An envelope with money that Alexei had given to her for emergencies. Their passports.

Two pistols lay strewn across the floor. Alexei's and the one from the young man who lay next to the broken door with a hole in his chest. She could not take them with her. She knew where she could escape to and could not take the guns along. Not on a plane she could.

But where she went would be plenty of weapons available.

While David tried connecting with Tel Aviv, Amos placed the briefcase on his desk. He expected a complex lock, a code, a number combination, some high-tech stuff. But none of that. Two clamps, that was all. The briefcase wasn't even locked.

He opened it.

"I'll have Yalom on the phone right away," said David. "With the good news."

"Bloody hell!" said Amos, looking in the briefcase.

The head of Division Head Yalom appeared on the computer screen. Open collar, no tie. The Division Head never wore a tie.

"Gentlemen," he said. "Good morning! May I assume you have completed your assignment? And with success?"

David turned to Amos.

Amos pulled up a chair to the computer desk and sat down.

"We have the briefcase," he said.

"Good. Can you open it?"

"It's not closed. There is not even a lock. Anyone could open it."

"Why bother with a lock when even the most complicated can be opened by a fat guy with a screwdriver. And any complex lock will give away that something important is inside."

"It's empty," said Amos.

Both David and Yalom looked at him in surprise.

"The briefcase?" Yalom asked.

"The briefcase we just recovered is empty," Amos explained, feeling stupid. "Of course it's empty. If there is no lock on it, then it is a piece of cake for those who took the briefcase to hide its contents somewhere else."

"It's empty," Yalom said, visibly trying to keep his calm. "Do you have any idea where the contents is?"

"We left two bodies in that house," Amos said. "One is probably the man who took the briefcase from the plane. The other is a young Arab man."

"You didn't check to see if either of them had the data card?"

"There wasn't time, chief. I had to get out of there."

"Go back."

Amos shook his head. "It's probably crawling with police there now. This is rather something the embassy could do."

"The embassy will not be connected with a shootout in a Brussels suburb between a Russian mercenary and a nondescript youth with a north African or Arab background," Yalom said sternly. "There are no Israeli citizens involved, and we will keep it that way. But we want our stuff back."

"We can find out if there was anyone else in the house, sir," said David. "If the data card was hidden elsewhere, we might later return and find out, after things cool down."

He wanted to be helpful.

Yalom stared at him like they were in the same room.

"I'm getting the best people I have to solve this case," Yalom said. "A young Arab? This confirms our worst fears."

"What can we do?" Amos asked.

"Nothing. You do nothing. Officer Amos, you sit on your ass and wait till I give you an explicit order."

And with that, Yalom ended the connection.

The two men have nothing to say to each other. The office was eerily silent.

"I messed up," Amos said after a while.

David didn't reply. There was nothing to say.

Anna still had her Jamaican passport as well as Lucy's. A sort of present from when she was married to Terrence. Dual nationality. She had kept it, but never thought it would come in handy.

The passports had not yet expired.

Now, at six in the morning and in Brussels Airport, she was standing at the desk of an American airline that could arrange transit for her to Kingston. Yes, ma'am, no problem. Couple of hours before your plane leaves. No luggage to check in?

It meant flying to Florida first, but as long as she didn't leave the airport, there would be no problem with American immigration.

Two tickets. Half price for Lucy.

She paid in cash. Not an eyebrow raised. Nobody seemed to find it strange that a young mother and her daughter would be in an airport at this ungodly hour.

A little later, they found themselves in the empty transit zone. Only one coffee shop was serving, with seven customers.

She and Lucy, unhindered.

Lucy, who was playing with the locket Alexei had given her.

The medallion, he had called it.

"Lucy, can I have a look at that, girl?"

"Alexei?" Lucy asked. "Weh im deh?"

"He's dead, dear girl." Not beating about the bush. Not with Lucy.

Lucy looked at the locket. She said nothing.

"Can I take a look at it?"

Lucy gave her the locket. Anna opened it. Jesus and Mary. Cardboard images. A superstitious man like Alexei? Probably got it from his mother. For protection against evil forces.

But not against bullets.

She pried Jesus free. Nothing. Then Maria.

There was a black piece of plastic stuck to the silver behind Maria. A data card, such as those used in cameras and telephones. A data card.

What had Alexei said? Something valuable? What both the Arabs and Israel wanted?

She pushed Maria back into place and closed the locket.

Lucy had been watching.

"You need to hold onto this," Anna advised her. "It is very valuable."

"Yes," said Lucy, "it's Alexei's."

Anna leaned back. Alexei was dead—murdered. She and Lucy were on the run. Suddenly it all dawned on her. Suddenly tears welled up in her eyes.

Lucy looked at her. "A wa do yu?"

"Speak Dutch, child. When we are in Jamaica, you can speak Patois. And what's wrong with me? What do you think?"

Lucy bowed her head.

"I'm sorry," said Anna.

"It's not your fault," said Lucy. "Are we going to see daddy now?"

Yes, Anna thought. We're going to see daddy. We're going to that damned idler of a father of yours, against my will, but because I have no choice.

# 2

Commissioner Jennifer Vassell was white, British, and a woman, and therefore at a threefold disadvantage. The rest of the police corps—almost the entire corps—was Jamaican, black, and male. So she was a minority of one. Upon her arrival in Kingston, she had acquired the skill of biting the bullet. Or at least dodge it. So far it had helped.

She now stood in front of the large whiteboard where the photos of the victims and their information were neatly grouped together. Sheets of paper with the summary of young and incomplete lives.

Eight victims.

Until now.

Eight girls between the ages of twelve and fifteen.

All of them black girls, which was not unusual in Kingston. The only white girls, or Asians, children of diplomats or foreign businesspeople, would be in schools in the idyllic green neighborhoods of Constant Spring or Stony Hill, where it was much more difficult to kidnap them. Ninety-five percent of the city's inhabitants were black.

Statistically speaking, the victims all being black was not an accident.

And yet the dead girls had not been slum children either, which were always easy prey for perverts and traffickers. Instead, their parents all belonged to the upper middle class. The girls went to decent schools. Almost all of them wore a uniform of blue and white, including the pathetic and completely impractical short socks.

They had been respectable. Not sluts who some people could expect to end badly.

How Vassell *hated* this way of thinking. As if those at the bottom rung of society simply had no value as human beings. Destined to be someone's victim, one way or another. *Hated* that!

There were a lot of similarities between the victims, and their background was one major item investigators would have to take into account.

But there were no other clues; nothing pointed to a specific perpetrator.

Whomever the kidnapper-murderer was, he worked meticulously, made no mistakes, left no traces, and he must have been invisible. He did not claim responsibility for the murders either. He had not written a letter to the parents, the police, or the press, nor had he left enigmatic messages with his victims.

And that's why he hadn't been found yet. He was a ghost. He was made up of air and mist. And of speculations.

Vassell looked out of the large, dusty window where, in the corners, flies were caught by black spiders. The view outside was not pleasant. The Jamaica Constabulary Force's Homicide and Narcotics Bureau was located on Spanish Town Road, on the west side of Kingston, in the middle of an area with warehouses, factories, a highway, parking lots, and a couple of popular nightclubs. Los Angeles, someone had said, but without the skyline. In a city as grim as LA's worst neighborhoods. Here the Bureau had a spacious building available instead of the very cramped one they used to occupy in the center of the city. But the building was gray and badly maintained, and there was nothing but asphalt and concrete all around instead of a park or grass. No roosters crowed here in the morning. Here, nature was far away.

Moreover, if you wanted to go somewhere, you had to drive. The forensics lab, for example, was on Hope Boulevard, at the other end of Kingston. This did not exactly make cooperation between the detectives and the science people easy. There were also no pubs or bars in the vicinity. Nowhere where you could get a drinkable coffee.

Vassell had moved here from London some years ago, and the JCF leadership had more or less embraced her, primarily because of her experience with the Metropolitan Police of the British capital.

Not because she was a woman.

And not because she was white either.

But mainly because she was a good detective and knew how to solve difficult cases. Here she was, and she survived.

She had proven herself to be a more than decent diplomat as well. She needed to be diplomatic, on account of her background. She would not want to annoy or offend the powers that called the shots in the force, at least not if she could help it. But if she wanted things to go her way, she acted effectively and without remorse.

The Chief had given her this case, which wasn't an obvious choice after all.

A particularly sensational case, even here in Kingston, where murders were almost as commonplace as traffic accidents. The city with the highest crime rate outside the United States.

Children were no exception on the lists of victims.

Damn Kingston, hot and sultry and always ready to reward your slightest mistake with misery and grief. Where even words were sharp enough to maim you.

Crime was everywhere. Drugs, smuggling, prostitution, extortion, and corruption. The usual violent cocktail.

However, this case was different.

First of all, because of the way in which the perpetrator killed the children.

The cruelty he displayed indicated a truly sick mind. Such was the opinion three psychiatrists unanimously expressed in the press. None of them had wanted to cooperate with the police. Not on a case like this.

Vassell knew something about sick minds, but she was not pleased with statements of this order. Going public with such ideas was not helpful to the investigators and herself. Things were heating up amongst the population. A mob had already lynched two suspects in separate incidents, turning the search for the murderer into a witch hunt. Both men were later cleared, but too late to save their lives.

And the police still had no leads.

"We'll never find him," said one of the younger officers on her team. There seemed to be awe in his voice. He expected nothing less than the devil to have a hand in this affair. Everyone avoided talking about juju or voodoo, but still it was on anybody's mind. The Devil, no less. And you can't stop the Devil from doing his work, can you?

Vassell hated those superstitions. Even though the killer might be inspired by the religion of his ancestors, he was nothing but human. Cunning and calculating, careful, and extremely committed to his crime, but a human being nonetheless.

Just a human being of flesh and blood.

Who would sooner or later make a mistake.

Who sooner or later would leave a trace. Or be seen by a reliable witness.

Or would become overconfident.

But so far he had done none of that.

Until now he was a ghost, a spirit, a wizard.

Sergeant Porters poked his angular head past the meeting room door. "Gov," he said, "Dr. Smith just called. He wants to get on with the autopsy this afternoon. If you want to be there?"

Hell no, Vassell thought.

Seven autopsies. Seven bodies, seven atrocities, and they had led the police exactly nowhere.

And now number eight.

She had no more tears left. She had to step outside when confronted with the earliest victims. Out of disgust, because her stomach couldn't hold it, and to cry a bit. As if she hadn't seen a body cut open before. But these were children.

But she had to do this one. She had to be present for this autopsy, just like with the others.

She owed it to the victim.

You only get to know the sick mind of a monster when you become acquainted with his work.

"I'll be there," she said.

As if this was all she had come from London for.

London.

She had left because they had made it clear they no longer needed or wanted her. The Metropolitan Police no longer had room for an opinionated detective who could and would not work with others and had made too many political enemies. They claimed dismissal was the only option, and she would lose her pension. So she chose relocation, as far away as possible, allowing her to keep her rank and pension.

And so she ended up in Kingston.

Kingston, Jamaica. The largest English-speaking city south of the US. A million inhabitants in a poor and beastly brutal country. Where the police kill almost as many people as criminals do.

A place at the same time so attractive to tourists. On account of the beaches and the music. But also for sex and the drugs. Those tourists, major sources of income, would remain carefully shielded from the poverty and the violence. They never get to see the real Jamaica.

Kingston. A spacious, modern city with new office buildings and wide avenues. A city as sweet and smooth as the best rum. But there was the other Kingston: the neighborhoods you wouldn't want to visit as an outsider, slums with drugs, prostitution, murderers who kill for a hundred dollars, people traffickers, serial rapists, and child molesters. The scum of the earth, in the same city as the rich neighborhoods and the fancy office districts.

Two worlds in one.

Kingston, Jamaica.

Where now a murderer was doing his gruesome work.

Dr. Smith leaned over the dissecting table. On it lay the naked, black body of a young girl under the strong off-white lights. Straightened hair over the ears, a small nose, narrow hips. Ethiopian descent. Dr. Smith wore a face mask and goggles. Not because he feared being infected, but because the three people behind the observation window would not see his expression.

This was still not routine for him either. He usually dissected grownups or older people. People who already had a life.

"Keep it so this laywoman can understand," Vassell said. "Would you, doctor?"

"I'll limit the jargon," said the doctor.

Next to him stood an assistant, an older man wearing identical protection. Probably for the same reason.

Somewhere a radio was softly playing a samba.

"He used that sharp knife again," said the doctor. "I'm almost certain it's a surgical scalpel."

"Which you can buy in thirty places in Kingston." This lead had already come to a dead end. Just like the other leads. There were virtually no other. Nothing led to the murderer. Yet.

"And she was still alive," said Smith. "When he did all this."

"Okay," said Vassell. She actually preferred not to know. However, she had to. She needed to know in detail what happened to the girls. Each horrifying small and seemingly trifling detail.

"Both *labia majoras* were removed. Clitoris removed. No bodily fluids in the vagina. No penetration."

Vassell swallowed. It was tough to watch. The words were worse. Next to her stood Sergeant Porters, and beside her the massive figure of Deveaux, the prosecutor in charge of the case. Neither of them was happy to be here, although this wasn't the first victim they saw being dissected.

"He's gone deeper this time," said the doctor, leaning over the opened body. "Damn a lot deeper."

"Bled to death?" Deveaux inquired.

The samba music turned into something that resembled ska.

"Eventually, yes. But she probably died of shock. You can't imagine the pain she had to endure. But he didn't seem rushed."

"Did he use other instruments?"

"Just like he did on some of the other victims. He knows a thing or two about anatomy, but you already are aware of that."

"Thousands of people may know a few things about anatomy," said Sergeant Porters.

The three people behind the window did not move.

The doctor leaned deeper. Blindly grabbed a pair of forceps. Searched the body. Took out a small object, like a miniature egg.

"Beetles," he said. "These are the eggs."

"Beetles," said Deveaux. His voice sounded wet.

Vassell continued to look at the doctor.

"Damn busy critters. Reproduce like hell, eggs by the hundreds."

"How long?" Vassell asked.

"I don't know for sure," said the doctor. "But he had her with him for several days before she died. And all this time . . ."

"Experiments?" Deveaux wanted to know.

"In his own twisted way," said Smith. He explored further. "He avoided her most vital organs. To prevent her from bleeding to death too soon. He wanted to keep her alive as long as possible."

"But that incision alone . . ." said Vassell.

"He initially sedated her," the doctor said. "I just checked the analysis of her blood," he explained.

"But not long enough. Not during the whole . . ."

"No. After a few hours, the stuff wore off. Then came the pain. And the shock. But she lived for several days after she was abducted."

Smith now stood up straight.

"Are you sure you want to be here?" he asked, addressing no one in particular.

"Have you finished?" Deveaux asked. His bald, black head shone with sweat. Even with the air conditioning on full blast.

"Not yet. However, I will provide you with a comprehensive report as soon as possible."

"Differences from the previous victims?"

"Only in the details. He's learning. He learns how to keep them alive longer."

"Jesus," said Sergeant Porters.

* * *

Vassell and Porters had driven all the way to the other side of Kingston to see the body and hear what Doctor Smith had to say. They had taken the route along the harbor, which was the fastest at that time of day. Large, rusty seagoing vessels were loaded with the country's treasures. Immense cranes hoisted containers. Hundreds of minuscule humans moved among large machines.

What the doctor told them was nothing new, except that the killer got better at what he did. Which was not what they had wanted to hear.

But as lead detective, Vassell had to witness every autopsy. She needed to know in detail what the murderer did to his victims, and she had to make sure Dr. Smith followed up on every detail, no matter how seemingly insignificant.

What with these beetles he had found, or at least their eggs? What sort of beetles were they, and where could they be found? How long did it take them to lay eggs? What was special about those beetles? What was their natural habitat?

Dr. Smith was going to put it all in his report, but it was up to Vassell's team to figure out the rest.

"Those beetles can be found almost everywhere," said Desy Foote, sergeant, still quite young, and one of the few women on the team.

Vassell had asked for more women on her team. Because all of the victims had been girls, and parents connected better with female detectives.

And because women simply handled certain things better than men. Especially those macho men here in Kingston. But she wasn't going to say that out loud. She couldn't afford to make such a statement in public. Macho or not, she needed the men on her team.

"Find a specialist and ask him the pertinent questions," she suggested.

No, it wasn't a suggestion. It was an order.

Most of the men who worked for her had a problem with her giving them orders. Because she was a woman, British and white. She was aware of the problem. She ignored it as much as she could. They would bend or crack, as far as she was concerned. They would click their heels and be on their way before she had even finished her orders. Or face consequences.

That's how the team was supposed to function.

Not the entire team was present. Half of them were somewhere in the city, searching, inquiring, and interviewing people. Questioning neighbors and relatives of the murdered girls. Girlfriends. Teachers. Friends of the parents. Relationships. Colleagues.

This was done by groups of detectives led by inspectors Ross and Thomson, veterans in the profession.

We're casting as wide a net as we can, Vassell thought, because we don't know where to look.

"Sexual mutilation and murder," Vassell said. Repeating what she had said before over and over again, so that no one would misunderstand what was going on in the murderer's mind. She had brought sandwiches and tea for the whole team. Soggy sandwiches and weak tea, but in this climate that couldn't be helped. "Humiliation and violation, and invading what is most intimate and personal to them, that's what he's after. But he doesn't rape. He is not concerned with the act itself, but with what his actions bring about. His motivation stems from the outcomes of his actions. First of all with the victims, but also with those who find her, us, the public, and her parents. He wants to defy our deepest fears. He does that because he hates.

He is someone who harbors a deep hatred for women and is looking for easy victims. A coward. Maybe impotent." At first, the investigators had shrugged their shoulders. Psychology had been wasted on them. Not anymore. They had come to understand her analysis could only be correct.

She had solved enough cases in London to be able to create a profile all by herself. She had also taken two specialized courses with the FBI. They all knew that.

That was also why she had been welcomed here in Kingston by the JCF leadership. The ordinary police officers, however, were not that much impressed. That was changing, but slowly, in her favor. All too slowly. Even now, using psychology as a means of capturing a murderer was not how these officers functioned. They knew all there was to learn about murderers. Needn't the input of some woman from London to tell them how to catch a murderer. Search until you find traces and evidence and collect witness statements. Then pick someone up, someone who fits your general idea of a suspect, and you work them long enough until you get a confession. A confession, sufficient for the judge.

If it were up to them, not one but at least four murderers would already have been caught. Enough black sheep around. Enough people who would easily fit the vague profile. Child molesters abounded, in Jamaica—at least as far as the detectives were concerned.

But she wanted conclusive proof before anyone was accused, even though the pressure from above to solve the case was enormous. She knew how some of her team felt about her very different approach. But the tide was turning in her favor. She knew how often former cases against murderers had been thrown out of court due to lack of evidence.

"But he is also," she continued, "someone who has at least a basic knowledge of human anatomy."

And he's smart, she thought, with the killer in mind. You don't play this game for so long if you're not intelligent. And well prepared. She was convinced that the man might have killed before. Before he started with these girls. This was not his first foray into that particular field.

She had put some of her people on unsolved murder cases from the past ten years.

But at once found out how useless that was.

Homicide over the past ten years in Kingston, in Jamaica? And unsolved?

Come on, gyal, where do you start? You're not taking this seriously, are you?

Most murders on this island never got solved. Never really.

Unless there's a high-profile victim involved.

But even a quick review found no similar crimes, not in the past ten years. There was murder in Kingston, but almost always for opportunistic reasons or within the criminal sphere. Gangs, drug-related stuff, and the like.

No serial killers. That only happened in the United States. Girls?

Occasionally children died, even murdered.

But not in meaningful sequences.

So back to square one.


She finally returned home, late. She had a flat in the somewhat shabby Ceddar Hills where she could just about afford a place with her rather modest salary. What had they said in London? Same pay grade? That had been an outright lie.

On the way, she bought an Indian curry dish.

Her street: a few three-story brick buildings, divided into flats, and clothing stores, workshops, and a garage, all mixed together as was *de rigeur* in such neighborhoods of the capital.

Rarely was the environment a balm for sore eyes. It wasn't exotic either, except for the smells and the music.

The neighborhood had gotten used to her. The people around knew who she was. She could buy bread and vegetables in the local shops without being hassled like a tourist would. In a few places, where she ate more or less regularly, they already knew her preferences.

That had taken a while, but now they knew her.

She parked the car—an unmarked but nevertheless official Toyota Land Cruiser—in the small courtyard behind the building where she lived, and closed the gate. Then she walked inside. Her apartment was on the third floor. Food smells from the neighbors often drifted past her balcony and even into her bathroom.

A shower. Sweat, dust, and the aura of dead girls. Fortunately, there was always hot water.

She heated up the curry in the microwave while watching the news on TV. A local channel with local politicians. Always the same conceited politicians and always the same meaningless talk. "Yu need a matie, gyal," said the old woman in the shop. But Vassell didn't need a partner. No man had to water her garden, as the local expression went.

The only thing she did was work. Always working. Except for six hours of sleep and a couple of hours a week for groceries and dry cleaning. She would read a book, go to sleep, then go to work. It had become routine.

What would she do afterwards, if and when she retired? She hoped to be able to return to England. She wouldn't be able to buy or rent a flat in London. Certainly not. A cottage, if necessary, in Devon. Somewhere without serial killers. But leave here for good? Back to England? That was an illusion. Once Jamaica, always Jamaica. That's what her colleagues told her.

You'll never get out of Jamaica. You can't get it out of your blood.

By then, on her retirement, she might have been wagga wagga. She tried to prevent that. Fat. Sloppy. Unpleasant. She didn't want to let herself go, but in this climate it was difficult to jog or go to the gym. Even a gym with air conditioning, of which there were few around. Only in the more expensive neighborhoods. She would look forward to such a treat. If she had the time.

Not now. Not with eight dead girls in Dr. Smith's fridge. Or in the ground already.

Deveaux had asked her out a few weeks ago. He asked her out! In his own somewhat awkward way. Something to drink, a bite to eat maybe? In one of those expensive restaurants frequented by an official like him? In St Andrews? Deveaux, the gruff prosecutor?

She had apologized. No time. Too many problems on her mind. An hour, he suggested, to discuss current affairs with him. She didn't have an hour. They met for ten minutes in her office. And later again in Dr. Smith's dissection room. Skillful black hands over black bodies. But everyone looks the same on the inside once you peel away the skin.

She certainly didn't need that image—the skin folded back.

She turned on the TV.

A program with music and dance. American. Of course.

Another channel. There wasn't much choice. A TV series. American again.

She turned the TV off again.

The curry tasted like cardboard. She didn't eat much. She threw away the rest and drank some more cold white wine. She knew she had to be careful with alcohol in any form. Problems usually started with cold white wine. They didn't end with cold white vodka. And then there would be a repeat of London problems. Problems that could not be solved with cold white vodka.

She wouldn't allow to happen what happened in London again. She had promised herself to keep everything under control. Promise? Promise!

The mosquito net in the window, the bedside lamp on, and then in bed with a book. She avoided looking at the clock on the bedside table. She still wanted to read.

But a few minutes later she was asleep.

Dust and heat woke her. She looked up, night still in the corners of her eyes. The book was on the floor, next to her slippers, carelessly open, spine up, dead bird. She placed it on the bedside table, where the clock said quarter to seven. She thought she should sleep more hours. But sleep was so useless. Lost time.

Breakfast of toast, marmalade, and coffee. Not just any coffee. Blue Mountain. One of the few luxuries in her life: Blue Mountain coffee. The island's most exotic export product.

Got you addicted, this stuff. And in the rest of the world, you'd pay a hefty sum for a packet of this coffee. Here Sergeant Foote had found her a local supplier, a decent price for her.

She allowed herself one cup a day. Without sugar, without milk. Black and strong.

At the office, Sergeant Porters arrived at the same time as she did. He shook her hand formally, a ritual she had introduced here. Better than a nod. Or salute, for heaven's sake. Some of the senior officers insisted on a salute from their subordinates.

Not her. A salute, like in the army?

"When can we expect the reports from the neighborhood survey?" she inquired.

"I finished a couple of them yesterday afternoon," said Porters. "But don't be surprised, Gov', if there's nothing new to be learned. No one pays attention to a passing schoolgirl, no, not even today, these days! And someone who does pay attention to a schoolgirl runs the risk of being beaten up. These days, for sure. People are tense. People afraid too."

There was a psychosis going 'round, if you had to believe the sergeant.

However, he was the right man to handle the large amount of information that flooded in and get her a general picture of the situation. Of what was going on in the streets as well.

She knew what to expect, however. From those reports.

Schoolgirls seemed to disappear without anyone noticing. They start off at point A and never reach point B, and between those two points they are invisible. They just dissolve into nothingness. And then, afterwards, are found dead.

This was the problem she was dealing with.

Even after eight murders, still no one paid extra attention to what happened to schoolgirls. No one took measures to offer them more safety. There was a lot of anger concerning perceived police ineptitude, but no one was considering their own responsibilities.

Although that was what the press asked for: measures to prevent another victim. Well, there had been yet another victim, and neither the police, nor the school boards, nor the judiciary, nor the minister had come up with measures to protect all those other tens of thousands of schoolgirls from an invisible, elusive, but bloodthirsty predator.

Tens of thousands.

Which were almost impossible to protect.

Unless the schools, all of them, closed indefinitely and the girls were locked indoors. Which suggestion had actually been made. But no one took it seriously.

"Again, we took a close look at all the victim's relatives and family friends. They have all been vetted. Nothing. Bloody nothing! Not one of them as much as a porn addiction."

The theory that murders often happen in a family context did not apply here. But Vassell still let her detectives interrogate relatives every time.

She sighed.

She didn't want to spend another day at her desk. Waiting for a ninth victim. Because that's what they all ended up doing. Hoping the man would make a mistake.

"Foote!" she shouted.

The sergeant appeared, fresh and alert as ever. "Ma'am?"

"We'll take a service vehicle."

"Where are we going?"

"To the place where the eighth victim was found."

"Donna," said Foote.

"What?"

"Donna Markham," Foote said, eyeing her. "That's the girl's name."

"I know, Foote," Vassell said irritably. "I know damn well what her name is."

Mrs. Markham was at home; her husband was not. "My husband is at work," the woman said. She stood in her living room in a floral dress and an apron with advertisements for a beer brand, and semi-leather slippers. "And tomorrow the wake starts."

Vassell didn't see any photos anywhere. No photos of the family. No photos of Donna. No photos of travel and holidays. Tomorrow the wake. Without a body.

"Im en say it would be better to go to work, im," Mrs. Markham continued. "Then he didn't have not to think about it all the time."

But your husband, Vassell thought, does not think twice about leaving you alone with your sorrows. This place, memories of your daughter, even if you've hidden them from sight already. So that doesn't bother him.

As everywhere in Jamaica, different social rules applied to men and to women.

"It won't bring her back," said Mrs. Markham.

They sat down in the drawing room. It smelled of thyme and garlic. The furniture was old. Maybe from grandparents. Nothing was ever thrown away.

Mrs. Markham had offered them tea or a glass of sparkling. The two policewomen had politely declined. She drank ginger tea herself.

"What was Donna usually doing when she wasn't at school?" Vassell asked.

It was a common enough question. One had to start somewhere. Vassell could guess what the girl would be doing in the school. Other detectives were working on that. They interviewed school friends, teachers, and maintenance staff.

What she was up to out there when not in school, however, might have given the police a better chance of finding a suspect.

"She was just hanging around," said Mrs. Markham. "Not doing much about the house. I say, A wa do yu? But never lifted as much of a finger in the house. Tiicha say: you homework to do, but never did. Aai di siem, she good gyal."

"Where was she hanging out, ma'am?" Desy Foote asked, notebook in hand. That she didn't use. In which she wrote nothing down. There was nothing wrong with her memory, and afterwards she always wrote flawless reports.

"The gym. Sports club. A youth club. This things."

"Who did she meet there?"

"Girlfriends. From school. She did not know anyone outside of school.

"Did she mention names? Girlfriends?"

"Not often. First names, yes. I only know them by their first names. They go to school there, those girls. You know who is in her class. All friends in the same class. All baan ya."

A closed world of teenagers, incomprehensible to adults. All from here—no foreigners. Vassell had already understood that much. Often the same pattern. Middle-class girls who went to the same types of schools.

All victims had that in common. The same kind of schools. The same lifestyle. The same social class.

But those similarities had not led anywhere with the other victims.

"Which gyms? Sporting facilities? Which youth clubs? Give my sergeant the details."

Sergeant Foote wrote down the names Mrs. Markham gave her, as far as she knew or could remember. Some of the club names Vassell recognized. One or two other victims had also been there.

Another clue.

But a clue of what? Leading to what exactly?

They had already checked out those gyms and clubs. Staff and visitors. Just too many people to keep an eye on.

Too much information.

Too few clues. Or none at all.

Mrs. Markham refrained from commenting on police efficiency. Other parents hadn't been so diplomatic. Vassell understood parents had plenty of reasons to complain. But it didn't help.

A million people in Kingston.

More than three-quarters of them were old enough, and not too old yet, to have committed the murders.

A needle in a particularly large haystack.

On the way back, in the car, after several more questions with meaningless answers, Foote said. "Not until he makes a mistake, Gov."

"I know, sergeant," Vassell said.

"And he will make a mistake. Because too much success will make him careless. Then we move in on him."

But when, thought Vassell. When will he make a mistake?

She could only hope it would happen soon.

Terrence Mason threw the wrench in the tool bin. "You better get a new car, Charlie," he said to the heavyset forty-something man who was drinking a bottle of beer on the sidewalk. Condensation beaded on the brown bottle. It said Red Stripe on the label. Terrence had his stash in the cooler in the garage. The regular customers knew that.

"Them wheels are going to take me far yet, partner," said Charlie. "All around the earth. What you need is belief! Damn faith in your own abilities, man."

"I can tell when an engine is rotten, Charlie."

"Well, he isn't."

"No? Did you smoke that jackass rope again?" Terrence had seen Charlie tampering with the raw tobacco that the man himself grew in some garden and smoked, in the manner of poor people, rolled into a ragged stem. You never knew what was on those plants. Bugs, or sprays.

"You just don't want to do it, man!" Charlie replied, taking a sip from the bottle. "You tell me!" The beer went down well but had no effect on the man.

"I'll take that whole engine apart and put new parts in; that's what I'll do," Terrence threatened.

"That will cost, I assume?"

"Plenty. Cho, man! What do you actually want? Do you want those wheels to still serve you or what?"

"Years."

"Or else a completely new engine. But the carcass is also rotten."

"I'm not buying a new car. You're not doing a bandulu business, are you, Terrence?"

Terrence looked at the wrench in the box. People kept talking. He had been accused of scams before, usually as a tease. Bandulu business. That was rather part of the expensive garages, where you didn't even dare take your car. Now that was a rip-off. That's why people came to him. Because they didn't want to be ripped off. Because they had no money. Because their car was rotten. Usually all three motifs at the same time.

"Expect seven hundred dollars, Charlie."

Charlie lowered the bottle in dismay. "Sebm onjrid?"

"That engine is really at the end of its life!" Terrence said. "Funeral coming."

"Well, damn," said Charlie.

"Ask your boss for an advance."

"An advance? On what?"

"Don't know. On your wages. Doesn't he pay you enough? Or not at all?"

"You mean the municipality? He pays a pittance. Regular work, yes, but for a pittance."

"You also do something, right? For that other man?"

"Mr. Harkaway?"

"The man you work for on your own time."

Charlie nodded. "Mr. Harkaway is rich, but not a generous man."

"Just ask him for some money. He's bakra, isn't he? Ask an advance on your wages."

"Seven hundred? How much do you think I earn from him?"

Terrence grinned. "What about your other dealings, Charlie?" He immediately raised his hands. "Well, no, I'm not interfering in your life. Not in your finances."

"Make it five hundred."

"The spare parts cost what they cost. And I don't work for free."

"Pfft. Alright then. Seven hundred. Do you give a guarantee?"

"That car is already falling apart, Charlie. Within a week. In a month. The engine will be the best part of it."

"You're a magician, Terrence. Really and truly. Everyone says it."

But Terrence wasn't.

A magician.

He was a mediocre mechanic. No more.

But in this neighborhood that was enough.

He could fix a car or a washing machine if he had to. Not the modern electronic stuff; he didn't have the instruments for that, but the old mechanical stuff, he could handle that.

Charlie slid the empty bottle in the crate with other empties. He took another look at the car, an old Toyota, waved at Terrence, then walked away.

Charlie was OK. You had to be able to get along with him, but he was a good guy. He had a decent job. Not like other people here in Trench Town. The port was close by, so it absorbed workers. But many young people here had nothing to do. Nothing official job, and none coming either. So they started doing other things. Things Terrence didn't like.

But this was Kingston.

Here you lived according to the rules of the street.

And that was what he did.

Charlie was lucky. An easy job at the municipality. And some thing with that philanthropist. The rich man in the large villa in the north of the city.

Mr. Harkaway was stoosh, upper-class, and white. Bakra!

Yep, Charlie worked for the White Man.

And he said, "Working for the White Man and making me

good money. Everyone else is jealous. White Man gives money to schools and clubs. What is wrong? I can eat jerk chicken with rice every night if I feel like it. And drink my beer. Good life, cho!"

Of course Charlie was right. Terrence would do the same.

Didn't Mr. Harkaway need a mechanic?

Terrence locked his garage door. He needed to. Tools and parts were attractive to thieves. That's why he kept his stuff always firmly locked away. That's why he kept a gun under his bed.

Not an idle precaution in this neighborhood.

People knew he had been to Europe. And so they looked at him as a man who had money.

He lived above the garage, in an apartment. As he climbed the stairs, he heard Tabita humming in the kitchen. She had entered from the back, through the veranda. Although the view from the veranda was not spectacular, it was a great place to spend a cool evening and enjoy a beer. That was quite something in this neighborhood. You could smell the tamarind, the lima beans, and the steamed fish that the neighbors made.

Tabita was making ackee and salt fish for her and Terrence. She had poured herself a can of ginger beer in a tall glass.

When he walked in, she welcomed him with a beaming smile. The most beautiful woman in town was in his kitchen making Jamaica's national dish. Life couldn't be better.

He kissed her on the neck and poured himself a glass of Ting. No beer for him. Not yet. Maybe later.

He had washed his hands in the garage but now did so again. To show her how neat he was.

"Good day?" he asked her.

She worked as a receptionist in a hospital in the center of the city. Made a decent living. They might have been able to buy a better apartment in another neighborhood, but then he would lose the garage. So they stayed here.

For the time being.

Everything in Kingston was for the time being. Provisional.

She swung her hips to the music on the radio. It was a channel devoid of advertisements and news. After work, all she wanted to do was listen to music. After all that whining from patients.

"Patients. And what's worse, their relatives. People think anything is possible. This is modern Jamaica, they say. This is like the US of A. Why is this and that not possible? Always whining. Never satisfied."

That's why she didn't want any whining on the radio.

Not while she stood in her kitchen preparing food for her husband.

Terrence took a few sips of the soda.

"That's a drink for kids, Terry," Tabita admonished him.

"I like it." It wasn't for children. Everyone he knew drank it.

"You like everything sweet."

"That's why I like you so much," he said, kissing her shoulder. Her flesh was firm.

"Good business today?"

"Charlie came to see about his car."

"Oh!"

"Right," he said. "It will cost him seven hundred. I won't do it for less. That car isn't worth it, but Charlie wants to keep it anyway."

"He had an accident with it."

"I have to talk to him about those brakes. That too."

"Charlie is stingy."

"Mmm. Charlie is like everyone else. Things cost a lot. Like cars. People have very little money left to live on. To have fun."

"Charlie has a good job."

"It's still seven hundred dollars, honey," Terrence said.

"He can knock on his boss's door for more money."

"Mr. Harkaway?" He knew the council wouldn't grant Charlie a bonus.

"Yes. I don't understand why the man can't show a little generosity. A benefactor, isn't he?"

"The white man cannot be trusted," Terrence said. "You knows that."

"I don't trust the white man," said Tabita. "I don't trust men as a general rule."

"Well, I can't blame you, gyal."

"I am not your gyal. I am your wife." She took the pan off the heat. "Finished. Just sit down at the table. Bring me another beer."

He had not yet had time to read the newspaper, but he knew that Tabita would not like it if he did so at the table. Paper and words were less important than she was. He was inclined to agree with her. But he also wanted to read the newspaper.

She scooped out the food. Rice was added, and the special sauce.

They ate. Her gaze drifted to the newspaper, which lay neatly folded next to his arm.

"They don't find anything," she said.

He looked at her.

"Those girls. The murderer."

He followed her gaze. A blurry photo of the place where the eighth girl was found and her portrait. The newspaper clearly had no other photos related to the case.

"Police are worthless," he said.

"Who does something like that now? These girls?"

"The devil's bidding."

She shook her head. Dense curls. Aromatic movement. "Don't say that, Terrence. If the Devil is involved, you must not speak his name. You must never speak his name. That's bad."

"It's not voodoo, girl. No obeah either."

"You spoke of the Devil."

"Only in a metaphorical sense."

"Metaphorical! You, with your expensive words. You wanne remind people you were in Europe. Cho! The man who was in Europe. Him a Big Man! Can use expensive words! In a moment you have to wear a suit, done up like Lenin or James Brown!"

"A human being who behaves like a Devil. Is what I mean."

She shook her head again. "The Devil is in every man. Look into them eyes. The eyes, man! Of course girls die. Every man who looks at them may kill them!"

"We're not all bad," said Terrence. He knew Tabita's sensibilities. He knew her past.

"Most men are."

"What should we do then? All the men in prison?"

"Too many dangerous men are walking free in this country."

"There are never enough prisons, Tabita."

"Ah!" In the meantime, she continued eating. The discussion had no effect on her appetite. "Let people police their own neighborhoods. With knives or guns. The Devil will then no longer be seen around."

That's why two innocent people had already been murdered. The desperation and anger of the audience. Always bad for society. However, this was not Europe. This was not a country like the one like where he had lived. The Devil indeed walked the streets here. Maybe Tabita had seen it right.

That's why he had a gun and closed all the doors and windows at night.


The next day Charlie was back. To look at his car.

"I'm not ready," Terrence said. Bent over the Toyota's engine. "Not ready at all."

"I didn't think you would," said Charlie.

"Why are you here then? Are you keeping an eye on me?"

"Just about."

"Don't you have anything better to do? Working for the boss, for instance?" Terrence gave Charlie a cold bottle of Red Stripe. He drank a Ting himself. Not ideal for thirst. Too sweet. Tabita told him he would get diabetes.

"My boss needs help. Not the municipality. That other boss."

"Help?"

"A few extra men," Charlie said. "For the garden."

"Really?"

"Yes. Would you like it?"

"What?" Terrence straightened up. "What would I like?"

"Working for Mr. Harkaway for a day or two."

"In the garden?"

"In the garden."

"How much does it pay?"

"Sixty dollars a day."

"Well. That's decent enough. Two days?"

"Yes. Just work to do in the garden. Nothing complicated."

Terrence liked that. He would be able to work on the Toyota for another hour or two in the evening. That's how he'd keep Charlie happy, too. That engine would be fixed in due time. Sixty dollars for some yard work—that was a nice extra.

"Okay," Terrence said. "Do I have to bring something? Tools?"

"No, Mr. Harkaway has all the equipment you need. He's all set."

"And he trusts just anybody in his garden?"

"Only people I know. He trusts me."

That made sense, Terrence thought. Someone had to do the work. It was likely that Mr. Harkaway had something like a park around his house. A rich man. White man. Could easily afford sixty dollars per day per head. He couldn't let that park become wild.

Terrence left a note for Tabita in case he was late back and locked the apartment and the garage.

A short while later, Charlie returned with a van. Terrence climbed in. They drove away, north, along the hills and towards the green hills.

Was nice to get away from the city. Terrence thought it was a good idea. Get away from the dust and exhaust fumes. From the crowds.

When you were rich, you could afford not to live in the city.

When you were rich, people looked up to you.

They didn't look down their noses at you like you were a lowlife or a criminal. Rich people always got respect. They could go anywhere and be anybody. That's what money did.

Terrence had once dreamed of such wealth when he had traveled to Europe. He had dreamed of being able to make money there. By singing, playing music, or performing.

Life would have been different from then on.

But nothing had come of the dream. Too bad. At least he had seen a small part of Europe.

He was now content here. With his workshop, with Tabita, who had a decent job. Between the two of them, they were happy enough. He was also glad that Charlie offered him this job. For sixty a day.

Mr. Harkaway did indeed have a park around his house, big enough for several families to get lost in, and Terrence wondered: how does a man earn that much money?

"Trade," Charlie told him, as they were handed their tools by a big niega with a bald head. "The man buys and sells things."

"Well, we do that too, don't we?"

"Different stuff than us. And on a different scale. That man fills entire seagoing ships with stuff that he sells to the United States."

"There is money in that sort of things."

"There is money everywhere," said philosopher Charlie. "You just have to find it. We haven't, for sure."

They worked in the garden for the day, occasionally with the bald niega giving directions. It wasn't hard work. And it was outdoors. Terrence liked that. He didn't understand how people could work in an office all day long.

At one point, around noon, Charlie stopped. He stood up to look at something.

Terrence did the same and followed his gaze.

A car had stopped at the villa.

A white Mercedes. Of a type that Terrence would never be able to repair in his garage.

"Is that him?" he asked.

A man had gotten out of the car. From this distance, they could tell he was perhaps in his late forties. Straight figure. Big too. White, of course.

He had driven himself. He was alone.

"That's him," said Charlie. "The man himself. The boss man."

Terrence looked at Mr. Harkaway. He wanted to be rich. But then again, he didn't want to be a white man. The white man was doomed. His race was doomed. He had brought that upon himself, that doom, by wanting to be the ruler of the world. By oppressing other races.

Mr. Harkaway was a stranger on this island. He would be driven away one day.

Terrence wouldn't want to take his place for anything.

"Just the car," said Charlie, who had never owned anything but third-hand wrecks.

Terrence bent back over the plants he was working on. He continued to work. That's what he came here for.

Terrence returned home after five. Tabita was already there. She was cooking rice and a red chicken curry. He quickly took off his clothes, took a shower, and put on other clothes.

"Were you off to work or what?" she asked.

She had read his note.

He showed her the six ten-dollar bills.

She grinned. "And tomorrow?"

"Yes, again. But that'll be all. Maybe Charlie can arrange something more for me later. The man we work for lives in a large house with a park. There is a lot of work to be done there. Charlie says they use the same people as often as possible."

He grabbed a Ting from the fridge and sat down to eat.

Tabita sat down and scooped out.

"A woman she call for you," she said.

He looked at her. No, it didn't sound jealous. But with Tabita he never knew for sure. He looked at other women more than often enough. He talked to them. He loved women. Sometimes she was jealous when this went on too long.

"A woman?"

"Yup."

"What did she want?"

"You."

"Who was she?" He wondered which woman would call for him. Someone with car problems? He almost never had female customers.

"She spoke like a stranger."

"Did she say her name?"

"She wanted to talk to you," Tabita said, taking a bite of the hot curry. "*Terrence*, she asked. *Terrence Mason.*"

"That's me, all right. What did she want?"

"Speaking to you."

This could go on all evening. He put down his fork. "Tabita?"

"Mmm?"

"What else did she say? Did she say her name? Did she say what she wanted from me?"

"She gave her name."

"Yes?"

She was actually playing with him now. But his patience had limits.

"Anna Weiss," said Tabita. She pronounced the name as if she had pebbles in her mouth instead of curry.

"Anna. . . ?"

"Weiss." Tabita looked at him. "Do I know her?"

Terrence remained seated with his gaze on her. "Anna Weiss," he said.

"Yes, Terrence. No matter how many times you're gonna say it, that was the name she gave. I'm not crazy. Who is she?"

He looked outside for a moment. Why did they eat in the kitchen and not on the porch? That now occurred to him. He hadn't noticed, but Tabita had set the table in the kitchen, not on the veranda.

Because she didn't want the neighbors to hear this conversation.

Because she didn't want to hear them arguing about another woman.

So Tabita expected problems.

Anna Weiss.

Terrence knew the name all too well.

"Where did she call from?" he asked.

Tabita looked at him. He saw passion in that look. But not the right kind of passion.

"I told you about her, Tabita," he said empathically.

"Nothing I remember, Terrence. Nothing the name tells me."

"Yes. The woman I lived with in Brussels."

Tabita looked at him, frowning.

"In Europe. When I was in Europe. The woman with whom I lived. That was before your time, Tabita."

As if that made up for everything.

"And now she shows up here," said Tabita.

"Here?"

"Yes."

"What do you mean, here?"

"She's here, in Kingston."

"She's here in Kingston?"

"That's what she said. Don't play echo with me, Terrence."

"Did she leave a phone number?"

"No. She will call back. What is she doing here? Why does she want to see you?"

"I don't know anything, Tabita. Really. I'm just as surprised as you are. It's all in the past."

"As you would say . . ."

"It's all in the past. I haven't seen her in years, not since I left Brussels."

"Maybe she come here on holiday," said Tabita.

Anna on vacation in Jamaica? Terrence couldn't imagine. Unless very radical things had happened in Anna's life. Unless she won the lottery, for example. Or married a rich man. Anna rarely had a job, rarely any money. Neither of them had had much money back there in Brussels.

"She's calling back?"

"That's what I told you."

Terrence said nothing more.

"Terrence, I don't want that woman in this house."

"There's nothing going on between her and me, gyal."

"I already told you I'm not a gyal," Tabita said.

"Sorry. But again, there really is nothing going on between her and me. I didn't even know she was in Kingston."

"But you do want to talk to her."

"Was she alone?"

"How could I know that over the phone?"

"Naw, you're right . . ."

"What do you mean, alone?"

"I already told you I had a daughter with her."

"Ah, the daughter! Yes, you tole me. And so the lady comes here with the daughter. But not in my house, Terrence. No way. She not come here, her."

He understood.

He would have to see Anna on neutral ground. But why on hell was she here?

The sun had already set when Anna called again. Now Terrence was the one who answered. He looked at Tabita, who was watching TV. She ignored him. But he knew she wouldn't miss anything of the conversation. Not a word.

"Is that you, Terrence?"

Anna's voice. After so many years. Yes, to hear her again really meant something to him.

"It's me, yes," he said.

"Oh, thank God!" She sounded really relieved. And then another voice. "Hello, daddy!"

Terrence at once got a lump in his throat.

"Daddy?" In English, like Anna.

"Lucy? Is that you?"

"Yes, it's me. How are you, daddy?"

This will never be okay again, he thought. There's no way back from this, was what he thought. He would burst into tears.

He would be reduced to a blubbering fool right there. No, he had to keep it together, with Tabita listening.

"Girl, how wonderful to hear you."

"You too, daddy."

And then Anna's voice, a little impatient. "Terrence, we need your help. That why we're here, in Kingston."

He didn't dare repeat what she'd said, 'cause Tabita didn't need to hear. "Tell me why you are here?" He made it sound as friendly as possible. As casual as possible. Why did they need his help? In what sort of trouble were they for them to travel half the world?

"Not over the phone," Anna said. "Can we meet somewhere?"

"That's . . . a bit difficult right now."

"It's really important, Terrence," Anna said. And then, in a different tone: "Are you alone?"

"No," he said.

"You're married," Anna concluded. "And she's there with you. The woman I spoke earlier."

Smart girl, he thought.

"I understand. I'm sorry, Terrence, for taking you by surprise. But we have no choice. We are not here as tourists."

"That's what I suspected," he said.

"We had no other choice. Things happened."

"Things always happen," he said cautiously.

"Bad things. Very bad for me and for Anna."

Sounds of Anna in the background.

"And you need me," he said. Clear enough for Tabita to hear. He was now looking at her. He couldn't read her look. But he knew what she was thinking. Not in my house. That had been clear enough.

"I don't know anyone else in Kingston."

"Then why are you coming here?"

"Not over the phone," Anna said. As if she were an internationally wanted spy.

"Where are you?"

She mentioned the names of a hotel and a street. Close to the airport.

Why close to the airport?

Because she didn't know the first thing about Kingston. Because she had nowhere to go. Except him.

"I'm coming to you," he said.

He ended the call.

"You go to see her," said Tabita.

Passion in her eyes. Jealousy, mainly.

"She is in trouble."

"Everyone is in trouble. You and me and everyone else. And no one solves these troubles for us. What should you do now? Taking care of your ex and her child?"

"It's my child too, Tabita."

"You have not seen her in years, Terrence."

"I can't abandon her."

Tabita waved at him. "Go. I don't care. I'll go to bed alone. Don't wake me. Sleep on the couch."

He grabbed his jacket. "I'll be back soon," he promised.

"You stay away from her pum-pum," Tabita said, using a colorful term for vagina, a word she wouldn't use in the clinic.

The Best Western Hotel stood on West Avenue, just a short distance from the airport. It looked like an oversized shoebox and had a deserted parking lot in front of it. The two men at the reception eyed Terrence suspiciously. He wondered what kind of customers came here. Not someone like him. At most, they mistook him for a taxi driver. But they were suspicious anyway.

Don't ask for me at reception, Anna had said. I'll wait for you in the bar.

And Lucy? He wondered. Would she be waiting there as well?

The bar was almost empty. The wrong hour. Too late for some, too early for most. The place was clammy and warm. Maybe the air conditioning wasn't working properly. It wasn't a particularly good hotel, nor was it particularly expensive. The carpet was almost bare in some places. Door frames would do with a lick of paint.

Anna was sitting at a table. A little further away, a girl wearing a red dress was watching television.

Both looked up when he entered.

The girl got up and quickly walked towards her mother.

My little girl, he thought, involuntarily.

Quite a big girl already. How old? Twelve, he calculated. The girl was twelve.

Damn!

He walked towards them.

Anna got up. She said nothing. She wrapped her arms around Terrence, as if he were an old and long-lost friend.

He wasn't. Not old, anyway. And he was no longer her friend.

But here under these circumstances, she was happy to see him.

They sat down at the table. He ordered drinks.

They didn't know what to say.

Except Lucy. Who had been eight when Terrence left them and came back to Jamaica.

"I've grown, haven't I?" said the girl. "Do you still recognize me?"

It was a strange thing to say. But he accepted it.

"You're still the same," he said. "Just a lot taller." Then, using a different tone, he said, "I'm sorry, girl."

Lucy nodded. Their final conversation before his departure had been challenging. She understood he could no longer stay in Brussels with them. No job, no means to support himself. And that they in turn could not come to Jamaica. And then, just like that, he was gone.

It had been difficult for Anna. For Lucy, even more so.

Here in Kingston, he had started his life all over again. But he had regretted leaving them behind.

"Why didn't you just let me know you were coming?" he said. "Then I could have picked you up and taken you to a better place than this. Since when have you been here?"

"Since this morning," said Anna. "We took a plane to Florida and then over here."

"But you're not . . . on vacation? I suppose you're not."

Of course not. No one came to this hotel on vacation. And where would he have taken them? Not to a fancy hotel, which he could not afford.

"Something serious happened in Brussels," said Anna. "We had to leave in a hurry."

"Alexei is dead," said Lucy.

Terrence looked at his daughter, trying to remember who Alexei was.

"Alexei lived with us," Anna explained. "He was involved in something. Something important. He was shot dead in my apartment. People were after him. Lucy and I, we are in danger."

"Why would you be in danger? And who was this Alexei? What did he do to get hisself shot?"

"Just take my word for it, Terrence."

"Drug-related stuff?"

"He did all kinds of things," Anna admitted, quickly glancing at Lucy. "And one of those things got him killed."

Terrence did not like the fact that Anna and especially his own daughter were involved in crime. Or had been associated with someone who was.

"Why did you come here?"

"I wanted to get as far away from Brussels as possible," said Anna.

"Well, this is far."

"Yes. So I thought of you. And we still had our Jamaican passports. They have not yet expired."

"Were you in danger as well?"

"I don't know," said Anna. "I think Alexei had something in his possession that he stole from some dangerous people." Another look at Lucy.

"Oh, Mom," said Lucy. "You know what Alexei did!"

"Yes, girl, I do. Well, not exactly. I don't know what the fuss was about. But just before that, Alexei gave this pendant to Lucy." Anna showed Terrence the silver locket. "There is something hidden in it. I think that's what those people want."

"Well, then you just give it to them."

"The man who came to our apartment is dead too, Terrence. Both he and Alexei were killed, I guess, by a third party. So I wouldn't know who to give this damn medallion to even if I wanted."

"Even if you wanted?"

"It's probably worth a lot of money."

"Oh!" Terrence said. "Now you need to explain me a bit more."

She told him about the robbery on the plane in Brussels. "I suspect Alexei was involved. And that the thing in the medallion also has something to do with that."

"Maybe you're jumping to conclusions too fast, girl. Thing is this: you ran away, and you don't know why."

"Two dead men in my apartment. And another man who disappeared after the incident, with the briefcase. And then a car driving off. I had no reason to hang around any longer. Not going to wait for the next uninvited visitor. Not going to wait for the police either."

"Yeah, well, I understand."

But she had traveled all the way to Jamaica, based on . . . Whatever. Because she thought she was in danger. As she might be.

"What's in that locket?"

"Does it matter?"

"Maybe. You asked for my help. I'm here."

She gave him the locket. He pried it open. "Behind the picture," she said.

He folded the picture away. "A data card?"

She took the locket back from him. "Now you know as much as I do."

"A phone card?"

"Those cards are used for a lot more than just phones," she said.

"I know, gyal. This is Kingston, but we are not backward."

"Sorry."

"No matter. What do you want from me?"

"A place to hide."

"Against the rain?"

She grinned. "Against the world." She looked at Lucy. "I don't want anything to happen to us."

"You're worried about nothing," he said. "Someone has lost their data card. If I can find me a decent computer, I can see what's on it. Who owns the thing? If necessary, we will post it back. Get rid of it."

She knew it wouldn't be that simple.

"Where can you arrange something for us? To stay, I mean?"

Damn, he thought. I do not know anything. There is no one I can ring the doorbell. There was nowhere for her to stay.

Except in his own apartment.

Not in the apartment itself, but in the workshop. Enough space. Quickly organize two sleeping places. For a few nights. Until they found something else.

And explain to Tabita. That too, yeah.

Tabita didn't like it one bit, as Terrence knew she wouldn't, but didn't show what she thought about the unexpected visitors. "So you are Anna," she said, sounding as neutral and welcoming as possible. But Terrence knew her well enough. Tabita wasn't pleased with the ex-wife. And the daughter.

Yet she was not going to kick the two out. "I'll arrange something," she said.

In a room next to the workshop, which was tidy because Terrence sometimes worked there on his accounting and invoices, she put down two camp beds and took some blankets from the wardrobe. "Primitive," she admitted. "But for the time being, it will have to suffice."

"Thank you," said Anna.

"Thank you, ma'am," said Lucy.

She meant it.

Terrence wasn't going to tell Tabita why Anna and Lucy were here, even though there may not have been any danger. He kept their Brussels story to himself. At least, that's what he planned to do.

While the two visitors organized themselves, Terrence and Tabita were back in the kitchen.

"I'll get them some water for the night," he said.

"Look my husband, all worried," said Tabita.

But it didn't sound accusatory.

"She looks just like you," Tabita admitted.

"Hopefully not. She looks more like her mother."

Then they were silent again for a moment.

Terrence realized that Tabita understood all too well that this was not just a family visit.

"Why exactly are they here, Terrence?"

The question was inevitable.

"Problems at home," he said. "In Brussels, I mean."

"Problems? What kind of problems? Does she have a husband? Is it husband problems?"

"She had a friend. The man is dead now."

"Dead."

"Something fishy, but you needn't worry, girl," he said.

"You're not going to tell me the details."

"No. I don't know much myself. They fled because there was danger. They come here because they have Jamaican passports and can therefore enter the country without any problems."

"Passports?"

"From when I was married to her. She got Jamaican nationality when I married her. The girl too."

Tabita thought about that. "If it's a problem, will they bring it down here to my house?"

"To our house."

"If I'm in danger, it's my house," Tabita said. And then: "Maybe we need some guys to protect us. Don't you know some guys?"

Practical Tabita, Terrence thought. Always ready to solve the problems without asking why too often. "I don't want to ask anyone for protection. It is nothing, don't you fret about it. She imagines it all—those problems."

"But the man is dead. So she tole you. Did she imagine that?"

"Gangsta business. In Brussels. Won't blow over here. Brussels, far from Kingston."

"It's blowing over here," Tabita said. "If their problems are accompanying them here, Terrence, I'm not sure I want to know. Gangsta business. I don't want to know. It's dangerous enough here in Kingston, life is. Suppose it concerns drugs. Or human trafficking. You know that stuff: people involved rarely are nice people who let things blow over."

"I'll find out. But not now. They have traveled for a long time. They are exhausted. They want to sleep. Tomorrow. Then we'll see."

That evening he took extra care to ensure that the doors and windows were closed properly. And he loaded five rounds into his gun. He slid the box of extra ammunition in the drawer of his bedside table.

He didn't sleep well.

The next day he made breakfast for Tabita, Anna, and Lucy and then left with Charlie for Mr. Harkaway's villa. There he worked in the garden all day long. He was paid another sixty dollars.

The bald black man said that he could still come to work the day after. Charlie would take care of the details. Maybe then he would get some more money—maybe seventy dollars.

The bald black man seemed to think that sixty dollars was not much money for a day's work. He was probably right, but it meant something to Terrence. Sixty dollars was a comfortable amount to take home. Seventy was even better.

It wasn't hard work. Not for him.

At home, Anna and Lucy sat in the wild garden behind the house—behind the workshop, which had been closed all day. Tomorrow he would continue working on Charlie's Toyota. Today he didn't plan to do anything. He put the money away in the tin box where he kept his savings. Tabita was standing in the kitchen, preparing dinner. For four people this time.

"She offered to help in the kitchen," Tabita said.

"You didn't let her," Terrence noticed.

"Not in my kitchen, no."

"She wants to do something. Because we allow her to stay here. She doesn't want to take advantage of us."

"How long will they stay?"

"A couple of days. If that's okay with you."

Tabita said nothing and looked outside at the woman and the girl.

"She looks like you," she finally said.

"She must look like someone. Personally, I thought she looked most like her mother. I still think so."

We've already had this conversation, Terrence thought.

"She is your daughter. Look at her. How could you leave her behind?"

Terrence said nothing. He had asked himself that question often enough in recent years. He had left a part of himself in Brussels.

"Was that difficult?"

"The hardest thing I ever did," he admitted.

"You're a bastard, that's what you are."

"Yes," he said. "It felt that way at the time."

"And now?"

"Still feel that way. Now that I see her, I realize what a bastard I was back then. And still am. Leaving my child behind."

"So now you want to do something for them," Tabita said.

Terrence looked outside. Anna was sitting on a chair, reading a newspaper. Anna hung around, looked among the bushes, at the flowers, but didn't go far.

"I want to find out what happened to them in Brussels," he said.

"Why?"

"No, maybe I don't want to. But they are upset. She had an affair with the man who is dead. He was murdered. They saw it happen. Then they flee here. Anna is convinced that she was in danger in Brussels."

"The question is: are they still in danger here?" Tabita said.

"I don't want them to be seen by the neighbors," said Terrence. "Them people ask questions. About who they are and where they come from. News gets around."

"You can't hide them for long."

"A few days, Tabita. Till I find them a solution."

"Your gun was still under the bed."

"Yes? And?"

"It's loaded. With a child at home. That's not a good idea."

He took a deep breath. If they stayed, he would have to take care of some things. In that respect, Tabita was right.

"And when people do ask questions?" Tabita wanted to know.

"Then they are friends. From me, from the past. Europe. Visiting."

"Well," said Tabita. "People believe in fairy tales."

Division Head Yalom took the glasses off his nose, folded them, and placed them on the desk in front of him, neatly next to the German fountain pen and the black leather diary in which he had just written a few words.

It was warm in the office. It was hot in Tel Aviv and in the rest of Israel. It would be hot for weeks to come.

The air conditioning in the office did not work properly. The air was thick and heavy.

Yalom didn't care. It worked equally well at any temperature.

"You are certain that the information is correct?" he said.

The man and the woman sitting across from him on those uncomfortable wooden chairs both nodded with conviction.

They wouldn't be here if they weren't convinced.

You didn't end up with Division Head Yalom if you weren't sure of your case. If you hadn't questioned every detail multiple times.

"And why is that?" Yalom asked.

The man, who appeared to be very young, said, "We assume it was out of fear. The woman undoubtedly learned that the Russian had something in his possession that he had stolen. Something valuable. And she took that object with her."

"We are of course speculating within a margin of certainty," said the woman, who was a decade older than the man. "We can only speculate at this point because we obviously cannot question the person involved."

"No," said Yalom, "because if you had interrogated her, this damn problem wouldn't exist at all. Then we had the card back. Then this case would be closed."

The man and the woman remained silent.

"Jamaica?" Yalom asked.

"Thirteen years ago she married a Jamaican who lived in Brussels," the man said. "A year later there was a child, a daughter. Eight years later, the man left for Jamaica again. He did not take his wife and daughter with him. They stayed behind. Difficult social conditions. Women's ever-changing relationships. No stability. Weak social position too."

"Relationships," said the woman. "Alexei, the man from the robbery. Who we suspect was the one who took the suitcase from the plane."

"And who killed the Russian?" the man inquired.

"A splinter group," Yalom said. "The Warriors of Allah. Saleh ibn Khalid al-Fuhan. Small group, big money—we know where that comes from. More money now, thanks to the stolen diamonds. They will go after her. Al-Fuhan is a fanatic but, at the same time, a strategist. He knows how to hurt us."

"We can send some katsa to Kingston," the man suggested. "To recover the stuff."

"Not the one from Brussels, of course," said the woman. "Because he messed things up."

"No," said the man, "not the one from Brussels."

"We might have someone in Jamaica," the woman suggested.

Yalom raised both hands. The man and the woman were silent.

"We do not send katsa," Yalom said.

"Shouldn't we then . . ."

"We're sending a kidon team," Yalom said.

The man and the woman were silent.

A kidon team.

Even they wouldn't have dared to suggest such a move.

Division head Yalom made a gesture. Both officers understood that they were being excused. They got to their feet. They nodded briefly to the division head and then walked out. Out of the office. Into the hallway, where it was cooler.

The man took off his jacket. There were sweat spots under his arms.

The woman dabbed her forehead and nose with a tissue.

"A kidon team," he said.

"This is really serious," she said.

They both hurried out of the building as quickly as possible, as if they didn't want to be infected by the devil that lived there.

# 3

The Jamaica Air DC-10 taxied to the terminal and finally stopped in front of the concrete barrier.

Inside the terminal, behind the glass, a handful of immigration officials waited, bored as usual.

The luggage hatch opened while the passengers disembarked, blinking against the harsh light. Men in blue overalls climbed into the belly of the aircraft and lugged suitcases and backpacks onto a conveyer belt.

Nothing out of the ordinary.

The passengers walked down the stairs. Tourists, mostly. Some businessmen flying first-class.

The asphalt was hot. The sun scorched every surface. Everyone wanted to enter the airport building as soon as possible, where hopefully there would be air conditioning.

The officials quietly did their work, screening passports.

The two men and the woman, who were not traveling together, had Canadian passports and appeared innocent. Tourists, actually. All three were young. They possessed the athletic appearance of individuals with ample financial resources and the leisure time to work on their physical health.

Their papers were in order. They had reservations at a decent middle-class hotel. There was no reason to suspect they were anything other than tourists.

The threesome followed the other passengers through the building after getting their luggage. They stopped in the hall but didn't follow the tourists to the buses. Nobody came to meet them either. Neither did they walk to the line of taxis.

After making sure no one was paying attention to them, they went outside together.

One of the men entered a car rental agency and arranged for a large, new passenger car, a Ford Taurus. They stowed their luggage in the booth and got in the car.

They drove a little further down the access road, toward another building on the airport grounds. That building housed a Greek transport company. They accosted the foreman and showed him a document. The man took them into a shed. Moments later, the two men loaded a steel suitcase into the back of the Ford Taurus. Then they drove toward Kingston. They had gathered the necessary weapons and equipment to carry out their mission.

At the Kingston Mercure Hotel, they each took a room on the same floor but not next to each other.

An hour later they were sitting in the bar with a Coke or a local fruit juice.

Although they continued to dress casually, their appearance no longer resembled that of tourists. Slacks, polo-shirts, trainers, all in subdued colors.

The tall, thin man in his mid-thirties with straight black hair was the leader. His passport listed his name as Adrian Beckers, but his true name was Kerem, which translated as "vineyard." His family used to be called Weingarten and came from Germany, but his father had his name translated into Hebrew.

A new country, a new name, his father had said.

As usual, the members of the team only knew each other by their surnames.

As a member of a kidon team, you didn't want to get too personal with your teammates. That made making difficult decisions easier.

The woman's name was Erez, and she clearly had Mediterranean roots. She was tall and moved with the grace of an athlete, which she probably was. Chayat, the tailor, was a younger man.

"We also have the third party to watch out for," Kerem said, in Hebrew, a language he was sure nobody around would understand. Nevertheless, he spoke softly.

"These people undoubtedly stand out even more than us," Erez said. None of them mentioned that party by name.

Kerem looked at her. "You're not exactly lily white either. Or black."

She grinned. "I am a wealthy Canadian tourist whose family hails from Lebanon. That was a long time ago. No one takes offense to that, right? Third-generation Canadian?"

"Then it's time to do some sightseeing," offered Kerem.

"Why are we sent?" Chayat asked. On the journey, he had given some thought to this question and how to phrase it.

It had been a very long flight. With two transfers. He had been thinking about that question all the time.

"You know what the assignment entails. Recovery of an important asset of our government," Kerem said. "Wasn't that clear enough?"

He was irritated by the young man. Did he fall asleep during his briefing in Tel Aviv?

"No, I mean, why us? Why not regular field agents?"

Erez looked around. But they were all alone at the bar. There was little likelihood of anyone overhearing them. It didn't seem like the Kingston Mercure was very popular during this part of the year.

"You mean, why kidon?" Erez said.

"I leave that to Yalom," Kerem said.

He didn't question an assignment. But send a kidon team? Such teams were usually only employed if an enemy of the state of Israel had to be dealt with. In a definite way.

Definite, as in: dead. A bomb in a telephone or under a bed. A raid on an apartment with silenced guns.

Yalom had only talked to them about recovery. The recovery of an object important to Israel.

And about a woman and a child who were involved in the affair.

Citizens. In the Mossad sense of the word. Not enemies. Even Mossad made an effort to avoid involving citizens.

Recovery of an important property. Chayat was right: why a Kidon team. But Kerem was not the sort of operative who would need to question the legitimacy of official orders. He was doubtful about sending the three of them but kept his opinion to himself. Orders were carried out, period. That's how Mossad worked. Maybe Chayat had a problem with that premise.

However, what bothered him more was the blind spot. They remained unaware of the involvement of others. After the Brussels affair—a mess, by the way—one could expect anything. A local katsa who had been unable to bring a simple assignment to a satisfying end. A shootout, two bodies, and too much involvement of the local police, the Belgian state security, and the press.

And a hostile organization with seemingly sufficient resources to rob a Swiss plane in a well-guarded airport. Must have been professionals.

They had been informed who the opponents were. The

Warriors of Allah. Saleh ibn Khalid al-Fuhan. Kerem had never heard of them before yesterday.

But that's how things usually went: terrorist organizations sprung from the infertile soil of many of the Arab countries and in refugee camps to join the already long list of enemies of Israel. As usual, it was linked to Al Quada and most probably financed by rich Arabs. And by the stolen diamonds.

And then Mossad was dragged in and had to solve the problems.

Mossad. The Shield of Israel.

But now they were stuck here with a blind spot: were there other interested parties on the ground in Kingston, and if so, where?

He looked at his watch.

"Let's get some sleep," he proposed. The journey had been long. Jet lag always was a problem under circumstances like these, but they would have to get to work tomorrow morning nonetheless.

"Do you have anything to tell me about those eggs yet?" Vassell inquired.

Sergeant Porters looked up from his desk. "Eggs?"

The other sergeant, Foote, rose to her feet. "That was me, Gov'. Beetle eggs, the doctor thought. I have . . ."

She rummaged through her desk. Pulled out a sheet of paper.

"I got an email from the Institute of Physics. This sort of beetle is found almost everywhere on Jamaica. Horrible little creepers. Opportunists. Lay their eggs where it suits them. A real plague."

"Okay," said Vassell. Who didn't need to hear the details about the breeding habits of the native beetles.

"Weren't we going to visit the place where Donna Markham was found, Gov'?"

"We certainly do," Vassell said.

They hadn't come to it the day before, after the visit to Donna's mother.

She hadn't felt like poking around in the girl's sad ending.

But it had to be done.

She had shortly been there, where the corpse was found.

Corpse, she thought. A little respect, girl. It's not a corpse; it's a body. You hope for the same respect later, when you are dead. You hope not to end up on the steel cutting table. You hope there is no existence after death.

But then she had barely looked around. The forensics people still had to do their work. It had been late. She was tired. She was discouraged. Yet another corpse.

"Just get the car keys, Foote," she said. "We'll move out right away."

A little later they were on their way in an unmarked car.

"Porters can be a little difficult sometimes," Foote said from behind the wheel.

Porters, Vassell thought. Should I care about Porters state of mind? Was she supposed to be a social worker for her people? Did they need looking after?

"Does he have a reason to do that?" she asked. "Difficult?"

"He feels like he's passed over."

"Passed over?"

"You know what I mean, Gov'," Foote said. "Like just now. He is a man. He's a Jamaican. He has a problem with women in leadership positions. Or women who perform better than he."

"He'll do what I tell him to do or fuck off," Vassell said. She looked at Foote. "As every sergeant must. Why would I make any damn exceptions?"

"Sure, Gov," said Foote, hands firmly on the steering wheel, paying attention to the traffic.

Which was necessary, given the way the rest of Jamaica was driving.

But Vassell knew what was wrong with Porters. Deveaux, the prosecutor, had told her. It's not that you're a woman, he said, and it's not that you're fucking white, because that's an exotic misunderstanding. What matters is that you were given a leadership position and command of this investigation, while being new. No, he told her, don't shake your head, Vassell; you're new to anything Jamaican. You don't know the culture. You are an anthropologist with a strange tribe. The finesse of Patois escapes you. You can barely read the expression on people's faces. You don't understand why they can't find suspects. You are a passerby to them. You'll go back to London at some point. They stay here, rest of their lives. They can only dream of London, even if they don't want to go there. They know they are not welcome there, but they still dream. And then you arrive. Do you understand their feelings?

No, she didn't. They could have London all to themselves, as far as she was concerned.

The place where the body was found was a vacant lot. On one side a warehouse with rubbish, on the other side a half-collapsed house.

Trench Town at its worst.

There seemed no one around.

The killer knew how to pick his spots. Every time somewhere he could be damn sure he wouldn't be bothered.

No snoopers anywhere.

Not even at night.

Especially not at night.

"It's a good thing the dogs didn't get to her first," Foote said as they walked from the car, which was left on the road, towards the vacant lot. Glass and pieces of brick crunched under their feet.

Vassell was worried about the dogs.

The next victim, she thought. Maybe the dogs will find her first.

It was strange that each of the victims had been found anyway.

She had mentioned this to Deveaux.

The very fact that we are finding the bodies, she told him, indicates that he wants us to find them. He wants us to find them. He wants the bodies in the press. It is a challenge. He's an exhibitionist. That's why he does this. That's his motivation, among other things.

She'd seen a few cases like this in London.

And she knew how this would end.

If he was an exhibitionist, he would finally get caught. Because he would continue to push the envelope. And that would end badly for him. Or at least it had ended badly for most psychopaths. It should have ended already sooner. Eight victims. But she should not compare the situation in Kingston with Londen. Less resources for the investigators, for one thing.

But basically she would be confronted with someone whose motivations would not be very different than in London. Sexual gratification. Cruelty. Or the total absence of human feelings. A truly twisted mind.

She knew she needed a profiler. Problem was the absence of profilers anywhere in Jamaica. Not much demand for that sort of job. Crime and law enforcement were of a different nature here than in London. Or in the US, for that matter.

The vacant piece of land was larger than she expected. She hadn't been back here since that night.

To the rear stood some houses, mostly rickety and poorly

maintained. Roofs made of rusty corrugated iron like the scales of a prehistoric beast. Uneven walls of concrete and brick blocks, half eaten by rot. She saw a faded billboard, clothes hanging to dry on a rope, and two women passing with a plastic basket on their heads.

A part of the site was cordoned off with multicolored tape, although that was useless around here because no one would respect it.

"Can those beetles be found around here?" she asked Foote.

"Do I know anything about beetles, Gov'? Am I the local beetle expert?"

"Well, you tell me. You were born here. I'm a white immigrant. I do not know anything."

Foote grinned. "Beetles live everywhere on Jamaica. This is beetle country."

She frowned, pushing through the construction debris and sand with the tip of her shoe. Hardly any grass to be seen, and that on an island where nature was everywhere.

"Maybe not here," she said.

"The body may have been somewhere else, long enough for those beetles to lay eggs."

"Those critters lay eggs almost immediately in everything that . . ." She did not complete her sentence.

In everything that can serve as a food source for small beetles.

A detail Vassell didn't want to think about.

But the beetles would only lay their eggs in a dead body, or so she assumed. Not in a living one.

That's all she knew about those damn beetles.

She took out her cell phone and dialed a number. "Porters?"

"Yes, Gov'?"

Everyone used that method of address. She wanted them to say ma'am, but so far it had not really caught on.

"Beetles. Eggs in last victim. You know what I'm talking about?"

"Yes, I read the report."

"Where do we find those beetles? Where did they come from?"

"Everywhere," said Porters.

"No, not everywhere. For example, not here, a barren piece of land in the city. Concrete debris, sand, no greenery."

"No, probably not there."

"Where then?"

"Wherever there is food and water for them. Or they can't survive. Take it from me. They are not picky, but they need water and the green stuff."

"Okay," she said. "Thank you."

She closed the connection.

"Porters says: not here," she said. "Green and water. Otherwise, no beetles."

"Seems logical," Foote said. "If I were a beetle . . ."

Vassell walked around. She knew forensics did a solid job. But no one had looked for the beetles because Dr. Smith hadn't found them yet. That only happened during the autopsy, and then forensics had already finished with the crime scene.

"Is it important?" Foote asked.

"The body lay somewhere else, long enough to attract beetles and for them to lay their eggs."

Foote nodded. "That might certainly be the case. We already knew she wasn't killed here. Too visible. Too public. Especially for what he did to her. Ditto for the others."

Yes, Vassell thought. The killer liked to keep things intimate. He would prefer secluded spots, obviously.

"So he has a place where he can do his thing," Foote concluded. "A private spot, far from everything and everyone."

"Brings us no closer to our man," Vassell said. "All over Kingston will be places where a man can go about whatever his business is and not be interrupted. Including murder."

Places where none of the neighbors would bother him, she thought. No social control of any kind. Not in these neighborhoods anyway. Or the wrong kind of social control, where crime is systematically ignored. Where crime is an accepted part of life. Although, perhaps, not torture and murder.

"But then he arrives here to get rid of the body," Foote said.

"No. Not to get rid of the body. To prepare it for us to find. He's an exhibitionist, remember?"

Foote studied the surrounding area. The houses on the other side of the barren landscape. The women who had already disappeared.

"The neighborhood survey turned up nothing," she said.

"There's hardly any neighborhood," Vassell said.

"And people don't talk to us."

Not even when this is about the safety of their children, Vassell thought. What a mess. Things were bad in a place like Brixton, the London suburb. In the socially deprived area of all British communities, and even in the countryside. Social standards and levels of poverty and crime all went the wrong way after Thatcher, even after New Labour. After the financial crisis, after the austerity measures.

But here, in Kingston, the gap between hope and madness was even greater.

She got an email from the Chief, inquiring about the status of the investigation. Chief Colin Vandermeer, Kingston's police chief and her immediate boss, a hardliner, and definitely old school. The marshal of the old regime at the JCF. She didn't answer him right away.

She would answer him later, whenever she felt like it. As far as she was concerned, she would ignore him as long as possible. Screw him!

She wasn't going to tell him that much, though.

She could, if needed, flatter his vanity and provide him with wordy but meaningless reports on the investigation so that he could inform the press if required. That might keep him off her back, she hoped.

The thing, however, was that they were all waiting for number nine.

A girl who was still alive and well, somewhere in Kingston, but who would soon be dead.

Not just dead.

But also tortured.

And left behind.

With beetles invading her body.

Several times already, members of her team had walked the entire route that Donna Markham had taken, or should have taken, the day she died. The route she would have followed all the previous days and weeks. Home, school, and back.

But she hadn't always followed the same route. It turned out she had different routines. One day she went to a youth home. The other day she visited a sports club.

Or hung out with friends for soft drinks, watching boys. Maybe sneak out to the movies. Things her parents didn't always know or need to know.

Donna Markham had no established habits. Her life was controlled by chance. By coincidence. By unforeseen events.

Yet the killer had found her.

Which meant he had followed her all the time and had kept tabs on her and her movements. From the school, a club, whatever, to the place where he could kidnap her without being seen. No one knew exactly where she had been that afternoon.

The detectives assumed he had followed her after it had gotten dark and then, at some point, decided this would be her last day. The last day of her freedom and of her life.

He was a patient man. Well prepared. Very motivated.

The worst possible opponent in this terrible game.

He wouldn't make a mistake any time soon, as long as he kept to his routine.

Commissioner Vassell stood in front of the whiteboard with the photos, names, and details of eight girls. The board was full now. A ninth victim would mean they had to bring in a new board.

No, she thought, there should not be a number nine. We, the police force as a whole, would not survive a ninth victim. Things would get out of hand.

What a creepy, inappropriate thought.

She wasn't concerned about her career or her job. She cared about her team. That team wouldn't survive a ninth casualty. The Chief would dismiss the team. He would appoint new people. New ideas too—another approach. And then those new people would start all over again.

But what new people?

From other departments? Drugs and Major Crime? Immigration officers?

And there would also be a new chef. Someone would take her place.

She was not going to let that happen. She would be the one who, with her team, caught the monster. She would get face-to-face with him and then . . . What would she do? Smash his face in? Break his legs? Cut off his balls?

She was angry—exactly what she needed. Her team needed to be angry too, but at this moment they were not angry enough.

Committed to the task, yes, but not emotionally involved. Except for some.

There had been a suggestion earlier on that the murderer might be a woman. A woman grabbing girls, dissecting them, cutting them up, and finally leaving them in some godforsaken place. No, Vassell had been certain, from the start, that it had to be a man. Female serial killers were rare and only killed for specific reasons, like getting even with men. Very few, if any, ever killed other women. With this level of brutality, it could only be a man.

An intelligent man.

As such, a formidable opponent.

Maybe they had already seen the killer.

One theory said that such a killer, of this caliber, was always around when the police discovered the body and when forensics did their work. As a spectator. An onlooker.

Another theory said that the murderer forced himself on the investigators, for example, as a witness. This allowed them to closely monitor the shortcomings of the investigation.

There were many theories. None of them could be tested.

After the fourth victim, she had asked the officers to discreetly take photos of the public near the kill zone. The photos were then examined closely. The faces in the photos compared. Always looking for the same spectator.

It had achieved nothing. There were a few ideas; there were a few people who seemed to be around again and again, but in the end the detectives didn't find anyone with more than a normal morbid interest in the bodies and in the work of the police. All suspects had a valid alibi.

There were no letters sent to the newspapers either. No cryptic messages were left on the victims' bodies, referring to the impending apocalypse. Nothing of the sort.

The few similarities in each of the eight cases told a lot about the murderer's preferences: age, social class, Kingston, schoolgirls in uniform.

It was unthinkable that the killer left no trace at all. And yet, that seemed the case. However, the fact that he worked so meticulously proved that he belonged to a specific class of people.

The average Kingston resident couldn't pull this off.

The detectives probably would not need looking for someone from a ghetto.

Not an idiot, not a slacker. Not someone driven solely by instincts or hatred.

The beetles offered no indication of a specific place where he was active. Still, he had a secluded spot all to himself; so much was certain. But how did he transport his victims from there to the places where they had been discovered? So far, no indications had been found. Tires left no tracks on the places where he dumped his victims. He probably knew that.

This time she took Porters and Goodman, another of the detectives, to visit Donna Markham's school. They had already been there, and the detectives had interviewed everyone, especially the teachers and staff. But doing it again might not be a waste of time—at least in Vassell's opinion. Not everybody shared her optimism.

Maybe it's a student, Vassell thought.

But that seemed very unlikely.

She was expecting a grown-up man in his thirties or forties. Maybe older if he was in good physical condition, but certainly not younger. Although she wasn't a profiler, her common sense dictated that such crimes required a certain level of maturity.

Maturity. Patience. Resolve. Self-control. Certainly nothing you would expect from a kid.

The director, Mrs. Channer, received them with some restraint. Almost sixty, gray curls, thick glasses, irregular teeth. Clearly not happy to see the detectives again.

Vassel knew where that reluctance came from. Bad publicity for the school to have the police come calling all the time. It would be bad publicity for the six schools the eight victims had come from.

"She had no friends meeting her that afternoon," Mrs. Channer said. What Vassell already knew. The investigation had reached a dead end at that point. None of the staff knew where Donna had gone. Her friends didn't know either.

But her friends probably hadn't known everything.

"Had there been tensions in the classroom between her and other pupils?" Porters inquired, glancing at Vassell.

"There are always tensions in the classrooms," Mrs. Channer said. "But not of such a nature that . . ." She made a despondent gesture.

After eight victims, everyone who was questioned made the occasional despondent gesture.

"No, of course not," said Porters, again looking at his boss.

"And no one said anything about habits suddenly having changed?" Vassell wanted to know. "None of the friends noticed that Donna had recently started behaving differently."

Mrs. Channer shook her head.

No, thought Vassell, that's not something they would share with the staff.

Numerous boys and girls in the class had already answered the question, but without success.

But Vassell was clutching at every straw.

The problem with Donna and the other victims was that they weren't special in any way. They didn't stand out. They were average. They enjoyed a certain amount of freedom, for as much as their parents allowed, but they did nothing unusual. Nothing punishable. Nothing objectionable. They were just good girls.

Good girls.

Why did he pick out good girls?

And how did he know they were all good girls?

Because he knew them personally. At least to a certain extent.

The killer knew each of the girls—that's as far as they'd gotten in their investigation. He knew who they were. He didn't just randomly pick them up from the street. He was prepared every time. That required long hours of observation.

"We have asked you before, but are you certain that no suspicious persons or vehicles were spotted in the days' or weeks before Donna's disappearance?"

Mrs. Channer shook her head. "Like what I said before to your detectives, ma'am. We don't pay much attention to what goes on outside the school. We are teachers, and so we teach. Public safety is police responsibility. And clearly one where you have failed."

Stupid cow, Vassell thought.

But she didn't say it out loud.

The previous interrogations in the school had already yielded nothing. Then why was she here? Because there really were no other clues? Because she believed that repeated questioning of people around the girls could help to unearth important details. Witnesses used to forget things; remember them later.

Beetles. School principals. School uniforms. Wastelands. None of it led anywhere. At least not right now. But somewhere in there, the identity of the murderer would be hidden. He certainly was no ghost.

"You don't use security cameras?"

The director shook her head. "We are not a prison, ma'am."

Probably no budget for that kind of thing. This wasn't London.

Teaching, Commissioner Vassell, is what we do here.

No results so far. Next step would, again, be a visit to the family. Not that Vassell expected tangible results from the conversations with the immediate family. All these girls had proven to be unremarkable, and there had been no issues at home. In any case, she wasn't seeking a relationship with a specific girl. That didn't match the profile she had in mind.

They said goodbye to the director.

"Drive me to the forensic lab," Vassell said as she walked out with her sergeant and Goodman.

"Would you like to examine the body?" Porters asked.

That was a stupid question, Vassell thought. He seemed a little too eager for another medical examination. She should keep Porters away from the bodies.

"Something is missing," she said. "Or wrong, I don't know."

"We have thoroughly investigated the eight victims," Goodman stated from the backseat. He belonged to an older generation and was used to different police practices than those Vassell wanted introduced.

Practices which he had used to some success in the past, but not always ending with the right defendant before the judge. Porters, on the other hand, belonged to a younger generation. There was hope for him, Vassell thought.

"We vetted them with the resources we have," Vassell said. "That's not the same as having certainty."

She knew there was talk of voodoo. Again.

And fingers were pointed at certain shady characters in Trench Town or Allman Town.

Well-known ominous figures who claimed to have other-worldly powers.

As long as the process only killed chickens, there was nothing wrong with it.

"Please call Dr. Smith," Vassell asked Goodman. "Tell him I have some questions for him."

That could have been done over the phone, but she wasn't keen on returning to the office as yet.

"He's expecting us," Goodman said after the call.

Porters parked the car in front of the forensic institute. It looked neat and modern, unlike the police offices. Relatives of victims were supposed to identify their relatives or friends here, so the place was kept in almost pristine condition.

Vassell got out of the car. The two detectives followed her inside.

Doctor Smith received them in his spacious office, which exuded intellectual tranquility. This, along with his professional demeanor of handling the deceased with care and respect, was intended to soothe the grieving relatives.

"You told me there were quite a few discrepancies in the time frame of the killer and his victims," she asked him.

He had poured coffee.

"He keeps them for between five and ten days after their abduction. These are his limits."

She had read that in his reports earlier. And she could count. She could use a calendar.

Between five and ten days.

But apparently Smith needed to stress the point with her, for whatever reason.

"You haven't figured out why yet?"

"I don't think there's a specific reason for that, at least not a medical one," Smith said. "In some of the cases, they had been dead for two or three days before they were found; in other cases, less than twenty-four hours."

"So there's not really a pattern."

"You don't need to concentrate too much on a pattern, Commissioner. It's probably a matter of logistics. How long he can keep them fresh, so to speak. But you don't read my reports?"

"I certainly do." However, she seemed to have missed something. Logistics. She hadn't found that specific term in his reports.

"His kidnappings are not opportunistic. You know that as well as I do. He is prepared. He knows his victim. But then he may not be able to start working on them straight away because he first wants to find a suitable location. A hide-out, whatever, or maybe some place for other, practical reasons."

"You noted that he let them live for at most a day once he. . . ."

"After the first, er, procedure, they only survive for a day at the most, yes. He has the means to regulate their pain to prevent them dying of shock too soon, even after heavy blood loss. He'll be prepared for that. He's a sadist, Commissioner. Of the worst kind. He enjoys what he does." Smith leaned forward. "Maybe you should look for him within the medical profession."

"We thought of that too, but interrogating everyone in Kingston with some medical knowledge is beyond your means."

"You'll have to narrow down your group of suspects."

"Twenty-four hours."

"When he waited longer, he kept them alive with all kinds of sustenance. Never the same stuff, either. He is careful. We don't catch him because he only buys his food in that one specialized store."

"And Donna's case? Did that reveal anything abnormal?"

"No. Same as the other seven. She lived another four days, was tortured for the fifth, and then lay somewhere for two days, not cooled, and only then was dumped. Hence the beetles."

She didn't need to be reminded of the beetles.

"I'd rather have them a bit more at a distance from you, Terrence," Tabita said in a whisper, like a conspiracy.

She simultaneously glanced at Anna, who was playing with Lucy in the garden.

Or at least in what passed for a garden. Nobody in his right mind would be calling it a garden. Except here in Kingston.

"There's nothing between us anymore," Terrence said. "All that is long past."

"Well, that's what you say, big man." She sounded accusatory. Suspicious too. "That's what you say."

Terrence knew his Tabita. Dare he look at another woman? That night, he slept on the couch. And perhaps many nights. That's how she would treat him.

The other woman was currently sleeping on a camp bed nearby, in the office. With their daughter.

"And she has to find shelter somewhere else," Tabita continued. "Not here."

"I agree, woman, I fully agree."

"A job too."

"Well, yes. A job, of course. What sort of job?"

"I don't know what," said Tabita indignantly. "It's your problem. What was she doing in . . . where is she from?"

"Belgium."

"What was she doing in that city?"

"Belgium is a country. Like Jamaica. She lived in the capital. Brussels. I don't know what she was doing there. Not much, I think. Living off benefits, I would guess."

"Pfft, benefits. Just hanging out, that she do. Nothing. She be parasite. Here I would say: gyal, smadi got to work! People on benefits? Let them work. What can she do? She has a mind and two hand, she not?"

"Maybe in a bar," Terrence suggested.

"A white gyal in a bar? A wa uno a say? Why not make her a whore right away? Where's your head, Terrence! Naa, man!"

"All right! You are clear enough!"

"So?"

"I'm looking around for her."

"Ask Charlie. He knows people. He knows more people than you. Better people too."

"Charlie?"

"Hear this, man," Tabita said empathically. "If she stays here with her kid, she needs a good job. She's fucking white. Should I ask around the hospital?"

"She has no . . ."

"Qualifications?"

"No. I do not think so."

"You can know. You had her in your bed. Without qualifications. I ask around. You ask Charlie."

"It depends on how final this is," Terrence said. "I mean, all this."

Tabita glanced outside again. The garden wasn't much. She never put any time into it either. Only rich people had time for a beautiful garden. Not in this neighborhood.

"It seems to me," she said, "that it is quite definitive. This coming here. But you never know. She doesn't have her roots here. People always go back to where their roots are."

Like me, Terrence thought. And that's what Tabita meant. His roots. In Jamaica. And with her.

It was a warning not to suddenly forget his roots, now that an old flame had shown up.

"I'll talk to Charlie about it," he promised.

He did that the next day. Charlie knew about the white woman and the child who now lived with Terrence and Tabita.

No secrets in this neighborhood. Certainly not for Charlie. Word got 'round.

That's what Terrence was worried about. What if people, nasty people, were looking for her? Who was overhearing the gossip? But what happened in this neighborhood usually stayed in this neighborhood. You could usually count on that.

"A job? Can't be anything," said Charlie.

"No?"

"Nobody sees a white woman just doing anything."

"Tabita said that too. Not in a bar, for example."

"Oh no, not at all," said Charlie, concerned. "Not in a bar. Not as a cleaning lady either. Not in a store. Something classy. Do not you think so?"

"Eh go so," Terrence said in agreement.

"You know what? I'll ask Mr. Harkaway."

"Yes?"

"He has a large villa. Several girls work there. For the rooms and the kitchen. Maybe he wants a white gyal to serve the guests. He certainly wants that. Looks classy, white woman serving."

"It's a possibility," Terrence offered.

He thought: We will never get rid of this, classifying people because of their skin color.

In Brussels, he had been the odd man out. Here Anna was the stranger.

In this neighborhood.

"You ask?"

"Give me a day or two," Charlie promised. "And that girl of hers—she has to go to school?"

"At some point, yes."

"Sure. To school. She is half black. That's less difficult."

Kerem, the leader of the kidon team, had spent two days at various public services looking for a relative of his, Anna Weiss and her daughter Lucy, of whom he had only two older photos. The whole family wanted to know what happened to them.

No, we're sorry, sir, but we don't know anyone by that name, and there is no one with those names in our archives. White, you say? From Belgium? No, we can't help you. You family?

Erez and Chayat individually searched for the mother and daughter in various locations such as hospitals, schools, hotels, and motels. And without attracting too much attention.

After three days, they were having lunch together. Without results.

The hotel restaurant was mostly deserted. Only some older couples who wanted to avoid the heat outside. And who would soon be taking their nap.

The three Israelis barely had time to sleep.

But they were trained for this sort of effort.

The lunch was extensive. They needed the food as a sort of comfort.

"We don't have many clues, and things are not improving," Erez said. She was wearing jeans and a men's white shirt, which she had bought at a local store that same morning. She also had a pair of large sunglasses pushed on her head.

"We can't expect much more help from Brussels," said Kerem. "Their info is sketchy at best."

Brussels had failed to provide much useful information. The state of the local archives was a disaster. Who and what Anna Weiss was, remained a well-hidden riddle. A riddle that was the result of bureaucratic incompetence.

She had been married; they knew that.

But they couldn't even find out her husband's name.

A child. Jamaica. So there was a good reason why she came to the island, and not just because of the passports she used.

For a moment, the team assumed that the passports were simply fake.

But why had Anna come here?

No, the reason was simple: she had been married to a Jamaican, with whom she had a child. She had now come to her ex-husband for protection.

The Jamaican embassy in Brussels had declined to provide any information.

Mossad had no local agents in Kingston they could count on. No informants, no katsa. Jamaica was a blind spot as far as the Mossad was concerned.

"We'll find them somehow," Chayat said. Who was young and therefore had too much confidence in the future.

"It's taking too long," said Kerem. He knew how impatient division head Yalom was.

The man had not made contact yet.

But three days would soon prove to be too long. An inquiry could be expected any time soon.

And sure enough, at the same moment, his cell phone vibrated.

He glanced at the screen.

"The great Manitou himself," he said. "I'll take this discreetly."

He got to his feet and looked for a quiet corner. "Chief," he said. Polite. Not that Yalom cared.

"You'll soon have company," Yalom said on the other side, in Tel Aviv.

"Company?" Kerem thought: an extra team? Because it takes too long?

"Two gentlemen of Syrian origin are on their way to Kingston, via Geneva and Florida. They arrive tonight. Our intel tells us that they are involved with the Warriors of Allah. They will not be on vacation to enjoy the sun and the booze. They probably found out you are over there, or they managed to find a trace that leads to Weiss and her daughter."

"What measures do you want us to take?"

"Find the woman before they do, and get me the data card. It's really no more complicated."

"It's not really possible at the moment," Kerem stated.

"Why not?"

Because if it was that simple, Kerem thought, we would already be back in Tel Aviv. "We don't have any clues as to the whereabouts of the couple, chief. We know she must be here, but at this moment we have no idea where. This place is complex, and the people are unapproachable."

"A white woman on a predominantly black island, Kerem," Yalom said. "How hard can that be?"

"If she ended up in one of those ghettos, we won't find her at all."

"Find her."

"Sure, chief. We'll do. But in the meantime, what about the two visitors?"

"You don't have time for them. Ignore them."

"Unless they get in our way."

"Then you deal with them at once."

"I can't spare anyone from the team for observation," said Kerem. He hoped for extra help.

"That's your problem. Solve the case as you see fit. You have the authority to do so. But keep in mind that you will need to remain in Kingston until the object has been recovered and that you must act with the utmost diplomacy and discretion."

Which meant that they could not afford a confrontation with

the two Syrians, could not use force, and certainly could not eliminate the two men, unless in such a way that the local police or security services would not notice.

That was what Yalom meant.

He didn't even have to say this in so many words. Mossad policy. But at any moment, that policy might need to change.

"Is that clear, officer?" Yalom asked. "Recovering the object is your priority."

"Understood, Director," Kerem said. Still polite.

Yalom rang off.

Kerem looked at the blank screen.

He now had one extra problem, which he could do without.

Two Syrians.

Two terrorists. And his boss told him that, officially, he was not to mess with them. *Officially.*

Damn mess he got himself into. What sort of information was to be found on that data card anyway? It had to be important to a lot of people.

He walked back to the table and informed the two others.

That same evening, Kerem and Erez stood like a couple in love in the arrivals hall of the airport, under the steel arches that supported the glass roof, next to the American Airways desk.

From there, they had an excellent view of the arriving passengers.

They knew which flight to keep an eye on.

The two Syrians entered the hall together. They wore casual clothes and could pass for any Middle Eastern tourist.

Except that virtually no tourists from the Middle East came to Jamaica. Too expensive, too much sin, too black, too many Americans and Germans.

An immigration officer examined their passports and visas for a long time but found no reasons to deny them entry.

In the meantime, Erez had already taken several photos of both men with her phone. She immediately forwarded these to Chayat's computer in the hotel, who then consulted the Mossad database.

The Syrians arranged a rental car and drove into the city a little later, followed by the Israeli agents.

A hotel in Vineyard Town. Kingston Palace Hotel. Three stars, at most, Kerem estimated.

A terrorist organization with a large budget but frugal with foreign expenses.

"We're not going to shadow them all the time, are we?" Erez wanted to know.

Kerem shook his head, and they drove off again. "No. Tomorrow we will continue our search for the woman and her daughter. Now we just have to make sure we are not followed."

He doubted whether the Syrians knew about him and his team.

However, exercising caution would not be a bad idea.

It took Charlie two days to find a job for Anna and a school for Lucy. "Now what do you do about the price of that engine?" he asked Terrence.

Terrence gave him the keys to the Toyota. "I'll charge you four hundred for the spare parts, and that's it."

Charlie reached into his pocket and pulled out some bills. "The girl will have to wear a uniform," he said. "School rules."

"Then that's what she will wear."

"And your gyal too, if she wants to work for Mr. Harkaway. Some sort of uniform."

"She is not my gyal."

"As you say. People talk. They think there's sinting going on between you. But hey, it's nobody's business. The child is yours, it shows. People think you're a nice guy to want to take care of a white woman and her child. Others think you're crazy."

"People are free to think what they want," said Terrence.

"You live off the people here," said Charlie. "They your customers."

"Still none of their business. But don't tell them I said that."

"No, I won't. But still pay attention."

"They will be out of here in a few weeks, if not sooner. That job, that pays?"

"Good enough," said Charlie.

"For an apartment?"

"Modest. Barely. She needs a man. Can't stay in Trench Town either. What did you think? That people want a white neighbor? They are not used to white neighbors."

"People think with their butts rather than with their heads."

"You live off those people," Charlie said.

"You already said that."

"I can't say it often enough."

"I'm not ignoring your good advice, Charlie. Glad you took care of those things. If your car is still giving you problems, I'll do you a favor too."

"A new car?"

"Don't test your luck," Terrence said.

Anna nodded upon hearing the news about her job. She had rarely done any real work, but she understood she couldn't live without here.

"I can do that," she said.

Yes, really, she meant it.

"Long days," Tabita warned.

"There is always someone to drive you," said Terrence. "I don't want you on the bus."

"And Lucy?"

"The school is a 10-minute walk away. She'll make it. She's not as white as you. She stands out less."

"That is very reassuring."

Clothing was arranged, although not new. The school supplies turned out to be easy to find for little money. Lucy didn't object. She realized that she would go to a school with all black girls and boys. And in a language she barely knew, even though she had learned some English and Patois from her father during the first eight years.

"You haven't forgotten that yet, the language," said Terrence. "What we talked among ourselves."

"She hasn't forgotten," Anna said. Who did not object to the school.


Donna Markham's body was released, and buried by her family just hours later.

Vassell parked her car well away from the other vehicles, on the large parking area behind the graveyard.

She wanted to be at the funeral, but not too obtrusive.

She knew how difficult it had been for the relatives of the previous victims to accept the presence of police officers and investigators. She wanted to avoid a scene with Donna's parents.

And she also wanted to stay far away from journalists and photographers. Because they would use the funeral to highlight the powerlessness of the police.

She had arranged with the editors of the largest newspapers and TV channels to provide her office with photos and images of those present at the funeral. This would cost her dearly, as the media would not provide such services in return for nothing, even when compelled by a police order. She would deal with that problem later.

"He might be there," she had told her detectives earlier. "He might want to witness the parent's grief. He's not going to miss the opportunity, and he might have done so before. That gives us the possibility to compare faces. See who sticks out, who was present at more than one of the funerals."

A murderer present at his victim's funeral? She knew what her detectives thought about her outlandish ideas (their term). She'd seen too many American movies. In reality, none of this would happen. A murderer foolish enough to. . . ?

She ignored their remarks. They would have to work their way through hundreds of pictures, and an hour or two of video. It would be in vain, most likely, but she wanted to pursue every sensible idea.

What she didn't like were the officials, politicians mostly, who made sure their presence was noted by the press, as a matter of good citizenship. She hated them for their public display of egotism. Even the Chief was there, of course. And she noticed Deveaux, the prosecutor, William Gunst, deputy mayor, and the energetic Brian Cisco, president of the Supreme Court. Some of them had been, at times, accused of corruption, but of course none were ever found guilty. Then there was the financier and benefactor Harkaway and John Harrison, the president of the trade association. And so on. And so on.

As if a public and well-known figure were being buried. Not a simple schoolgirl.

The spectacle drew a crowd, of course. The police kept most of the onlookers at a distance.

Vassell looked at the hundreds of faces and wondered if he was there. She pondered what exactly his presence would bring. What sort of kick? If she knew that, if she could gain insight into his demented mind, she might perhaps be able to build his profile. She would be able to see what sort of bastard he was.

But for now she had to get herself under control. She could not allow herself to make this personal. If she got emotional about this monster, she would not be able to approach the problem on a rational level.

And a murderer like this could only be caught by applying rigorous methods.

Later that day, in the main incident room, she and several of the detectives looked closely at the pictures and images, trying to compare faces with those from earlier funerals. And indeed, some spectators showed up more than once, something that was to be expected.

There's always an audience for this sort of spectacle. Those who came out of perverse curiosity. Those who came to so-called support the grieving family. Those with nothing better to do—which meant a substantial part of Kingston.

They would try to identify the most obvious ones, but it would be all needles and haystacks. And it was far from certain the murderer would be present at all. Would he make that sort of mistake?

Probably not, Vassell thought. He's the Devil incarnate. He's voodoo. He's invisible and untraceable.

Vassell thought about doing a detour before heading back to the office. The team was expecting her, but she considered switching off her phone so she could not be disturbed while taking a bit of time for herself. Needed that. Thinking—and trying to think clearly—was ever so difficult in an environment with so many people acting busy.

Behind the cemetery, a park opened onto the hills that in turn provided a view of the Blue Mountains on the northeast side of Kingston. At this instant, she would dearly hand over a pile of money just to be able to go on vacation in those mountains.

Climbing on her own, with no more than a backpack and some provisions, and not being obliged to meet people.

But this was not going to happen.

Only one man actually prevented that.

Public pressure and her own hierarchy would make sure that the person leading this investigation would not have as much as a moment of peace.

She knew what was said behind her back. The same as what the newspapers occasionally implied. She was British, a woman, and white, and why was she entrusted with this case? Hadn't there been a more suitable candidate? Jamaican and, yes, black?

They were right, of course, as she would be the first to admit. All those disapproving voices were right. Why was she leading this bloody investigation anyway?

She wasn't happy with this particular situation. A female officer in charge? If she failed—and perhaps a number of people wanted her to fail—not only would the finger be pointed at her personally, but every other female officer, including those outside her team, would suffer the consequences. If the team, under her command, could not catch this murderer, no other female officer would ever be put in charge of an investigation of this size. Perhaps of any size. All the prejudices against women in the workplace, particularly in the police force, would be proven to be true. Women simply were not able to lead. Only men could.

And what about white people? Let's not start about white people in charge.

In Kingston, in the whole of Jamaica, crime enforcement was still considered a matter for black machos, for the sort of men who upheld the old police mentality. Crime had to be solved with violence, because that's the only language criminals understood and appreciated.

Violence.

A drug dealer caught in the act? Cut off his thumbs. A rapist who didn't understand the lesson after the first time went home minus his dick and balls.

If he managed to return home at all.

But the mentality had been changing over the past decade. Police officers became more restrained, violence an exception and no longer the rule. Criminals were brought before courts more often and condemned to long stretches in prison. What previously had been common practice now became socially unacceptable.

Several police officers were skeptical about the effectiveness of the new approach. There was a certain old guard who considered a more humane approach to criminals and crime a mistake. People like Chief Vandemeer and even Deveaux were among those opposing the new regulations. These men, who had not shied away from violence in their youth, later became experienced police officers or prosecutors. They were actually looking forward to the restoration of the old ways.

And then arrived a senior female and white officer from London, destined to lead one of the most challenging investigations since long. Who was supposed to solve the sensational and very public case against a perverse sadist.

Yes, Vassell knew what was at stake here. And it was about more than just her job.

Near an impressive chestnut tree, a bench invited her. Further on, people were strolling and conversing, giving the impression that the world was at peace. Perhaps it was for them. Some of them might be the bigwigs who had attended the funeral. She sat down on the bench.

Could she trust any of the bigwigs?

Would any of them get her out of trouble and save her career if or when the ax fell?

No, she would rather not think too much about the *what ifs*.

She didn't need their kind of help either. If things ended badly here, she might just move back to London and do something else with her life.

Like in private security.

There was money in that.

Or teaching.

But then she would never lead a criminal investigation again. And that was exactly what she put her heart into. Despite all the difficulties and stress, this was what she lived for. Private security? Catching industrial spies or staff embezzling company funds? It all seemed rather pointless. It only helped the rich get richer, didn't it?

Although she wasn't exactly helping the poor here either.

Not the way the investigation was going now.

That enough, girl. Pull yourself together. Stand up. Go to your car, drive to the office, go through all the files again, read the reports all over again, go through the conversations with family members. Look for significant details you may have missed before. Read the profiles of the victims.

Eight victims.

She would not allow a ninth girl to be found. To her, this now was a personal matter.

Only an hour later, she was at her desk again. With her were her two lead officers, Ross and Thomson, who usually were on the road all the time, each with their own team of detectives. Two old school officers. She knew she needed them, in spite of their tendency to stick to the old methods, because they understood the city and its inhabitants much better than anyone else.

"Either a new approach," she said, "or we start the investigation all over again."

"All over again?" said Ross, not impressed. Vassell knew very little would ever impress him.

"With the same people?" Thomson asked.

They could have been brothers: tall and sturdy, in their fifties, graying stubble on the top of their heads, hands that walnuts feared. Hands that had often come into contact with criminals' faces or other body parts.

"And what would that new approach be?" Ross inquired. Keeping it neutral.

"The army, and a curfew?" Thomson suggested. "With tanks and stuff?"

She knew he didn't mean any of that, even though the idea had been out there in the press. A curfew. For how long? Nobody had made any serious suggestions.

"We need a better profile of the killer," she said.

She realized that she was kicking the shins of both investigators, figuratively speaking. She had done that before, the kicking. No problem, she thought. She wasn't after their friendship. She only wanted their best efforts.

"We know what his profile is," said Thomson.

"No, we only have a rough idea of his profile. Which isn't a profile at all, really."

"Well, you said it," said Ross.

"Yes, that I do. We talked about this before. After the fourth victim, remember? The Chief doesn't want to hear about it. Profiling. Too American, he said."

"It is."

"Exactly," she said; she couldn't help but sound vicious. "And here in Kingston, we do everything our way, not the American way."

"Or the British."

"All right. I get it. And after the sixth victim, I made that comment again. We still knew nothing about him at that time. And neither do we now. I don't see any photos of suspects on the board. There is fuck all about him on the board."

"We know what kind of man he is," Thomson said.

"And, detective, what kind of man is he?"

"Smart, but a brute. Vicious. Hates women. Perverse and well organized. Patient and, well, smart. Smart enough to evade us all the time."

"Right," she said. "See, that's what I mean. How many people do you think fit that description? In Kingston? Possibly all over Jamaica?"

"We assumed at some point he might be a foreigner," Thomson suggested.

She had heard that comment before. Some people, including a number on her team, hoped the murderer was a foreigner. That would confirm certain prejudices. That would also be politically appropriate.

"I said to the Chief: this is not enough. Tens of thousands of people in this city fit that profile."

"Yes, we said that too," Thomson agreed.

"Which means," said Vassell as patiently as possible, because to her it seemed they were going round in circles. "We're not going to get anywhere with a profile like that. Which it is not—a profile, I mean."

"Like you said."

"Yeah, like I said."

Ross looked at Thomson, then addressed Vassell. "What do you actually want?"

"I'll send for a specialist from London."

Ross said something under his breath.

"What?" she asked.

"A white man," he repeated. That wasn't the word he just used.

"I don't give a damn, Ross, what the color of his skin is. As far as I'm concerned, he's Chinese. Can he help us to create a better profile? After eight victims? If the answer to that question is yes, then we should have done this earlier."

"People aren't going to like it," Thomson said.

"You mean your people."

Thomson shook his head. "Everyone in this building. It means we have failed."

"We have failed, that's exactly what we did," Vassell said. "We failed collectively. We fail every day, time and again. That's why eight girls are now dead. Eight dead girls and as many burials. We failed them all, these girls. What are you going to say to the parents of the ninth victim? Well, Ross? What are you going to tell them?"

She knew he didn't deserve this. She knew he worked hard to achieve results. Just like everyone else in this building.

She sighed. "I'm sorry, Ross. It's nothing personal. I know what people have been doing in recent months. Hard work. Lots of overtime. Taking a lot of shit from everybody. But even then, we are nowhere. We have to get help."

"Can we keep this out of the press, Gov'?" Thomson asked, clearly wanting to calm things down.

"Ross?" Vassell asked.

"Yes, Gov'. I'm sure you are right. We worked our butts off, and we still got Jack shit."

"So you can explain to your people why we are asking for external help?"

"I can do that, Gov'. I think I can."

"And as for the press, Thomson, we'll keep them out of it. This remains between us. The whole team. I hope everybody keeps mum about this. I'll have to ask the Chief for permission, though. The bills will really add up. Profilers don't come cheap. But the whole thing remains between us."

"And what do our people do in the meantime?"

"What they always do: turn over all the stones to see what's underneath. Refocus on the families. What did the girls do? Who did they come into regular contact with? Who do they have in common?"

The two detectives rose to their feet.


Terrence knew someone who would want to rent out an apartment, not far from where he lived. Purely a matter of safety, he told Tabita.

"For my daughter," he explained to her. "I don't want her to walk half the city; you know it is not safe these days."

"You still have it in for the mother," said Tabita. "And don't you lie to me, Terrence! Not about that!"

He saw it in her eyes: she hated him right now. Might not last long, or it might, but he felt he hadn't deserved such a treatment.

"No, my wife, you are wrong," he said. "The kid is all my concern is about!"

"Oh, I thought you were a great man, but you're just like all those other men."

"I'm not like those other men. I've been with you for four years. And very faithful at that. Right from when I got back. Four years! That means something, doesn't it?"

"Why did you come back from Europe anyway?"

"I already tole you. I missed Jamaica. Could not get it out of my mind."

"Oh! You missed Jamaica!"

"No, really, I did. Europe is cold. There is too much white people in the streets. They look at you like you're a criminal, they do. I couldn't get a decent job. I was unable to secure funding to launch a business."

"You don't have a decent job here either!"

"Here I am my own boss," he proudly said. He was angry too, because she pushed him in the defensive.

"Boss of what? Of a crummy workplace where you fix crappy people's crappy cars. Big Boss Man! That's your entire empire."

"A wa yu say? My own garage! I take pride in that. It means something. That means a lot in this neighborhood. I being my own man!"

"The way you want it! So you are a successful businessman. And you have a black woman. And you want a white woman as well."

"I already told you . . ."

"Yes, you have nothing to do with her anymore. But the kid? That's your own kid. And you want your own kid close to you. Of course you do. And then you want the white woman close to you as well. And where does that leave Tabita? Eh? Room for two women? I do not think so!"

"Don't you get all that into your pretty head," said Terrence. "There's no way I'm bringing her into my home again. I'm done with her. The kid, you're right. The kid is mine too. I will make sure she's all right. I am responsible for her. And you will take care of her, because she is my daughter."

"Yes, right as always, big man," said Tabita, but her anger was mostly over.

"There is nothing between us!"

"Yes, I hear you!"

At least he had found an apartment for Anna and Lucy. Downstairs was a shop run by an elderly Asian couple. The apartment itself was small. A living room with a kitchen corner, a bathroom with toilet and shower, two bedrooms. Thanks to Terrence, the rent was more than reasonable.

But Lucy was sad about the new place. Sad and unhappy. It was a far cry from the old place in Brussels. The floor consisted of wooden planks, and running barefoot meant you got splinters in your feet. All since she was small, she had always enjoyed running barefoot. The walls were thin, and the place was noisy from the neighbors. The walls hardly had any paint on them, and the windows didn't close properly. There was no airco, nowhere in this neighborhood. It got hot.

But as far as Anna was concerned, there wasn't a problem at all. She only needed some stuff to furnish the apartment. Terrence would drag furniture in for her. But now she had to go to work and Lucy to school, in her newish uniform and all, which made her uneasy. Never had worn no uniform, for school.

Terrence drove the girl to school the first morning, but after that she had to walk. Ten minutes, tops. That's how she got to know the neighborhood. That's how people got to know her.

Then Charlie took Anna to Mr. Harkaway's house.

Anna was allowed to sit in the front seat of Charlie's Toyota, the car recently restored by Terrence, which now drove almost like new. At least for the time being.

"If you need decent work on your car," said Charlie, "Terrence is the man to go see. He is an excellent technician. Can fix anything on a car. Not those modern things with computers, but everything that is older but still in good condition, he makes better."

She looked at the villa and the park in surprise.

"Do I work here?"

"Yes, girl, you do," said Charlie. "There really are rich people living in Kingston. Not everybody poor like us."

"Mr. Harkaway?"

"You won't see him often. He does things with international freight, and he gives away money to hospitals and orphanages, and schools. Good man, him."

"And he's white, Terrence said."

"Yes," said Charlie with a grin. "Crazy, isn't it? A white man important in Jamaica." He looked at her for a moment. "It's a slave country, girl."

"A slave country?"

"Jamaica. The whole nieshan. We are all descendants of slaves. We, the black people. Of slaves who escaped and others who managed to start their own business, and others who came her from elsewhere. All slaves. We have a slave soul."

"You are no longer slaves."

"It's in the soul. God gives you a slave soul, and you have to make do with it."

He dropped her off at the door of the villa.

She stepped out in her neat black dress and black shoes and her bag with some personal stuff.

"See you later today," he said.

She didn't know how she was going to get here the next few days.

"Charlie will drive," Terrence had said.

But she couldn't expect Charlie to continue driving her. Maybe Terrence could lend her a car for a while.

She had heard what the rich white man paid. That was enough for the apartment and for food and clothes and the occasional extra, and maybe gas for a car. She couldn't buy a car, not even with the money she had brought from Brussels.

Although, maybe a really cheap car.

So far she had seen almost nothing but old cars in the city. Or at least in Terrence's neighborhood.

A thin, older black man welcomed her into the villa. "Mrs. Weiss," he said. "We were expecting you." His hair was frizzy white, and his teeth seemed perfectly groomed.

It turned out that he only spoke for himself, because there was no one else to welcome her.

He explained to her that she had to take care of the drawing rooms and the bedrooms, and, if necessary, provide the owners and guests with drinks, food, and cigars.

"Not difficult," he said. "Not hard work."

It took Anna a few days to find her way around the house, the living rooms, the large garage, the kitchen.

It took Lucy the same amount of time to learn her first words of Patois, if she wasn't already using Terrence's words.

Kerem, the leader of the kidon team, visited a number of police stations. He was looking, he said, for a relative, a young white woman with an infant daughter. He knew little about the pair, other than names. And the fact that they had recently arrived from Europe. However, Mason, the daughter's given name, was a common name in Jamaica. He didn't use the name Weiss, as he was sure the woman would not be registered anywhere.

Most offices were reluctant to help. One police officer however provided him with a list of local Masons. Armed with this list, the team went out investigating.

Kerem worried about the Syrians and what they would be doing in the meantime. Their presence was a problem he could do without. He had one member of his small team check on them every morning in their hotel. Sometimes they had breakfast; sometimes they sat over coffee or tea in the bar. Most of the time, they were simply missing. He had not the resources to keep a permanent eye on them.

"You know very well what we have to do in circumstances like these," Erez said ominously.

At a young age, she had lost her father during a war. That made her uncompromising. Exactly the kind of agent the Mossad needed as part of a kidon. Someone who would not hesitate to kill when given the order.

The other two knew very well what she meant.

Kerem was more cautious. He had killed a few people in his past. With a bomb, with a gun. Always on command. He had been in Iraq at the wrong time and in Egypt at the right time. He was the shield of Israel, although no one in his family knew about whom he worked for.

"If we cross that line now," he said, "we will create a situation that may be even less under our control."

The reputation of the Jamaican police was not stellar. The country had its own security service as well, which was mainly concerned with combating financial crime. Terrorism was not a priority in this part of the world.

However, the killing of two Syrians, possibly members of a terrorist organization, by three Mossad members in the heart of Kingston would likely be unacceptable. No amount of diplomatic fervor would be able to keep the Jamaicans off their backs.

And at Mossad, few people would be happy with the incident either. Certainly not because division head Yalom had not explicitly ordered a killing. In practice, it was often left to the discretion of the acting team commander to make such decisions, but Kerem wanted to be cautious.

"We cannot count on our embassy in case we get into trouble," he added.

"Shit, Kerem! They are terrorists!"

"What we have here is a long list of men named Mason, around the right age," Chayat interrupted. A change of subject was urgently needed, was what he thought. He was the youngest and most inexperienced of the team, but he hoped that the voice of reason would prevail.

"We need to split up; each take another part of the city," Kerem suggested, calm now. "Even then, a formidable task."

"There are neighborhoods we cannot safely enter, and we ask questions and hope to get out alive," warned Erez.

"Let's stick to the safe areas then," Kerem suggested.

"Nah. We need local help," Chayat suggested. He noticed the other two were doubtful of his suggestion. "A few people to help find the man. What about a couple of private detectives? Do they have them here? Someone who pokes around for us without stirring up too much dust."

"We can't do that."

"We stick to the story. We are looking for family members," Chayat argued. "That's what we tell the detectives."

"If we involve local people, they might question our story. Do we look like people who might have family members in this part of the world?"

"Mason might be married to a lovely Jewish girl from Brussels," Erez suggested. "There would be no reason to doubt the story."

"We can't possibly ask every man named Mason about his former wife."

"That former woman is white. When she walks around on the street . . ."

"Oh, that's how we do it. We walk around the street until we see a white woman, and we ask her if she is Anna Weiss."

"How much money do we have left?" Chayat inquired.

"A few thousand dollars."

"American?"

"Yes."

"That may not last us very long anymore."

"To do what?"

"As I suggested. Pay local people to find Mason for us. We are distant cousins of Anna Weiss. Why should that not sound plausible?"

"And we pay these people."

"Sure."

"Okay," Kerem said. "You and Erez play the family card. I'll keep looking separately. The story is unbelievable with the three of us."

They got to their feet.

"But we might run out of money quickly that way."

Kerem shook his head. "I will ask Yalom for additional funds. If the object is worth that much, he won't say no."

**4**

Rarely had Anna seen so much luxury, even in Brussels. And Brussels could be a pretty luxurious place, at least in a number of its neighborhoods.

The house itself was a detached villa that would not look out of place in any expensive European neighborhood. Two floors and a couple of extra rooms under the roof. Eight bedrooms, each with an adjacent bathroom and dresser. Two lounges and two dining rooms. An office, a library, and a smoking area. Two kitchens were larger than her complete flat in Brussels. The underground garage has the capacity to accommodate five or six cars. And even an elevator.

A house big enough to have an elevator.

Even then, there would probably be parts of the house she had not yet seen. Where she wasn't allowed.

Then there was the park. It seemed to have everything the ideal park—as she envisioned it—had to have. The grass had been carefully watered and mowed. The flowerbeds were laid out with mathematical precision. The trees varied in size and shape as they would under real natural circumstances.

Most of Kingston she had seen—except for the commercial center and the area around the airport—had the appearance of a third-world country, even if the city could boast a number of modern apartment buildings, wide boulevards, monuments, and parks. But most residents, she assumed, lived in ghettos.

Here, however, money seemed no problem. There was even enough for an extensive private park.

She herself was now part of that luxury: a housemaid. Only the very rich would have housemaids. It was a whole new experience, being employed and wearing some sort of uniform. She liked the black sleeveless dress, and when she discovered she got reimbursed for it, she bought two more. With the small white apron over the dress, she absolutely looked like a proper housemaid, as in the movies.

She hardly ever saw Mr. Harkaway. When he was home, he worked in his office or received guests in the salon. These guests usually were male. Business people, Anna assumed. He had another office in the city center.

She served drinks and snacks to his guests. None of the men spoke to her. The majority of the men were black, but occasionally there were foreigners, white people, or Asians. Mr. Harkaway spoke mostly English with them, sometimes French. She never heard him speak Patois, not even with the servants.

The old man, appropriately named Abraham, who had welcomed her, gave her instructions.

Could this be the career she would pursue for the rest of her life? She didn't know for sure, but for now, it didn't matter. She had no idea how long she would want to stay in Jamaica. How long until it would be safe to go back to Brussels.

But then, why would she want to return to Brussels? To what life would she be returning?

If she ever wanted to see Brussels again, she had to deal with the data card in the locket, which she had hidden in a hollow space between two wall panels in her apartment. What else could she do with it? What could she do with that data card? If she knew who the owner was, she would just give it back. Then she would be free again. At that point, she would no longer face any threats.

But those who wanted to get their hands on the data card had already killed for it. And had robbed a plane, no less. She was sure they would kill her and Lucy without batting an eyelid, only to make sure nobody knew about the card. She would never be safe.

But they would have to find her first. She realized, however, that her trail led from Brussels to Kingston. A trail of passports, plane tickets, immigration, and customs.

But here, in this chaotic and wild city, that trail hopefully came to a dead end.

Here, in this house, she had not used her own name, but Terrence's. Here she was Anna Mason. And of course Lucy was also registered at the school under Terrence's name.

That offered no certainty, however. They had been married in Brussels. Those people might have found that out.

But she was careful now. On the street, she made sure she wasn't being shadowed. She kept a lookout for strange men with an unusual interest in her. Terrence and Tabita would tell her if people were asking about her. She left the flat as seldom as possible but needed to go to work and buy groceries.

She looked up. Someone was playing Adele's "Rolling in the Deep" on a powerful stereo. The air trembled. She was polishing glasses that would later be used in one of the two salons.

Adele! She had only heard hip-hop and ska and reggae and such since she arrived here, and seen the not very female-friendly music clips on TV. Terrible music, for the most part. Someone playing Adele was a welcome change. Would it be Mr. Harkaway in his office? She had never spoken to him, only caught a glimpse. She was the maid, and was supposed to concern her with her job, nothing else. Make sure there were enough drinks in the bar, refill the bar from the stock in the basement, clean the rooms, air the beds, that sort of thing. Easy stuff, and Abraham was hardly difficult or strict. He gave her the instructions for the day and let her be. As long as the work was done properly, he made no comment.

Mr. Harkaway would be preoccupied with other matters than villa management. He wasn't married, at forty-something. A handsome man, Anna had noticed, already graying at the temples, classy, a tall man, and athletic. A discreet man, it seemed; she hardly noticed him around in the house. She wondered why such a man had not been married, or at least had a mistress. But there was no proof of female presence anywhere in the house.

Anna wasn't allowed to clean his personal bedroom, however, which was the exclusive domain of Abraham and of one of the older maids.

She tried to figure out how many people actually worked in the villa. Nearly a dozen, including those occupied with the park, she assumed. And there would be people who would be only occasionally employed, like Charlie and Terrence.

Her flat was not exactly spacious, and more primitive than the one in Brussels. Everything was different here, even the doorknobs and the light switches and the shape of windows and the way the afternoon light fell over the floorboards. She found out soon enough that living here also had advantages. The flat didn't need heating, saving a good deal of money. Food was cheap, as long as you didn't buy imports and went to the local market. Clothes were not expensive either. Lucy had to attend school properly dressed, but the uniform was affordable.

Terrence had given her some money for the books. She rarely needed to draw from her limited savings.

Brussels was far away. No asphalt in the street, no old stately mansions, no expensive cars. Stalls on the street, music everywhere, usually loud dancehall, sometimes also classic reggae. Young men with radios on their shoulders, like in the wrong kind of movies. Girls provocative in as little clothing as possible. Even in the pubs, people smoked ganja with unabashed abandon.

Lucy absolutely loved it. "Brussels was so boring, Mom," she said. "All those dour people. All those little rules. The place is cool, mom." Well, at least she's finding her place, Anna thought.

Life had suddenly changed into cool, as far as Lucy was concerned. She had no problem adjusting, not even with the children at school and the language. They probably found her exotic with her stories about life in Europe. About a hundred TV channels in a dozen languages, about the metro and trains, about snow and weeks of rain, about Belgian cuisine.

Oh yes, that too.

Commissioner Vassell had seen part of her team leave in recent days, mainly, if not solely, because Chief Vandermeer needed those people elsewhere. Smuggling, drugs, and prostitution. Burglaries, a few murders—the usual Kingston stuff. Incidents that needed manpower to investigate.

Now that the killer hadn't immediately found another victim (to everyone's relief, evidently), the Chief assumed Vassell had no need for so many detectives.

Which was ironic. They would be waiting for a ninth victim, without any means to stop the murderer. Evidently there was actually very little her team could do, and she at least kept Ross and Thomson, and her two sergeants, and some of the other detectives. But with each murder, more and more people had to be interrogated, and the amount of administration became staggering.

Although Donna Markham was barely in the grave, Chief Vandermeer saw no need to keep the entire team together, not the lot of it. He had been whining about the use of such vast resources in what seemed—to him—a lost cause. Vassell had complained, knowing it would not help. How could such a cause be lost? And what exactly did that mean? Were they going to let the man go on killing? How to explain to the general public?

She suggested, as an extreme measure, calling in a profiler from Londen, as she had discussed earlier with some of her team. Forget it, the Chief said. Too expensive, too much strain on the budget. Not going to happen.

She sulked for a day, but that didn't help matters either.

So she went out on her own. Took matters in hand. Went against regulations. She didn't even call from her own office but walked to a phone shop in town and asked for a connection to London. Which only cost her a pittance.

It took fifteen minutes before she got the right number from someone she knew at the Met. And from the same phone shop called that specific number.

On the other side of the connection, a tired and bored voice replied. A very British voice. Her memories of those times flooded back.

"Hesseltine," the voice said. "What could be urgent at this time of day?"

At this time of day?

It was late afternoon in London, Vassell assumed. Even the former colleague at the Met had not complained about her calling. Did things go downhill for Tim since he traded police for academia? Did he start drinking a bottle of wine after lunch or something?

"Tim? It's Jennifer."

Silence ensued. He tried to remember which Jennifer could call him at this hour. Late afternoon? Almost evening, even. She tried to imagine an evening in London.

"Jennifer?"

"Jennifer Vassell. From the Met. Formerly."

Goddamn, she thought; we worked together for a year and a half. However, not all the time. And not always under the best circumstances.

Not the best circumstances at all. And it had been more than a professional collaboration. He could not have forgotten. She hadn't.

Perhaps he didn't want to be remembered for that particular aspect of his life? Of what they had shared. Especially the promises they made—especially the ones he made. And the promises he had more or less extracted from her. She knew how hopelessly naive she had been. She liked him—more than just liked him, and even now she remembers that time fondly, but she had been so damn naive. She had not been alone in that relationship, and he was not particularly faithful or intending on a long-term relationship. Not with her anyway. She had walked away. From him, and eventually from London. But not only on his account.

"Oh, *that* Jennifer," he said, sounding as if he wanted to remain neutral. "Hi, Jennifer. Where are you hanging out these days?" She was relieved that his memory didn't completely fail him. But at the same time, he sounded like he was being careful. Jennifer. From London. That Jennifer. He carefully avoided emotional statements. But at least he was talking to her.

"I'm in Kingston," she said matter-of-factly.

"Kingston? Isn't that on the coast? Some tourist hole where . . ."

"Kingston, Jamaica."

Another short silence. He probably needed time to get a grip on the correct geographical dimensions of that statement. Then: "Jamaica?" As if he really didn't know where she had ended up. As if he really suffered from acute amnesia. He had known. People had told him.

"Yup," she said.

"I heard you left after that damn affair," he said quickly. Too fast. He didn't refer to their affair, but to an investigation that had gone pearshaped. "Sucks, actually. Completely messed up. But Jamaica? Why not the South Pole?"

"They don't need police officers at the South Pole until further notice. In the absence of crime."

"Oh," he said. "And in Kingston there's a lot of it, I guess."

That's it, Tim, she thought. That's how it is. Me fighting crime in some remote corner of the world. You still over there, in the heart of the Empire.

"Special mission, Tim," she said. "The ministry was kind enough to let me leave. It remains a former part of the Empire. Although that's not very obvious over here. Not how these people feel about it."

"Jamaica. Music, rum, beaches, and drugs. What do you actually do? Still, it's sensible work, I hope."

She didn't know what to make of that statement. Anyway, she was not going to waste time on an affair that had been. "I'm hunting a serial killer," she said.

Silence. Then, more seriously: "I didn't know you had them over there as well." He didn't say *another* serial killer. He didn't say that. He was too careful for that.

"Even this place is not immune to current trends in crime,

Tim." With a delay of three decades, Jamaica had followed the American trend in crime. Three decades, at least. And several dozen films on the subject. At last, serial killers had embarked on the shores of this paradise.

"That's bad," he said. "Pretty bad."

She thought, I'll limit myself to the facts. Just the facts. "Eight girls. Children still. And we find nothing on him. Absolutely no clues. Obviously we don't have the resources of the Met, but even then . . ."

"And you don't have me . . ."

She said nothing.

He didn't say anything more either.

"Tim . . ."

He was silent.

"Tim?"

"I'm not even going to consider it, Jennifer," he said tensely. Because now the conversation suddenly had become very serious.

She said: "I can't even ask you officially, because my boss doesn't want to spend as much as a dollar on a profiler. So I have to scrape together some money somewhere for your travel and your expenses, and so on . . ."

"I don't chase serial killers anymore. Left all that behind me."

"You're really the only one I know, Tim. Only one I can ask." That was, she knew, an unfortunate statement. Even more so considering their former relationship. But he had been the only one, in more ways than one, at that time.

"I don't do things like that anymore. You know that. The Met knows. Everyone knows it. And you know damn well why, Jen."

"Yes. Yes, I do."

"If you get too close to the fire, Jen, you get burned."

"Yes." They both had gotten burned.

"And that happened to me."

"I know," she said. She tried to sound empathic, but her heart wasn't in it. He was the one who had been able to walk away mostly unscathed. Although the Met didn't work with him anymore.

"I'm a fully employed academic, these days. I teach. For a number of hours a week, I drag myself to an auditorium and tell my students what kind of twisted, perverted minds some of their fellow humans have. I don't tell them about Evil, because I don't teach philosophy. I tell them about failed people and the horrible things they do."

"Tim . . ."

"And they go home, those students of mine, or to their dorm room, and they shake off my warnings about the dangers of psychopaths because they think it's all just academic. They believe that serial killers, serial rapists, and people who torture other people to death and do untold things to them are merely a matter of pure textbook theory . . ."

"Tim?"

". . . or at most something they see in movies."

"So far he has done all that with eight girls. The oldest were fifteen. Some were only eight or nine. Children, all of them girls. I want to prevent number nine from being murdered. Not on my watch, if I can do something about it. But there seems to be nothing I can do about it since we have no clues. And I really don't want to have to scrape number nine off a vacant lot, preferably before the rats and dogs come near her."

He didn't say anything for a moment. Then: "A vacant lot?"

"Yes. That's usually where we find them."

"He makes sure you find them?"

"Yes."

"Exhibited?"

"Not explicitly." She'd worked with Tim long enough to know what was on his mind.

"How not explicitly?"

"No attributes. Not really showcased. But not hidden away either."

"Ah. He wants to avoid the risk of traces. Attributes can be tracked. Shop, department store, wholesaler. Those sometimes keep data about their customers. So he pays attention to things like that. The dirty details."

"Tim?"

"I want to say something very unkind to you, Jen, but I have too much respect for you."

"Then just say something kind to me. I need that."

"You're in a lot of shit, aren't you?" He sounded like he really was paying attention now. Yes, she thought, now you're paying attention. Now your curiosity is piqued.

"We are virtually nowhere with this."

He sighed. Not loudly, but she heard it anyway. "Why aren't you?"

"No one noticed the girls before their disappearance. No one sees him deposit the body. No one sees him transporting the body. No one hears their cries. No one hears their cries for help, Tim. He's like a ghost. Which, probably, should not be too difficult in a city like this, but still . . ."

"He has his own place, where he . . ."

"Yes, we have already gone through that."

"Don't you have people there in Kingston who . . ."

"Until recently, my officers used to beat suspects to get a confession, Tim. Things have improved lately, but that's what I'm dealing with. Detective work is still not exactly an intellectual pursuit over here."

"Too bad. And what are your further plans?"

"I have been able to get some younger detectives on my team. But nobody has any experience with serial killers. Most murderers are caught within a day, or they belong to a gang or an organization and are never caught, even though everyone knows who they are. The rest is domestic disputes gone wrong or bar fights with deadly outcomes."

"I think I see your problem."

"I guess you do."

"Jennifer . . . I'm merely a professor. A dull, boring professor who . . ."

"You were one of the best . . . No, you were the Met's best profiler. Period."

"Because there was no other."

"That's mainly the reason, yes," she admitted. She felt she could afford to be honest.

Silence.

He was thinking it over.

She remained silent, wanting him to make that decision all on his own.

He said, "I don't want it to be in the news, Jen. I don't want my name in the newspapers. Nothing about me and my background. I can miss all that, like the plague."

"You come here anonymously, Tim. I can make that work."

"By the way, I have taken the exams yesterday."

"Did you? Happy with the results?"

"In the field of criminal psychiatry? What do you think?"

"I assume the best students all want to go into business. Banking and insurance and stuff."

"You're on track. They all want to be famous and on television. They want enormous bonuses and buy a flat in central London, even those that have no talent at all. That doesn't stop them from being ambitious. Do you know how many students

I had this year? This field does not have a bright future. And yet more and more people exhibit serious psychological problems. Some of them have an innate criminal predisposition. Look at the US, where people like them can buy a couple of guns but not get proper treatment. They walk into a school and start shooting. It is a serious social problem, but no one wants to acknowledge it."

"How fast can you get here?" she asked.

Because she knew he had made his decision now.

Two days later. She woke up with a start and registered two things: her cell phone was buzzing like crazy, and the radio alarm showed her emphatically, accurately, and at the same time teasingly that it was three o'clock in the morning.

Even in Kingston, that was supposed to be the hour when even the ghosts would be sleeping.

She answered her phone.

The voice of Sergeant Desy Foote. Excited, wide awake, probably because she was on night shift.

And had drunk a lot of coffee.

"Number nine, Gov," Foote said.

Vassell immediately got out of bed and put her phone to her ear.

Barefooted to the bathroom, trying not to stagger and hit the wall or pieces of furniture.

What was she looking for in the bathroom? What on earth could she find in the bathroom at this point? Her own ugly, still sleepy face in the mirror?

Number nine!

"Where?"

"Darlington Avenue. Close to the Calabar High School."

"A schoolgirl?"

"Yes. Uniform. Wasteland. Totally his thing."

Within a few weeks, the school holidays would start. Schoolgirls would exchange their somehow prudish uniform for loose and often provocative clothes, summer clothes, bikinis, and shorts. They would flock to the beaches as on a mass migration. No more uniforms. At least not for about seven or eight weeks. Maybe the killer would take a break.

Or not.

She couldn't read his mind. She didn't believe murderers took breaks.

But until then, there would be schoolgirls everywhere. Until then, the murderer still would find his prey. That's what they are, Vassell thought. For him. That's what they are. Prey. Cattle. Meat.

"What do we . . . Do we already know when she disappeared?" Because she had heard nothing, received no report. No missing girl.

"Yesterday evening."

Vassell wanted to turn on the shower in the bathroom, even though she couldn't put the phone under the water. But she didn't.

Yesterday evening.

That was very wrong. The girl had disappeared the night before. And not earlier.

"The parents initially thought she was sleeping over at a friend's house," Foote said. "That's why we didn't know until midnight."

And you didn't call me earlier, she thought.

Another girl's gone missing, and you're not calling me. But how many girls went missing in Kingston at any given day? It happened with some regularity, but most of them turned up sooner than expected. No problem. Unharmed. And not dead.

"The local police didn't know until about midnight," said Foote, who read her mind—or thought the same she did. "They often have teenagers who don't come home for a night or so. Not possible to follow up on all of them."

However, that wasn't the point. What mattered was that the killer had changed his method.

He kidnapped her, and almost at once he killed and dumped her. Immediately, almost without a break. No more than five or ten days in between.

Why had he suddenly started working differently?

"Give me twenty minutes," she said.

She forgot about the shower, brushed her teeth, put some energy bars and a bottle of water in her bag, dressed, holstered her gun, stowed an extra magazine for the gun and a notebook and some pens in that same purse, took a quick look around the apartment, and left.

A quarter of an hour. She didn't even need her blue lights and siren to reach Darlington Avenue in record time.

Three o'clock in the morning.

Someone, probably Sergeant Foote, had called for several local police patrols and for the duty officer in headquarters, who had alarmed other detectives and the technical people. Not bad for a sergeant on night duty. Behind Foote, four sets of floodlights illuminated the area.

Concrete, twisted iron, bricks, gravel, and sand.

A dump, like so many in Kingston.

Nobody seemed to live close by. Darlington Avenue was a nice neighborhood, middle class, but the last stretch of it, on the northwest side, was still undeveloped. Or been built on and demolished some time ago.

Hence the mess.

There was a lot wrong with the way urban planning functioned and with the management of unused plots of land in this city. Nor did construction companies adhere to some strict code.

Foote in her uniform came to her at once. The uniform was something Vassell didn't insist on during normal service. But it had been smart of Foote to wear it during the night shift. That gave her a certain authority she as a woman would otherwise not have.

Up ahead, half a dozen patrol cars stood with their high beams on. An ambulance. The neutral gray van of Doctor Smith or someone from his team.

It looked like so many crime scenes she had seen in London. In terms of desolation, it made little difference.

"Is Smith around?" she asked Foote.

The sergeant grinned. "In person. I got him out of bed. He didn't object."

"Where is he? Where is the body?"

Foote led her to where a group of people were standing.

They made room for her. Of her own team, only Inspector Ross was here. Three people from forensics were working on the area in their white bunny suits. Pieces of the terrain were cordoned off with yellow-white tape.

Foote had done a remarkable job in the time between the discovery of the body and now. Vassell wondered why she hadn't been informed first, since all these people had been here before her. Anyway, she was not going to complain.

Smith joined her. "This was a rush job," he said. He was talking about the murderer.

"It was?"

"She's been dead for an hour, maybe two. He didn't really get around to torture. Strangulation marks and a few knife wounds in the abdomen. Then a stab through the heart. It was over soon. Thank goodness for her, the poor thing."

"Identity?"

"Marcelline Dennis. Her parents live in Pembrooke. That's

about a mile and a half to the west. So close. She didn't come home after school. Didn't leave a message. The friends thought she was with one of them, perhaps staying the night. Girls often do that."

That explains why the alarm didn't go off until after midnight.

"As it happened, yes. And your team didn't know until some local kids took a shortcut through this area and found the body. Otherwise, we wouldn't be here until tomorrow. Or later." He rubbed his head. "You would think that these young people would be much more careful after eight murders. But no, they aren't."

"Maybe it's not the same killer," Foote said.

"A copycat? I hope not," Vassell said. "Because then we're in for a lot of trouble."

"It is, however, not impossible," Smith said. "But it doesn't look like he left any traces either."

"Schoolgirl, uniform, black, wasteland. It must be our man."

"Most probably," said Smith, "but not necessarily. Anyone can get those details from the newspaper. An imitator. But my guess would be: our man."

"We need another full medical examination, doctor," said Vassell.

"Obviously. You'll get a report as soon as I'm done."

"How old is she?"

"Fourteen," said Foote.

"The parents have been informed?"

"They have. I had the family liaison officers see them at once. Are you going to speak to them as well?"

Vassell knew she had to see the grieving parents, and without delay, now that the memories about the previous evening and days were still fresh. She knew a confrontation would be unavoidable, as she would, once again, have to admit the police were still not able to catch the murderer. But this was her job, as senior investigating officer.

"Foote?"

"Yes, Gov'?"

"I want the entire team in the office by ten o'clock this morning. And make sure that those who were recently transferred to other departments are on the way back."

"No problem, Gov'," Foote said.

"And Foote?"

"Mmm?"

"You don't have to be there. You worked the night shift. Go to sleep after this. I'll keep you informed."

"I can't sleep, if it makes any difference to you, Gov'." She nodded her head to the people around the body. "Not after this."

Vassell nodded. "Your commitment is admirable, sergeant, but you're no good to me without sleep."

She went to see the covered body. Squatted down next to it. Smith pulled the sheet away from the girl's head. Only the head. A pretty girl. Smooth hair. A narrow nose. East African origin. All those Jamaican ancestors came from almost all over the entire African continent.

"Was she still clothed?"

"She was," Smith said. "Which also indicates he was in a hurry."

The other girls had only some of their clothes on. But they had never been completely naked. They had all still worn some of their uniforms. The killer probably meant this as a sort of message for the public and the police.

"Anything different from the other victims?"

"I would need her on my cutting table first, if possible, before I can answer that."

She got back up and glanced at her watch.

Her day had started early. He would undoubtedly finish late.

But before she spoke to the team, she had to pick Tim up from the airport.

He came on a night flight. Not because there was no other flight available or he liked flying at night, but because it made a difference in the budget. Her personal budget. She had wanted to send him the money, but he had told her that she could bugger off with her money. Nevertheless, he took the cheap flight.

"Do you know what the university pays me?"

"No idea, Tim."

"Much more than you earn there. Or so I assume. I'll pay for the flight. You make sure I have a bed and a shower. And I want to have a few good cups of that Blue Mountain coffee. It's the only luxury I want. One cup a day. Preferably in the morning."

"Will happen, Tim."

Budget or none, he chose a cheap flight.

A red eye from Florida, after first crossing the ocean.

Vassell wondered why on earth there were no direct flights from Europe to Jamaica, on account of all those tourists. Most of them, however, were Americans. And any direct flights were Lufthansa or Air France, so quite expensive.

He looked a bit dazed when he entered the arrival hall. He was wearing jeans and a sweater and a leather jacket and was clearly not dressed for the local climate. Apparently spring had not yet arrived in London. She would buy him suitable clothes if necessary. A wide choice of those were to have in Kingston for little money.

That's what she wanted to do. But she thought, I can't give him the impression that I want to mother him. He doesn't need that. And it would be grossly inappropriate.

They embraced. Spontaneously.

Which they would never have done in London. Embrace and all that. Not in public.

However, this was not London. This would never be London, she promised herself.

It was half past seven. She drove him and his terribly techno suitcase to an all-night (and day) bar in town, near the university, where they had Bleu Mountain, and he drank two cups while having breakfast. She stuck to one cup and water.

"Tell me the whole story," he said.

He was clearly unwilling to chat about health and relatives and people they both knew. He had never been good at small talk.

She said, "We discovered the ninth victim this morning." She gave him the short version of the story.

There was an alternate version as well. She told him that too.

"A copycat killer?" he said. "That would seem unlikely. It's always possible, but still . . ."

"He changed MO."

"He did? That is meaningful. Unless . . ."

"Unless?"

"Unless," said Tim, "he does this on purpose. You rightly think that he is a very smart guy. And he will be. Otherwise he wouldn't have stayed out of your claws for so long."

"We've already gotten that far. We're not going to underestimate him."

"Good of you. One of two things. Either he changes his MO because an external cause forces him to do so while he had already kidnapped the girl . . ."

"Maybe he. . . ."

"Wait a second. Or he changes his MO to mislead you."

"Correct. But he . . ."

"He kidnapped the girl," Tim said, "and then something went wrong."

"Why you think so?"

"Because serial killers never, if rarely, change their MO. Unless they are in a learning process. But your boy seems accomplished on the first try. But even then . . ."

She knew where he was going. Somewhere she didn't want to go herself. "You mean these are not his first victims. He has killed before the current series."

"Probably so," said Tim. "Have you had cases like this before? With more or less the same Modus Operandi? But less intensive, not as many victims, maybe just one or two in a row, and then a long time nothing."

"Before my time." She hoped this killer wasn't leaving a trail of bodies, still undiscovered.

"Even so . . ."

"No," said Vassell. "I mean, the police and investigators may not have been looking for this kind of murderer in the past. Before my time, even five years ago, things were different, and you know what that was like. Because it has been like that in London, a few decades ago."

"I wasn't there, but I know what you mean. He may have kept himself busy for a while without anyone noticing. Do you have the manpower to dig through the archives?"

"I can't spare anyone."

"Too bad."

"But I have you."

"Yes," he said, "you have me. But I'm not going to go through those archives."

"That will not be necessary."

He glanced at his watch. "Will you take me to my hotel? When will you meet your team?"

Along the way, he looked carefully and thoughtfully at the city. The plank fences, the steel scaffolding, the unfinished flats, the painfully shiny glass of the new offices, wooden bridges, cranes, workers with yellow helmets, the dull puddles, the wrecked cars.

He made no comment. But he took it all in.

Tim's appearance at the ten o'clock meeting did not go unnoticed by the team. The second white face in the room.

Vassell knew she couldn't afford not to introduce him. There would be too much gossip if she didn't.

"Team," she said, "this is Timothy Hesseltine. He comes from London, where he teaches psychiatry."

"Criminal psychiatry," Tim said, standing behind her.

Good, she thought. That was the correction she didn't need. Corrected by her own guest. "Criminal psychiatry," she repeated.

Everyone kept looking at her, waiting, because no one knew how to respond.

A psychiatrist. On their team.

Someone from outside to observe them, maybe to evaluate them?

A civilian. And a goddamn psychiatrist.

"Tim specializes in the study of abnormalities in criminal behavior. He will help us draw up the most detailed profile of our murderer as possible. We found the ninth victim this morning, as you are all well aware. You just received the details. We are nearly back to full strength as a team, and we have a task ahead of us.

She repeated what she had already discussed with Tim, with an emphasis on the abnormal MO.

"He's under pressure," she said. "As we are. The idea for us is to increase the pressure for him as much as possible."

She expected reactions. She got them at once.

Ross said, "Is Mr. Hesseltine's appointment official?"

"No," said Vassell. "His presence is at my request and without cost to the department or corps."

"Where does he fit into the structure?"

"He reports to me, and I expect you to give him all the cooperation he needs. For his part, he knows the procedures. He has cooperated with police forces in the past. He knows not to ask the impossible of you."

Shuffling. Glances at each other. Whispers.

But for now, no one reacted with hostility.

That was quite something. Tim would be given the space he needed. For now.

"Let's focus on the matter at hand, people," Vassell said. "Inspectors Ross and Thomson are once again taking to the streets with their assistants. We know the routine by now. Let no trace escape us."

She knew news of the new psychiatrist would reach the Chief within minutes.

He called her just as she was consulting with Porters and Foote in her office, with Tim in the background.

"I hear you're offering shelter to a British shrink," Vandermeer said. "And want to include him in your team?"

Vassell motioned for the three to leave her alone. "That's right, Chief," she said after they had left.

"Who gave permission for that?"

"It happens on my own initiative, and it costs the corps nothing. I pay his expenses in full. As you may recall, we have indeed discussed this possibility."

"And I remember having said no. He is a civilian, and you are offering him access to information strictly reserved for members of the corps."

"He swore an oath in a British court to treat all official information as confidential, Chief. That also applies here. I definitely need his expertise."

"You went behind my back."

"That's right, Chief. But if I remember correctly, I was assigned to catch that serial killer by any means necessary. Absolute priority."

"By all authorized and officially sanctioned means, Commissioner."

"That's not what the memo says, Chief, with all due respect."

Silence on the other side. Then: "You're fucking brutal, Vassell."

"I'm sorry if it comes across that way, Chief. I wanted to work quickly and efficiently. Timothy Hesseltine and I know each other, and we worked together in London. We achieved excellent results there. Especially with abnormal cases like this."

"Oh, God, never mind. Find the damn murderer. I have to attend a press conference later today. A damn press conference. They tear me to pieces. Make sure I can say something meaningful."

"Tell them that we have made an important discovery about the killer's methods, which may lead us to him."

"Is that true?"

"Yes, it is."

"But you're not going to tell me what that is."

"No, Chief. With all due respect. The press doesn't need to know either."

"Your head will be on the block, Commissioner, if this ends up wrong."

He rang off.

She thought, If this goes wrong, several more girls will die. Why would I be worried about my head?

* * *

Kerem read the newspaper. He then pushed it toward Erez.

"Another child murdered," he said. "Another school girl."

"Barbaric country" was her only comment.

They were having breakfast. Eggs, tomato, cheese, brown bread, and fruit afterwards. Chayat had already had breakfast and had left earlier. They avoided being seen together, or tried to.

Kerem knew, better than the others, how long an operation like this could take. In the cinema, a team like theirs would catch their victim within twenty-four hours. But that was very far removed from reality. Their main weapon was patience.

"A serial killer," said Kerem.

Erez quickly skimmed the article.

"They've been trying to catch him for a while now," she said. She had read previous articles on the subject. "But they don't find him. Nine children. What a mess. Maybe they should call on our services."

"In exchange for Mason or Weiss's address," he proposed, not in earnest.

She grinned.

"If it's such chaos here, maybe we should call our Arab friends . . ."

"Forget it," said Kerem.

"I expect Yalom to contact us shortly."

"Why?"

"How long will he be willing to wait for results?"

"As long as the owners of the property aren't yanking his chain."

"I wonder what that thing is we're after."

"We don't need to know that," Kerem said. "Are the Syrians still around?" Kerem knew he would have to go out to certain parts of the city again, today, and chase a man called Mason.

Erez rose to his feet. "I keep myself busy with shadowing them."

She walked out in the street and took a taxi. She was annoyed by this whole assignment. There was no result, and she felt not at home in this city. Too hot, for one thing. A city partly modern and light, but at the same time a nightmare of busy narrow streets, old cars, cheeky young people, and overpowering food smells. And too many of the wrong Masons.

She gave the driver the address of the Kingston Palace Hotel. They took turns keeping an eye on the Syrians, making their observation less noticeable.

The two Syrians were having breakfast. Everything fine then. But this time, they had company.

Three black men sat at the table with them, engaged in conversation. The three burly men, each dressed in a neat suit, had sunglasses on their heads or in their breast pockets, a strikingly large watch on their wrists, and clearly a pistol in a shoulder holster.

Shit!

The Syrians had recruited local help. Probably of the worst kind. These men were not private detectives, Erez assumed.

She didn't hesitate and took a taxi back to the Kingston Mercure. Kerem was still having coffee.

"Three black men," she said. "Our friends from the Middle East have recruited local help."

"Not other Syrians?"

"No. Cleary Jamaicans. Exactly like we should have done."

"What kind of men?"

Erez described them.

"Local crime, hired muscle," Kerem surmised. "Which means someone gets impatient and told them to take this to the next level." He got to his feet. "I will contact Yalom."

A few moments later, they sat around the laptop in his room. The connection was made quickly.

Yalom leaned back behind his desk, in his shirt sleeves. "Tell me you have the object in your hands," he said. "Tell me about your successes."

"Not yet," said Kerem. "But the Syrians have hired local muscle. Exactly the kind of people we want to avoid."

Yalom looked at them for a moment. There was always a pause between responses because of the satellites.

But now he was probably considering his response. And his strategy.

Finally he said, "they must be stopped."

Kerem assumed he meant the Syrians. "By all means?"

"By all means. If you can't find the data card, neither can they. Our intel indicates that certain people in the other camp are becoming nervous. Something is afoot. Israel's enemies are stirring. Under no circumstances should the object fall into their hands."

"By all means," Kerem repeated.

That's all he needed to know.

Vassell's cell phone vibrated. She put on the speaker so Tim could listen in.

Doctor Smith. "I'll email you my report right away, Chief. But I thought I'd give you the shortened oral version."

"Any specific conclusions?"

"Our man continues to prefer sharp knives. A scalpel, most probably. But also a larger specimen, a hunting knife type with one smooth edge. Thousands of those on this island, so I'd guess this information is rather useless. And he used the same kind of knife before."

"Any other resources he used?"

"Does he need to? That scalpel has served him well every time. You surely remember the wounds of the previous victims. Nothing different this time. Never need heavy tools."

Tim made a gesture, attracting Vassell's attention.

"Doctor," said Vassell, "Timothy Hesseltine is listening. He has just arrived from London. He's a profiler . . ."

"A profiler? I assumed your Chief . . ."

"Never mind. I pay his bills. He wants to say something."

"Hello, doctor," said Tim. "No heavy tools, you say?"

"Not once."

"So he doesn't work from a workshop? Not, like, a garage or something?"

"A garage? No. Unless the garage is merely a quiet place where he feels safe. I think he deliberately chose these knives because we can't trace them, and certain types of rope that don't leave fibers, or tape that don't leave marks . . ."

"Everything leaves traces," said Tim. "Unless he used electrical cords to tie up his victims. Even in that case, the skin will bear pressure marks.

"We have indeed found those. Ankles and wrists—all very classic. Sometimes on the neck as well. But never anything that would be the cause of death. He let his victims die by cutting into them. And often quite deep, I'm afraid."

"He has a room big enough for this work, somewhere where he cannot be disturbed or his victims heard. He is not necessarily a specialist, but has learned something about human anatomy."

"Dr. Smith also came to those conclusions," Vassell said.

"Of course you did, doctor. I am convinced you have," said Tim. "I'm just summarizing. And then I have to get into his head."

"Getting into his head? Well," said Smith, "I wish you all the luck with that. I would not want to be near him, and certainly not in his head."

"Anything else we need to know, doctor?" Vassell asked.

"She died sometime after midnight, between twelve and two, and when she was found, she had been dead for no more than two hours. I couldn't be more accurate. It gives you a fairly defined time frame. No blood around, like the others. Genital mutilation, but this time not deep. Blood loss and shock as causes of death. She didn't survive much longer after he started working on her. I'll give her an hour at most. Let's hope it was faster than that."

"He used gloves?"

"Surgical. Minimal traces of talcum powder. Just like with the other victims."

"Thank you, doctor; I will read your report right away."

Vassell rang off. She looked at Tim.

He looked at her.

"I barely slept on the plane," he said.

"I've been up since three tonight," she said.

"The right combination for quality police work: stress and no sleep."

"As if we aren't used to this."

And then she shut up. She didn't want to go back to their earlier experiences. Which meant the things that had happened in London. Their last case together. A man who had cut open five boys aged around seventeen in a period of five weeks and sent their genitals to their families.

Tim had created a profile.

But he had made a fatal mistake.

The wrong man went to jail. The murderer killed two more boys in one night and then committed suicide.

They never commit suicide, Tim had said. People like that are too cowardly for that.

That was his second mistake. He was not given the opportunity to question the murderer. He had ventured into the man's head, but things had gone dramatically wrong.

He drew his own conclusions, left the force, and disappeared into academia.

And now he was here.

Once again involved in an investigation into a serial killer.

Because Vassell asked him to.


"There was a man at the door this afternoon," Tabita said. She had a chicken in the oven and was preparing a salad with peppers, onions, and tomatoes.

"A man?" Terrence asked. Most of the people who asked after him were from the neighborhood, and needed him for some jobs. Tabita's use of words implied that the man was a stranger.

"Yes. He asked about you."

"What kind of man? Police?"

"No. An almost white man. Dark hair. Southern European type. Italian? Don't know. He spoke strange English. No Patois."

"A wa im telling yu say, gyal? A strange man? What did he want?"

"I say: he not in the house, so bugger off! He was looking for a relative, he said, and thought it could be you."

"Relative? Like family member?"

"Yes. God, Terrence, you're so slow. Do you have relatives in Italy? Or elsewhere in the south of Europe?"

"No. Not that I know. What did he want with that family thing?"

"Maybe give money. Maybe inheritance. He asked about you. Asked if you had lived in Europe."

"And you said?"

"I told him you have no family. Not in Europe and not elsewhere. He took off. So no money."

"Weird. An Italian?"

"Maybe. Or from the Lebanon, Egypt, or Iraq. Dark, but not black. Nice, yes. And still young. Maybe I should have told him: come in and see if we can find out something you don't know yet, boy!"

"Tabitha!"

"Well, Terrence leaves me alone? So do I still do what I want? I have the day off, and Terrence he leaves me alone. What does he do all day?"

"Working for Mr. Harkaway. Sixty dollars a day for yard work."

"Sixty dollars? Working in the house where your white woman also works. She gave you a lemonade? Or was there more?"

"Tabita, I already told you . . ."

"Yes, Tabita, she believes everything Terrence tells her. And in the meantime, everyone has noticed something. Everyone has something to say. People talking behind my back. Terrence and his white chick."

"Did the man say anything about Anna?"

"A no dat man mi a talk. I'm talking about the neighbors. And our friends. The man I don't care about. People talk. Terrence, who crosses the line, he does! Terrence, who neglects his Tabita, he does!"

"People gossip. You care? They always done that, right? What do people do differently than before?"

She laughed. As only Tabita could. While she prepared the salad with everything God had generously spread over this land.

"I only care when Terrence is home and with me! Good now?"

It was good.

But the next day Terrence spoke to Anna about it. He had gone to ring the doorbell in the evening, at her apartment.

"A man came looking for you?" she said.

"Or for you," he said. "More likely."

"They know your name."

"Maybe it's a coincidence," he said.

"If it was a coincidence, Terrence," said Anna, "you wouldn't be standing here, worrying about the visit of an unknown man."

"Tabita says he was of the dark type. But definitely not Jamaican. Maybe someone from the south of Europe. Maybe even an Arab. Where did that stuff you brought come from?"

"I have no idea."

"And the man who shot Alexei? What did it look like?"

Anna remembered a North African. Or someone from the Middle East. She wasn't sure and hadn't had a good look at him. That boy had been dead. And full of blood. And she had been afraid. At the bottom of the stairs: a third man. She alone with Lucy. Of course she didn't look at the man very closely.

"Maybe the man came from the same place as that boy," Terrence said.

"Would they have found me? Here?"

"Not impossible. That depends on what resources they have. Alexei really didn't say anything about. . . ?"

"No. He didn't get the chance. The thing he had is valuable. I want to give it back, Terrence, but I don't even know to whom."

"You don't give anything back," he warned her.

"But what if they find me?"

"Tabita told him that I don't know anyone in Europe. He left again. There is no problem."

"How many people named Mason are there in Kingston?"

He grimaced. "I do not know. Thousands. It is a fairly common name. And if they only know my last name, they will be busy for a while. Would they have seen our marriage certificate? In Brussels?"

She didn't know. If they had, they would also know her name. She knew she was in danger. And Lucy, who was doing her homework and had just received a big hug from her father, was also in danger.

But there wasn't much they could do.

Maybe run again, but where to? She had nothing but the Jamaican passports. She needed a visum for most countries. And that would cost money and time. Which she didn't have.

"You look dejected, Mom," Lucy said afterwards, after Terrence had left.

"Always worry, girl," said Anna.

"Everything is fine at school," said Lucy.

"Oh, that's good. I'm glad you're integrating."

"It still is a strange language. I thought I learned a lot from Dad, but I don't understand half of what they're saying."

Well, what about me, Anna thought. She was happy that more or less standard English was spoken in the Harkaway house. She didn't have a problem with English. But Patois! Even going to the store was a problem. Lucy often accompanied her as a translator, even with the little she knew.

She had just opened the newspaper. On the first page: another girl kidnapped and murdered. She didn't show the paper to Lucy.

But at school, the kids would talk about it.

A dangerous city. Where she would rather not have come.

But it hadn't been her choice.


Anna had the impression there seemed to be a lot more police in the streets than earlier. Men and women in uniform, with rifles, and what looked like armored police vehicles. She could not really compare with the usual situation, but she assumed it had to do with the new murder. All this attention would be pointless and came much too late. It was merely a matter of the cops showing they were present and giving people what amounted to a false sense of security.

But then she heard what new measures had been taken by the authorities. Young people under the age of eighteen were no longer allowed to go out alone after ten o'clock in the evening. Places where these young people would usually gather after school would be closed. Patrols would also be on the streets, and the authorities asked civilians to watch the neighborhoods carefully for strangers.

It looked as if a revolution was in the air, and maybe it was.

Anna heard harsh voices over the radio, from ordinary people. She didn't fully understand what they were saying, but Abraham told her that people were angry because the police apparently did nothing about the series of murders, or at least were not able to find the murderer. All those measures no one really believed in drew more anger, and not only from kids.

The murdered children's relatives accused the government of negligence, but at the same time called for calm. Not that anyone in Kingston would listen to them.

Politicians tried to profile themselves as the guardians of public safety, as they usually did under such circumstances. They asked for more money for the police corps, even when, in the recent past, they had been opposed against extra spending on law enforcement. They called for more funds for child protection, for tourism, and for public housing—all the while knowing that those kinds of funds would never be available in Jamaica.

Anna recognized the pattern: the politicians were elbowing their way into the coming elections, gathering votes with promises, even ones they could not keep. Elections when? Anna didn't know, but she was sure the date would be written in large letters in the politicians diaries.

She knew this for sure: that she watched Lucy leave for school every morning with a heavy heart and was relieved when she safely returned home in the evening. No police in the street could take that feeling away.

Under no circumstances would Lucy go anywhere on her own after school. She was too young. And certainly not with a monster walking around freely.

However, she tried not to scare Lucy too much.

She had no fear for herself since she was well outside the scope of the murderer. Too old, wrong skin color. She had another problem to deal with: an enemy, invisible to her but who would perhaps already be observing her. And she could do nothing about that threat.

In the absence of a plan, she concentrated on her work in Harkaway House, where Abraham seemed satisfied with her.

To her surprise, Mr. Harkaway spoke to her that morning. She especially noticed his shoes: dark yellow suede moccasins with rough leather laces. Quite unusual, even—she assumed— in Kingston.

"You're Anna, aren't you? Where do you come from?" He sounded cultured, like a well-read man. He was well-read, she assumed. She had seen his library. Many of the volumes looked like they had been frequently used.

"Belgium, sir," she said. Of course she just told him the truth. Because he undoubtedly already knew, or at least could find out. You wouldn't work in his house if he didn't know who you were.

"Ah! Beautiful country. Hardworking people. Very different from Jamaica. This is a paradise, but not for everyone. And it is hard to find good and trustworthy help here."

"Yes sir."

"Maybe you would like to work for me in the evenings as well? I often receive guests for dinner. I need reliable people who won't spill the wine."

"I have a young daughter, sir, that I have to take care of. In the evenings."

"Of course you do. Children are important to all of us. They need a lot of attention. But why don't you bring her along?"

"Here?"

"Yes. Why not? If you work here evenings, she can come with you. Homework, whatever, and something to eat. They still have homework to do, I hope? I come into contact with young people often enough because of my foundations, but if you don't have a family yourself, you don't know how education works today." He smiled.

His hair was neatly combed back. He smelled faintly of an expensive aftershave. He shaved carefully. His skin was tanned, but not too much. His chin told you that he was able to make decisions and stick with them. That was the sort of man he was.

"I agree to pay well for evening work. I want decent people to serve me when I have important guests. What do you think? Will you consider my offer?"

"I think I will, sir," she said. She could use the extra money.

He nodded. "All right then. That's settled. Abraham will arrange the details for you. Here, your daughter will find a place where she can keep herself busy. And where she is safe."

"Yes sir. Thank you."

"How old is she?"

"Twelve, sir."

"Twelve. They grow up fast, don't they?"

"Yes sir."

That was it. An offer for more pay.

She couldn't afford to say no. Besides, it was good that Mr. Harkaway knew who she was. Maybe one day she would need him.

He was a man who cared about the community, she had heard. She could use a man like that, not as a friend, but at least as an acquaintance.

She took the elevator down into the basement with a trolley she used when she had things to move around the house. She had a list of drinks that needed to be replenished. Whoever those friends of Mr. Harkaway were, they could handle quite a bit of liquor.

And expensive drinks, too. Any of his party's would cost a few thousand dollars, she assumed. All for the sake of doing business, no doubt.

The basement was not a single room but a number of storage rooms with a separate hallway next to the garage.

In the garage, she noticed, stood a metallic gray BMW 6, a large black all-terrain vehicle, and a dark blue Mercedes E-series. All as good as new. To the side, she also noticed a not very new Ford Transit van, probably used by the staff to transport supplies. And yet another van, a somewhat more recent Mercedes.

The rest of the basement was a bit of a maze. She herself had been given a key for three rooms, where freezers and pantries were located. Food and drink. But also table linen, extra cutlery sets, tableware, glasses, and candles. Everything to throw a decent party.

She knew Mr. Harkaway himself wasn't much of a drinker, or so she had heard from the other servants. He was generous with drinks for his guests, though. And with cigars, which he had shipped in straight from Cuba.

However, there were more doors in the basement. She didn't have a key for them. Probably archives of Mr. Harkaway's companies. Or even more supplies.

Or maybe bomb shelters, in case of war.

You never knew with those rich people.

She placed the bottles on the trolley. Then she took the elevator upstairs. She placed the bottles into the unlocked bar. Mr. Harkaway did not want closed cabinets in his home. Except in his office.

In the kitchen, two girls were preparing supper.

Bottles of wine in the refrigerator.

Abraham entered. He looked around. Two couples came to visit, he announced—Americans who had been on the island for a few days. Business associates, Anna assumed. She never asked about who the guests were.

Deveaux made his appearance. Vassell was never thrilled to see him, and certainly not now. His presence served no purpose at all. She could do without the public prosecutor, always meddling as he was with police procedures. She could do without his attention.

But why was he here? They didn't even have a suspect in custody. There was no one to question, even if they had interviewed hundreds of people who had not seen anything and knew nothing.

However, he was old-school. Had always been part of the old regime. He believed in meting out justice with harshness. On the other hand, he did not believe in repentance.

But he was part of the whole public inquiry. And even more than Chief Vandermeer, he was following her inquiry meticulously.

At least he hadn't made any more advances. There was that.

The Chief, on the other hand, kept himself busy with the

usual official matters, at a distance from Vassell's team. He was usually to be found in his office, planning committees, seeing the Board of Directors, meddling with human resources, and so on.

But Deveaux could not resist meddling with the investigation himself. When he walked into the operations room, Tim was sitting quietly on a chair in a corner, reading through some reports on the different crime sites.

"Who is he?" Deveaux asked Vassell.

"Timothy Hesseltine," said Vassel. "The profiler from London. I got him here on my own initiative."

Tim said nothing but carefully watched Deveaux. Probably judging the man, as he usually did with people he met for the first time.

"And your Chief goes along with that?" Deveaux asked with a frown.

"He has given his consent," Vassell said. "In a roundabout sort of way." Which wasn't the same as consent, but she left it at that.

"How is the investigation going?"

"There are some new elements," she said.

"Such as?"

"I can't discuss them with you for now."

He wasn't in her chain of command, so he could fuck off for all she cared. She was past caring about what he thought of her.

He clearly didn't like that attitude one bit. "You must understand, Commissioner Vassell, that I usually am the one addressing the press. This is how things are done in Kingston, as I'm sure they are done in London as well. So I need details I can share with the reporters." He quickly glanced at Tim. "Details, Commissioner."

"I'll get you details if and when we know more about our man and when the information is relevant to share with the public." For Deveaux, it was a political game. One of public relations. But murderers read newspapers and watch TV as well as anyone else.

She assumed he was going to talk to Vandermeer about the attitude of his Commissioner, but she didn't care. The Chief would give her a hard time, but he would think twice about ordering her to involve Deveaux too closely with the investigation. There still were rules they all had to adhere to. And police officers in general were not inclined to allow a public prosecutor on their patch. Not even the Chief.

Deveaux stomped out angrily.

"Nice fellow," said Tim, after the door had closed. "A real sunshine."

"You know all about his ken," said Vassell. "We had plenty of them in London. Comes with the territory."

"I see you haven't changed at all and still know how to stand your ground."

"Yeah, but even then, I need results quickly."

"No," he said. "You needed those weeks ago. Or months ago. When you found the fourth or fifth victim. There is a psychological threshold."

"Oh? And we have exceeded that?"

"You did. After the fourth or fifth victim."

I didn't send for you for this kind of support, Tim, she thought. I need you to help me find the man. I sent for you because I remember your brilliant intellect and the way you comforted me when things got really bad.

He got to his feet. Walked to the other side of the room.

She followed him.

He stepped up to the whiteboard. Two white boards, actually, since one hadn't sufficed now that there was a ninth victim. That in itself was a defeat for the team.

He stopped in front of the pictures and the documents.

She had often seen him standing in front of similar boards in London.

Completely lost in thought.

As if he forced the photos and the details and the pictures and the maps to share their terrible secrets with him. As if he could communicate with all those inanimate things.

"Girls," he said.

"Yes."

"And young."

"Yes. He targets young girls. One of the very few things we know about him."

Porters and Foote had stepped from behind their desks, as had three other detectives on the team, realizing that new things were about to happen with the new man. They all joined Vassell and Tim.

"He's not really into young girls," said Tim. "He's not your garden variety of pedophile."

"He isn't?"

"Not necessary. What he's doing isn't sexual. He doesn't rape. He doesn't masturbate. At least not as far as I read in the reports I just looked at."

He had only just gotten here and had already gone through some reports and had analyzed their details. Vassell was impressed. Or not, because she knew what he was capable of.

"You haven't found any of his sperm anywhere, have you?"

"No. He leaves absolutely no traces, no DNA, nothing. But the bodies were moved around. And of course he touched them and stripped them of most of their clothes."

"He did. But he's careful so he doesn't leave anything of himself behind, and secondly, that's probably not why he kidnaps them. Not because he's into them. No sexual gratification."

"Power? Does he need to have power over them?"

"Disgust," said Tim.

"Disgust?" Foote asked.

"He hates women," said Tim.

"Well," said Porters, "that's clear enough."

"No, sergeant," said Tim, raising his voice, "that is not clear at all. It's not even obvious. Why do you say that? Because a male serial murderer kills girls? Is a man who kills another man a man-hater?"

"Well . . ."

"You're clearly not thinking this through. It's not obvious, after all. Rather, it is rare for a misogynist to express himself in this way. Killing women, I mean. Nearly all of them are cowards. And yet I think this is what is happening here. Because he is disgusted by women."

"He doesn't showcase them," Foote said.

"That's correct. He does not. But he does make sure they are found. Their corpse. Their dead body. That in itself is humiliating. He thus humiliates the victim and even more so their family. But first and foremost, the victim. For example, if he was only concerned with killing, he would make the bodies disappear."

"He tortures them."

"Yes, he does. He wants them to realize that he can do anything to them. He wants them to know there will be no rescue nor salvation for them. He enjoys the pain, and more specifically, their despair. That's why he keeps them alive as long as possible."

"Apparently so," said Vassell.

"And there you are. He enjoys power and pain in others, and

definitely in women. He is very dangerous. The most disgusting kind of psychopath."

"Does that lead us to a possible suspect?" one of the investigators asked.

"If you have a few suspects, I'd like to interrogate them personally," Tim said.

"We do not have any suspects to interrogate, I'm afraid," said Vassell.

Tim went silent for a few moments, deep in thought. Then he said, "He also has power over people in ordinary life, but not this kind of power. He must share that power. Sometimes he realizes that his daily power has limitations. Then he is frustrated. He's a psychopath after all. He can function well in society as long as he gets his way and while he can exercise his power. He belongs to the upper class. He's a fully paid member of your own upper class."

"God, that already narrows down the field," Vassell remarked.

And then she realized she had sounded sarcastic. "Sorry, Tim. I didn't mean it that way."

But Tim hadn't even heard.

"Don't look for him among relatives of the girls," he said. "He doesn't know these girls personally. They are strangers to him. But he kept an eye on them for a while. From a distance. He observed them. He chose them, probably carefully."

"He's a peeping tom."

"Not in the usual sense. His observation is not sexual but simply practical. He wants to know where and how he can kidnap them."

"And then he strikes."

"He does. He has a big car. A van. Some anonymous vehicle he can transport them in without standing out."

"Thousands of them in Kingston."

"He's from around here. He knows the city," Tim said.

"Thousands of people again."

Tim took a deep breath. "Give me suspects. Give me people to talk to. Give me potential murderers I can look in the eye and accuse of lies."

"We don't have any suspects," Vassell repeated. "That is currently our main problem."

Tim looked at her.

He said nothing more.

For now, he had done his job.


Lucy soon realized that she could easily find her way in school and with the other kids if she learned to talk like them.

English, that is.

But that was only as far as official communications were concerned. The children hardly spoke English among themselves.

She already knew she would have to repeat the year. Logical too: it was almost at the end, and she wouldn't even be able to really understand all the exam questions.

So that would not work out.

Repeat her year. The first year of secondary school. What a bummer.

She didn't like the situation, but Mom had convinced her that it didn't matter. The education program was less strict here than in Belgium, and she first and foremost had the language to learn. Which she would learn as much in the streets, with other kids her age, as in class.

English was a powerful stronghold. With difficult rules, which she wasn't even handed. So she took what she could. She had heard quite a bit of English on television at home—by which she still meant Belgium. So she had a basic grasp of the language.

English would work fine for her, given time.

The patois, on the other hand, wasn't even a real language.

Yes, it was a language, and there were even textbooks about it in the school library, but it was a fluid language, reinvented every day. Taken apart and put together again, every day.

That's how it seemed to her.

A language with English as a distant ancestor.

And so she started to connect with both languages.

For the time being, however, she played the role of clown. Out of necessity. The children found her amusing, especially when she spoke French or Dutch, languages they did not understand. Some children didn't even know that languages other than English or Patois existed. Boys and girls aged twelve and thirteen! How little they knew of the world.

The fact that she was from Europe and that her mother was white was also a source of amazement. Not because it was impossible, but what are you doing here at this school, gyal? Go weh! White mother you? Not in a rich school?

She was captivated by everything. Not only the language, but the music as well. There was music everywhere. Not in the class-room, evidently, but anywhere else. Streets and street corners, out of houses and pubs, out of office buildings and workshops, coming from the baker and the fishmonger. Sharp, rhythmic, loud, brutal music. Sometimes nostalgic and soft. On television: black men with big sunglasses and rasta hair, flashy cars, and girls with barely any clothes on.

Her mother didn't want her to watch these clips. Pure exploitation of women, she said. Ugly words. Rude behavior. Whores!

Gangsta.

Dance hall.

Sex!

But many of the young people Lucy encountered had high regards for those singers and musicians. They were true role models, popular heroes.

The girls in the videos, however, were negligible. Attributes. Flesh. And Lucy understood why this was demeaning, not only for themselves but for all girls.

Sex was also discussed freely. Not only in the videos and music, but also at school. In Patois, most of the time. *My brother, he run the pussy red.* Snickering at the brother's sexual exploits.

She didn't tell her mother things like that.

Sometimes she wandered around in the streets on her own. The school had a fence around it, but if you wanted, you could climb over it. She didn't, of course, as her mother had warned her.

There was a garden surrounding the school buildings, with flowerbeds, grass, trees. Serviced by two men with a van. It was always the same van, always parked on the same spot. She recognized one of those men: Charlie, Dad's friend. The one who got mom a job.

Charlie saw her and waved at her. She waved back.

At least someone in this town she knew.

The visit to Marcelline Denis' family was a repeat of the misery that Vassell had experienced every time with the families of previous victims. She was forced to make hollow-sounding assurances. The physical distance she out of necessity maintained from the parents, the aunts, the sisters, and the grandparents. The details in every household reminded of the irredeemable absence of the girl.

The horror she tried to cover with well-meaning words. The lies she told, of how their daughter had not suffered, while everyone knew otherwise.

The accusations about the inadequacy of the police she could not refute. More promises, more meaningless words.

She would do anything to be spared these visits. But Chief

Vandermeer had told her from the start that the head of the investigative team was supposed to see the relatives.

So here she was.

She brought Sergeant Foote, who still wore her uniform.

A black policewoman in uniform and a white woman in civilian clothes. Even that didn't help restore trust in the corps.

At his own request, Tim had stayed in the car. He was hunting for a killer. He wanted to be spared the confrontation with surviving relatives. If they had something useful to say, he would read it in the reports.

He noticed Vassell was visibly shaken when she left the house. He expected nothing less.

The two women climbed into the car.

Tim, at the back, said nothing. He didn't have to.

Vassell's cell phone pinged. She had just turned it on again when she left the house.

She pressed the green button but said nothing.

On the other side, a voice started talking. Neither Tim nor Foote could understand what was being said. Vassell looked straight ahead. "Okay," she said finally, and rang off.

"Good news?" Foote asked.

"An explosion at the Kingston Palace Hotel in Vineyard Town."

"Nothing to do with our case?"

"The Chief wants me to take a look. Foreigners are said to be involved. Syrians. Emergency services dragged two bodies out of a room. He suspects a terrorist attack."

"But nothing to do with us?"

"We already have half of Kingston's detectives on our team," Vassell said. "So the Chief judges that we can miss a few."

**5**

While Vassell and Sergeant Foote went to talk to the fire chief, Tim had a good look at the outside damage to the hotel. All in all, this seemed rather limited, in spite of a ragged and blackened hole in the facade, where that one room had been. Outside, on the pavement and tens of meters around the facade of the hotel, pieces of concrete, glass, wood, broken furniture, and a few rags that had probably been clothes were scattered around. Nobody passing by seemed to have been wounded, as far as he'd heard.

If there had been human remains among the wreckage, the fire brigade would already have removed them.

Two occupants of the room were dead.

Tim didn't need to speculate. He recognized a targeted attack when he saw its consequences. He was just glad to be spared the sight of dismembered bodies.

He sat back in the car with the windows open. However, he became bored and ventured out into the sun and heat. The interior of the car had been much warmer.

Vassell and Foote joined him a little later. Foote stowed her little notebook and pen in her purse.

"It's most probably a professional attack," Vassell said, eyeing the hotel again. "A bomb, according to the fire chief. He will need a professional evaluation, however."

"Undoubtably," said Tim. "Just enough explosives to destroy the room and kill the two occupants, exactly when they were present. Whoever did this, made sure the rest of the building remained more or less unscathed."

"Carefully executed," Vassell said.

"Two Syrians?"

"Yes. According to their passports. Tourists."

Foote grinned. "No Syrians will ever consider a holiday in Jamaica. They hate black people. No tourists, them."

"What is the plan?" Tim asked.

Vassell grimaced. "I'll put two or three people on this case. They'll have a look at the backgrounds of the victims, but that's all I'm going to do. I'll leave the rest to State Security. They will contact their embassy. And will probably try to find out if there are other suspected foreigners in the city."

"Suspected foreigners."

"Not you, Tim. Obviously. But when you say dead Syrians, you say, for example, American or Israeli agents at work."

"Oh, Americans," said Foote. "Plenty of them on the island. In droves they come here, on vacation."

"Not much else I can do. And what about you, Tim?"

"Not why I'm here."

"No, that's not what I meant. Do you still want to work with us on the investigation into that serial killer?"

"Has anything changed since yesterday?"

Vassell said nothing. As far as she was concerned, it wasn't about yesterday. It was about Tim. He had not come here because of her, but on account of the mystery surrounding the murders. She wondered, however, if their former relationship had motivated him in coming here as well. There had been implicit promises back there in London, but they had never really been a couple. There had been mutual attraction, but they both knew their lives would become unworkably complex if they really had pursued the affair.

Meanwhile, Foote had stepped away from them to exchange a few words with another uniformed police officer. Now she was observing her chief. Tim knew that look: the sergeant was trying to find out how things worked out between her Gov' and the newcomer.

Vassell opened the car door. "Let's go back, sergeant," she said. They climbed in the car, Tim in the back. Vassell looked at her watch. It had been a long day. She had to find a hotel for Tim.

She turned around. "Is your luggage still at headquarters?"

"Yes, hopefully," said Tim.

"Good. Drive us back, Foote. Then you can go home yourself."

They were stuck in traffic for a while, but eventually Foote dropped them off in front of the office, where some people were still at work. Vassell instructed Ross to assemble a small team to investigate the bombing. No other news had come in.

Then she had Tim stow his luggage in her car.

A hotel?

"I have an extra room, Tim," she proposed. "You can stay with me for a while, till I can arrange for a hotel."

Hoping this did not sound wrong.

"Jennifer," Tim carefully said, "I don't want to abuse your hospitality. A hotel would be okay."

She would have to pay for the hotel herself. Would be less of a burden on her budget if he stayed in her place. Was that the only reason?

"It's really no trouble," she said. "It's also easier. Transportation and all that. Coordinating our agendas. I'm doing myself a favor by keeping you near me."

So that was it. He stayed at her place. Which she would never have done in London. Tim in her apartment. Allowing Tim into her own personal sphere for a full night and morning and perhaps even several days afterward.

But she convinced herself that she had made the proposal purely for practical and financial reasons. She drove him through the city, both of them in thoughts. She was already planning ahead on how to organize her team around Tim. To allow him as much space as he needed to do his work.

She parked the car between two old and decaying palm trees. Several tiles lay loose on the sidewalk in front of the building. Some old women in colorful dresses and scarves were chewing tobacco and speaking loudly in their rapid and incomprehensible dialect. Further on, a boy was selling newspapers.

Her apartment. Neat, not specifically feminine (whatever that meant), almost exactly like the one she had in London.

"It's much more spacious than I expected," he said, approvingly.

He, of course, compared everything with what he had known in London, where flats of any size were difficult to come by. Where people were living in broom closets. Here, she had plenty of space, even a terrace, with some potted plants that deserved a better fate. The view, however, wasn't great. But where was the view anything but less great in Kingston? A nice view over a nice part of the city was expensive.

She made room for him and got him some sheets, towels, and a blanket he probably would not need. She moved stuff around from one closet to another, discovering she had too much of anything and needed to clean some things out. Her life would be less complicated with less clutter. The extra room was there when she rented the flat; she had no use for it but had put a bed in it anyway.

Why? No one will stay over at your place, girl.

But right now, it came in handy.

Afterwards they ate at a seafood restaurant at the end of the street, where Tim was surprised by the fresh lobster and extensive assortment of shellfish. And by the cold white wine that went with it. They had coffee, but not the Blue Mountain variety.

She realized he probably hadn't eaten much that day. At most a sandwich in the office canteen.

Then they said a chaste goodnight to each other in the hallway. She closed the door to her bedroom, something she normally never did. But she didn't lock it.

She fell asleep straight away. And then she woke up again. She glanced at the clock. Quarter to three. She was really awake, convinced that she wouldn't sleep again. If she had been alone, she would just walk around the apartment. Read a book on the coach. Couldn't do that now. Not with Tim in the other room. She didn't even turn on her light.

She listened. The walls were thin. Yet she didn't hear him. He didn't even snore.

And then, probably, she fell asleep again.

The morning radio broadcast reported extensively on the bombing. Officially, the government had no information concerning potential terrorists, which did not stop the media from speculating.

Witnesses in the hotel, a spokesperson for the fire brigade, and an anonymous source at the Ministry of the Interior all had some interesting things to say, although they probably knew nothing.

Speculation ensued everywhere. Gossip went widespread. Was Kingston now the new target of international terrorist organizations? Had the conflict in the Middle East now reached this peaceful region, which had nothing to do with all those

Arab situations? Would oil now become more expensive? And food? Should there be more police on the streets?

With that, the news of the ninth victim faded into the background for a while.

Which Vassell could live with.

There was an almost intimate atmosphere present in the small kitchen, with her and Tim at breakfast, something he was clearly aware of. Or was she misreading the signs? Still, he tried to take up as little space as possible. She wondered if her motives—or lack thereof—were all that transparent to him. Does he read motives that weren't there?

Her phone buzzed. A message from Porters. She held the phone up to Tim. "Look at this," she said.

POSSIBLE WITNESS IN DENIS CASE, it said.

"A possible witness?" Tim asked.

Vassell called the sergeant in the office.

"Someone saw a van near where the girl was left," Porters said, choosing his words carefully, as if he expected to be overheard by the press and public. "And at about the right time, too."

"We have a description of the vehicle?"

"Yes. We have a description."

"We'll come right over," she said. And at once she realized she had used the plural. We.


The witness was seated, with a cup of tea, in one of the interrogation rooms. She was a young woman who had voluntarily contacted the office, as any responsible citizen should. Not something most Jamaicans, however, would do.

"She called this morning, and I went to pick her up at her home," Porters said. "I'll drive her back too. She lives near where the body was found. Even works in the same school . . ."

"The Calabar High School?"

"Yes, Gov."

"Where Marcelline Denis went to school."

"Right," Porters patiently said.

"Did she know the girl personally?"

"No. She doesn't know any of the girls in that school. She works as a cleaner, usually after hours. Sometimes late. That night she was still out and about."

"A shitty job."

"No doubt," said Porters. "Lucky for us that she worked late that specific evening. She positively described the van."

"Okay," said Vassell. "I'll talk to her."

She entered the interrogation room with Tim. Made introductions but kept them short. The young woman, thirty, she estimated, had already seen enough police officers that morning. Frayed jeans, top made of glittery material, clearly no bra for small breasts, a small scar on her cheek.

"Tea oké?" Vassell asked to put her a bit at ease. "Do you want anything to eat? Breakfast?"

"No, thank you, ma'am," the woman said.

"Where were you when you saw the van?" Vassell asked.

"Carlisle Avenue, ma'am. Can't say the hour, sorry. After work, anyway. It was coming out of Darlington Avenue. Drove past me. With a speed, as if he had to be somewhere. Damn rush, at that time of night. Pursued by the devil hisself. Or being chased by duck-ants. Cho, man, I thought, cho, chill out a bit! Make accidents like that. Then down the small street. From there probably to Red Hills Road."

"Did you see who was in it, at the wheel?"

"No, ma'am. Well, just a bit. A man. Black. Im deh pon has'e, I thought."

"He was in a hurry, that was clear. Just a black man?"

"Yes. I didn't pay any further attention to it. I wanted to go home. Late already."

"Do you know what kind of van it was?" Vassell asked.

The young woman shook her head. "Not new. Closed, no windows in back. Dark green, gray, blue maybe—it's hard to see at night. With one thing on it . . ."

"A thing?"

"A drawing."

"What kind of drawing? A logo? That what you mean? From a company?"

"Yes, something like that. Logo."

"And a text?"

"That too, yes," said the woman.

"Do you know what kind of text?" Vassell asked, growing impatient but not wanting to show it. She noticed a small silver amulet between the woman's breasts. Protection against evil spirits.

"No," said the woman. "Just a text. Fast man! I think: a mad uno mad? That's how fast he was driving."

Vassell suddenly realized that the woman could not read. She was illiterate. The text meant nothing to her.

What had she seen?

Letters, a logo.

Vassell would not get more out of her.

"Can you draw the logo?"

"I can't draw well."

Vassell pushed a pad and pencil across the table to her. "It doesn't have to be perfect. This is not a drawing competition. We want to have an idea what kind of van this was."

The woman took the pencil, held it clumsily, and carefully, with concentration, drew a circle, a curl, a series of curved lines.

She stuck the tip of her tongue between her teeth.

Like a child.

Then she pushed the pad back to Vassell. "Something like that," she said.

Vassell looked at the drawing. She had no idea what it represented.

"Is it good?" the woman asked.

"And the letters. . . ?"

"Large and small letters, as is written on all those vans. Lighter color than the van."

"Good," said Vassell, getting to her feet. That's all there was to it. "You helped us very well. Thank you for coming in and talking to us."

In the operations room, she said to Porters, "Show her pictures of vans. See if she can pick out the right one. Make and model, that would help."

"I already did," said Porters, with a quick glance at Tim. "She doesn't recognize any of them. They are all the same vans to her."

"Okay. Take her back home then."

In her office, she looked at the drawing again.

Then she gave it to Tim. "Does it mean anything to you?"

Tim held the drawing at arm's length. Then he stood up, propped the sheet up against some books in Vassell's cupboard, and stepped back.

"She saw the logo from a distance," Tim said. "Maybe it wasn't clear. Maybe the van was dirty, and she didn't see the whole logo."

"It still doesn't mean anything. It's just an abstract logo."

"No," said Tim. "It means something. It is a stem with a leaf on it and a circle around it."

Vassell looked again. Squinted. "Could be."

"Or something else, of course. But that's what it most resembles."

"Could be," said Vassell again. "Does that tell us anything about the killer?"

"That he drives a van."

"It could be a coincidence, a van at that place."

"It may indeed be a coincidence. On the other hand, it is handy, a closed vehicle like that. And you already established he uses a vehicle to transport his victims. Or I assume you did?"

"Do you have any idea how many not-very-new vans are driving around Kingston? How many different small businesses there are, each with some logo or other?"

"No," said Tim. "I have no bloody idea."

"Me neither. But my sergeants will tell you there are a lot of them."

"Give them a copy of the drawing. Your sergeants. Let them show it to people."

"I certainly will."

Tim got to his feet. "I'm going to look at the files for a bit," he announced.

"Do your best," Vassell said.

When Tim was gone, she called Chief Vandermeer.

"The terrorism case? I gave that to some of my people to deal with it," she said.

"What is your assessment of the situation?"

"A homemade bomb that went off prematurely," she said. "The terrorists blew themselves up."

"Terrorism." He sounded relieved. The child had a name now. His lead investigator confirmed it. Things with names were no longer frightening.

"Yes, plain old terrorism. Now in Jamaica as well. Does not seem we can avoid getting involved in international politics. We will keep you informed."

"We need better border control," Vandermeer said. "Americans and Canadians and British and Germans, no problem with them. They are welcome here. But Syrians? What do they come here looking for? They have no money. You are right, Commissioner: terrorism. Better control of our borders!"

Well, she thought, one problem I won't have to deal with anymore, since the Chief has established that the bomb killed the perpetrators. Case closed, as it was. One less thing on her plate. She could direct all her detectives back to the main problem.

"But I'm not done with you," Vandermeer said.

"Chief?"

"Your friend. Hesseltine. Doctor Timothy Hesseltine."

"Yes? What about him?"

"I had him checked out," Vandermeer said.

Here comes trouble, Vassell thought.

"At some point he was no favorite of the Metropolitan Police, as I'm sure you know. He has been suspended, or he left on his own account—things are not very clear on that point. And I don't need to know. He returned to teaching. You have not told me everything about your man."

She could just about see his smug grin. "Tim was wrong about a perpetrator in a major operation. He made a professional mistake. What he does is not an exact science, not by far. It's not like *Minority Report*. Even for him, people are not always easy to understand."

"He was mistaken and someone was sent to jail, an innocent person. He no longer works for the police. And yet you have taken him into your team."

"One mistake doesn't obliterate years and years of experience and knowledge, Chief," she said. She was defending Tim now, of course she was. "On the positive side are the many murderers he helped catch. That's why I wanted him."

"You had an affair with him."

It sounded clinical, the way Vandermeer said it. It sounded as if something completely separate from her feelings, of what she once felt for Tim.

"That's right," she said.

"Is that why you wanted him to come here? Is there still something going on between you both?"

None of your business, she wanted to say. And it is personal. But she could not say that, could she? "Our relationship ended at some point," she said. Not that it had anything to do with their job. "And anyway, if I had emotional ulterior motives, chief, I would have asked him to come on vacation. Just a holiday. Old friends and all that. Not in his capacity as a profiler."

"Ex-profiler, not to put too fine a point on it."

"I'm actually the one paying his expenses," she said persistently. Well, partially, but that wasn't the point.

"But if he gets his name and picture in the paper or on television and it all goes wrong, I will be the one shoveling shit," he said.

I wish you would, more often, she thought. "Do you want him gone?" she asked. And she couldn't keep the anger out of her voice. "Because if he has to go and we still don't achieve results, the press will wonder why we didn't use all available resources to solve the case. Including the free expertise of a former top profiler from the Metropolitan Police in London."

"I'm keeping an eye on you, Vassell!" he snarled, throwing down the receiver.

Charlie opened the door of his van and let Lucy get in. "Come on, big girl, on our way to school. And happy about it, I hope?"

He spoke English to her. Keeping things easy.

"Thank you, Mr. Charlie."

"Oh, there are no mister here," he said. "Just Charlie."

He drove her through heavy traffic the short distance to the school, where he dropped her off properly. More or less in plain sight of other pupils.

"If it works out, I can also drive you tomorrow and later," he said. "I come here often, in this neighborhood."

"Thank you. I actually prefer walking," she said. "Getting to know the neighborhood. And people."

"As you wish. You're right, it's not a far."

"You work in the school's garden?" she asked. She was already getting used to English. Soon she would speak it perfectly, and Patois as well.

"I work in gardens everywhere, mostly for the City. Nice work. You can do that later too. Decent, healthy work."

"Maybe," she said. Later, she hadn't thought about that much. Later was like a foreign country.

"Of course you must. I personally prefer not to work behind a desk with a boss constantly watching over my shoulder. I like working with nature, outside, the sun, and the air."

"Thank you, Mr. Charlie," she said politely and walked to the playground.

He drove off, a cloud of dust behind him.

The girls on the playground glanced furtively at her. There were boys around as well, forming their own private clusters.

She ignored the boys. Had no idea how to talk to them and didn't want to. She had no use for boys, and usually they ignored her. But the girls, who had seen her getting out of Charlie's van, had more than enough comments to make.

"Your new boyfriend?"

"Isn't he a bit too old for you?"

"Not your father, right?"

"Not as black as him?"

She shrugged those remarks off. She wanted to say something inappropriate, but she couldn't think of something that was both appropriate and inappropriate, and certainly not in English.

"We got him," Chayat said.

The other two members of the team looked up. They had set up this meeting in a bar a few streets from the hotel, and Chayat was late. But there he was, all excited.

They had decided to lay low for a few days after the thing with the Syrians and because they might have drawn too much attention to themselves while acquiring the chemicals for the bomb. While it was relatively simple to assemble a powerful bomb using basic components, and they had procured their materials from various suppliers and shops, they still exercised caution. The most difficult thing to make was a reliable detonator. A timed detonator.

But it had been money and time well spent.

Of course the bombing was all in the newspaper. Certain people would be furious on either side of the barrier. And maybe more Syrians would arrive soon.

Or Saudis. Or Iraqis.

But that would take a while, and on top of that, Tel Aviv monitored electronic traffic between all concerned, so the team would receive a warning from Yalom well in advance.

Now Chayat stood with them at their table. He sat down quickly.

"I found him," he whispered urgently, sweaty, feverish.

"Him?"

"Right. The man we are looking for—who else? Terrence Mason. I'm sure it's him. This one lived in Brussels for ten years. Came back four years ago. He now lives in Trench Town and has a garage. Sort of anyway. People say he was married to a white woman back in Europe. Some say the white woman is here now. A lot of gossip. Interesting gossip."

"That's our man," said Erez.

"We have to be sure," Kerem said. He was the leader, he had to assert himself. And he wanted certainty about the identity of their target.

"We can shadow him," Chayat suggested. "He takes us to the woman."

"Carefully," Erez said. "We have to avoid to arouse suspicion."

"Yes," said Kerem, "we will be on enemy territory. Let's not forget where we are."

"And we stand out amongst the locals," Erez said.

"What about that ghetto? Trench Town? What can we expect there?"

"Dangerous environment."

"Oh," said Chayat. "Why would we not take a stroll there, being tourists and all?"

"No," Kerem said. "No. We cannot take any risks. We already took a major risk with the bomb. Maybe we pissed off certain underworld figures. Remember the guests of the Syrians? Perhaps they have lost a source of potential income. They may ask themselves questions like, who killed our new friends, the Syrians? Those kinds of questions we have to anticipate. The answers should not lead to us. We can do without that sort of attention."

"The police will be asking themselves similar questions," Erez said. "Again, more aggravation we can miss. But we needed to get the Syrians out of the way; we agreed on that, didn't we?"

"So," Chayat said, "we are in hostile territory. Aren't we always? As kidon?"

"Of course we are," Kerem said. "Should we therefore take

unnecessary risks? No. Remember: our only task is to recover the object. Nothing else."

"I assume," Chayat said, "we will be keeping an eye on the subject from now on?"

"Around the clock," Kerem suggested. "But how? Can we find shelter for some sort of stakeout somewhere in the immediate vicinity, with a view on his house?"

"I'm looking into the problem," Chayat said.

"All right. Take Erez and go look for places where we can establish a lookout. But don't speak to anyone. Find a vacant property. But be discreet about it."

Chayat nodded.

"And take your gun."

Chayat and Erez left.

Kerem drank his bottle of beer. He paid the bartender, who would undoubtedly not remember having seen them.

It was that kind of bar.

A moment later, he was standing in the street. He walked back to the hotel on foot. There he sent a coded message to Tel Aviv via his telephone.

A short message.

Nothing more was needed for the time being.


Terrence furtively glanced outside. The street was quiet, if a street in this neighborhood could ever be quiet. Two cars across the street shivered under the sun, their paintwork faded, their windows dusty. Equally faded awnings of nearby shops provided some shadow. Shop signs had been painted over, amateurishly. Two plump women down the road carried clothing baskets on their way to the launderette. Housewives with groceries hurried from shade to shade, trying to stay out of the sun. Nobody around who didn't seem to belong here.

He took a moments' break from his work, with still two cars needing repair. He had ordered parts for one, but the other would be on the road again tomorrow. He was the man who kept this neighborhood provided with more or less roadworthy vehicles.

Maybe he would have a few beers in the bar down the street later this afternoon. Not even Tabita would stop him. She wouldn't be home anyway, not until later that afternoon. He would make them dinner: oxtail, red beans and rice. A couple of bottles of Red Stripe. Maybe some soup as a starter? He would want to spoil her, as she did spoil him when she cooked.

He glanced across the street again. What exactly was he keeping an eye out for? What bothered him, except the heath and the occasional flies? Why did it feel like someone was constantly watching him?

It must be his imagination. You're imagining things, Terrence Mason. You're getting old and more paranoid than ever. Why would anyone be interested in you and in what you do in your little shop? You're not rich, and you're not dealing in dope or any other illegal substance. You're a nobody.

The only thing that set him apart from the rest of the crowd was the fact he had a white woman who had come over from Brussels to Kingston to seek refuge. But nothing had happened to her since she came here—nobody bothering her, nobody showing an interest in her except here in the neighborhood.

Still, he had the feeling something was wrong.

Anna was at work, he assumed, and Lucy at school. Things seemed in order. But he should have kept them here, in the house, in spite of Tabita. In spite of the complete lack of space for them. Then he could have kept an eye on them both, at least part of the time.

And he missed Anna.

Oh no, he thought. No, he could not go down that road.

He didn't want to be unfaithful to Tabita. A man will never be unfaithful to his spouse. Not a real man. He knew about the public image of men in Jamaica, but he wanted no part of that. They were all over TV and the internet and in movies and whatever, those kinds of men. He had learned a word: misogyny. The hate for women. Men hating women, because they were basically afraid of them. That's the public image of Jamaican men. But he knew plenty of men who hated that image.

And what about the women themselves? Why did they let this all happen? Why did they agree to play the role of submissive creatures, enthralled by the menfolk?

He had no answer to that question.

He knew he had been too long in Europe. He no longer really connected to most things Jamaican.

Anyway, he had a hard time getting Anna and Lucy out of his head. No, he didn't want to get them out of his head, certainly not Lucy.

He wondered if setting them up in a flat in the vicinity had been a good idea. If indeed she had made enemies, and they would have followed her all the way to Kingston, she would not be safe here nor anywhere else. He would have to hide her better, giving her a whole new identity, a new name. But he didn't have the money, and neither did she.

A car passed in the street. A fairly new car. Terrence kept an eye on it all the way till it disappeared behind a corner.

Did the driver look his way?

Was there someone in the back taking pictures?

Gosh, he got all paranoid.


After the third or fourth victim, it would have been easy enough.

Ross and Thomson and their teams would have grabbed a couple of suspects off the street. As they had done until a few months ago, when everyone was still full of hope about the outcome of the investigation. When the investigation was still new, and a final arrest was thought to be imminent.

But now, things were much more complicated. Unless Ross and Thomson were concerned.

The suspect that night was a young black man who had been in the wrong place, and not exactly at the right time. He had behaved suspiciously (according to the arresting patrol), and he had a past as well.

He didn't live in the right neighborhood and did not have the right kind of friends either. And a past of violence against women, rape, sex with minors. Not a nice guy, all in all, and therefore a very suitable suspect.

"We may have our guy," Thomson announced to Vassell.

She followed him to the basement, with its cells and interrogation rooms. A dark and gloomy place, stinking of decay. She hadn't been here often.

Thomson led Vassell into one of the larger rooms. Four men were already present, two in uniform and two plainclothes. This had been going on for a while, she noticed at once, with the blood on the floor and on some of the uniforms. And they even hadn't bothered wearing gloves. She knew at once that this situation was all wrong. There would be consequences later, for her and for the team. Why wasn't she called in from the beginning? But she wasn't.

The young black man lay stretched out on a sturdy table, naked. Not exactly the sort of sight she was happy with, to say the least. His body was bloody and showed the beatings he had received.

"Thomson, what the hell is going on here?"

"He wants to confess now, Gov," said one of the plainclothes officers.

"He wants to confess? What does he want to confess to?"

"The murders. All of them."

The young man tried raising his head and tried to speak.

"Tell the Gov," one of the uniformed officers shouted at him. "Did you kill these girls? Nine of them?"

"Did you cut them to pieces?" the other shouted. "Repeat what you just told us!"

Bloodshot eyes looked at her, pleading for help or for having this all stopped.

His whole body was shaking. Of course he would confess, Vassell thought.

"She the boss, she decides whether you live or die!"

The black man gasped but didn't speak. Probably could not.

Thomson's fist landed on his midriff. The man groaned deeply, trying to arch his body, but the two uniformed officers held him flat on the table.

One of the others had a sharpened bamboo stick in his hand.

"Thomson!" Vassell said sharply.

"Just a little while, Gov," said Thomson. "You'll hear him confess yourself."

"No. This ends right here."

They looked at her. What was going on? Didn't she want to have a suspect interrogated? Did she only want to follow procedures? Did this not go as it should? Was this not the same as investigative work that had been done here for years? Here, and in the UK? They knew about the good old interrogating techniques of British cops. Why was she bothered?

"Get him up, and get him his clothes back!"

"We sure he killed those girls, Gov," said Ross. "He confessed."

But they helped the man up and gave him whatever was left of his clothes.

"Take him to a holding cell," she said. "Get the doctor. No one comes near that cell except me and the doctor."

They didn't move.

"Now! That's an order!"

They moved. The black man went along naked, had to be supported, not friendly, but not too rough either.

She summoned Thomson into her office.

"What was that all about, inspector? What the hell were you doing?"

"An interrogation, boss. Just a suspect we're interrogating. We assume he's the man. Confessed and all. That's how we always done it. It gives results. People confess."

"A wa im telling yu say?" she asked.

He looked surprised for a moment. Disturbed too, as if the Patois belonged only to him. As if she had no right to speak Patois. Which, by the way, she never would have done.

"He told us he didn't know anything, Gov'. They never know about anything. All worthless bastards, them. Until we work a bit on them. Then they tell us all. Always been this way."

"Why is he a suspect?"

"In the street, he's walking around the area where we found the girl."

"And so? What of it?"

"Too much interest in the case," said Thomson. "At the wrong place. And that past of his."

"Too bad for him. Does he have an alibi for the evening?"

"I ask: what were you doing over there, where the girl was left behind? And where you been when she was killed? And he doesn't admit anything. Of course not. But he knows more. No, he doesn't confess. They never confess, them. Those kind of people. Always guilty of something, never done anything. Always lying . . . Until we . . ."

"Inspector Thomson."

"Yes, Gov'?"

"This unit, my rules."

"Gov'?"

"Suspects have rights; that's not only my rule; it's what the law says. We interrogate them, not torture them. No violence. No more violence, understand? Today there are lawyers, and there are organizations that deal with human rights. We're going to have problems because of what happened down there. But even if I wouldn't have to worry about lawyers, I would not want such a treatment of suspects. Do you understand? That is an important principle to me."

"Principle. Yes, Gov'. But principles don't solve crimes."

"You should know, Inspector Thomson, that confessions made under duress—not to call it torture, mind—are worthless in court. Now get out of my sight. We will be talking about this incident later."

After the fifth or sixth victim, Thomson had reminded her team that they were working according to moral and ethical principles, but still no killer had been found. But it seemed the lesson was soon forgotten by people like Thomson, who should know better.


"It is, of course, not a good thing to have nine victims, and still not a perpetrator in sight, or even a decent trail that might lead to said perpetrator." Tim stirred carefully his sweet tea and milk. "Now there's the description of the van, but I can't shake the impression it will not lead you anywhere." He looked up at Vassell. They were conferring in her office.

"This isn't London as we both knew it, Tim," Vassell said. "Or at least the civilized part of London. This is Brixton in the eighties, or Notting Hill in the sixties. This is Yorkshire in the seventies. Take your pick. People disappear, usually when they are connected to organized crime. Headless bodies turn up in unexpected places. Nice people go to church in the morning and to voodoo practice in the late evening of the same day. And I'm talking about people from the better neighborhoods."

She was, actually, angry with him. He should be supporting her, certainly after having heard what had happened earlier in the day. Meanwhile, the black suspect had been transferred to a regular cell and had been treated for his wounds. He had not yet requested a lawyer. Not yet.

"Why wouldn't you be looking in the well-to-do areas for your murderer?" he said.

"Why would I?"

"Well, because I can read your mind: a black man with an old van. You are thinking: getto. Lower-class areas."

"That man could have been anybody. Plenty of black men in vans around here. All of them innocent. Anyway, where do you want me to look?"

"He's probably not working some regular job where he has to clock in and out. No regular day job. Not working in an office with a boss. He might not have any obligations, as family goes. He has some independent profession. Maybe he is a prominent figure, someone who is not accountable to other people. He's not necessary lower class."

"Why all that?"

"Because our man observes. He takes his time to do that. He can afford to take his time. He's free, at least part of the time, to pursue his hobby."

"Hobby. He observes his victims. He ogles young girls and kills them."

"Yeah, but it takes time to do all that. Certainly long enough to get to know their habits."

"We already suspected that much."

Tim stopped stirring his tea and tasted it. "Oh," he said. "Then you don't need me."

"I need you."

"Why?" he asked. He seemed amused. He had her cornered now. To his delight.

"Who else can I have these sorts of conversations with? Those goons out there?"

"Your Sergeant Foote seems smart enough. And decent."

"Yes, she's one of the good people."

"Put her up for promotion."

"I certainly might consider it."


"Damn hot wife he has there," Chayat said. He and Erez sat on rickety chairs in a dilapidated house, dirt and dust and perhaps vermin everywhere, slightly opposite Terrence Mason's home and workshop. They had brought some food and a lot of coffee since they would be here for a while.

Erez stretched her body and groaned. Chayat admired her physique for a moment and then turned his attention back to their subject across the street. Erez looked attractive in her narrow black jeans and stretched T-shirt, but Mason's wife belonged to an altogether different category. She went through life minimally dressed, as was not at all unusual around here, except when she went to work and wore a decent outfit of slacks, blouse and a jacket.

"She works in an office somewhere," he concluded.

But once home, that suit came off, and Mrs. Mason appeared in front of the window in an extremely short skirt and an extremely short shirt, all dark flesh and dark curls and sexual provocation.

Chayat never had imagined he could fall for a black woman. And now he fell for a black woman. Although at a safe distance.

"What is she doing now?" Erez asked.

"Setting the table, I assume."

"Are they alone?"

"They are. The white woman is nowhere to be seen. Neither is the child. We may have found the wrong people."

"Nah. Keep an eye on them. He must be the right Mason."

"I hope she leaves the curtain open tonight."

Erez punched his arm. "Yalom will nail your balls to his wall if we don't come back with our prize," she warned him. "So keep them eyes peeled, mate."

"But in the meantime, here we are, in this dump."

"That's what it means, being part of kidon. We observe when asked, and we make sure the enemies of Israel do not get a moment's peace."

"This has fuck all to do with kidon work. This is not an enemy of Israel over there."

"Shut up and observe."

Tim looked outside, through a dusty window. What he saw was not exactly exotic: a more or less congested highway, a large area with neglected and blind warehouses. The city, a ghost a few kilometers away. He expected something different from Jamaica, something with beaches and palm trees and festive people. Lots of rum, too. But no, not a palm tree in sight. Hadn't seen a beach yet. Not that he was a beach person. He could perhaps do with a shot of rum later in the day.

"The man you are looking for is someone who can organize things," he said, turning to Vassell. "No, I assume he's someone who gets things organized. Someone with power over others. Someone to whom other people have obligations. Profound obligations even."

"Oh," said Vassell. "This is new. Haven't been there before. So again, we are talking about a few thousand new potential suspects, only different ones than before. Just what we need. Half of the upper class in this city has a network and has obligations, mostly financial ones. And you want them all investigated or what?" She turned around in her chair, facing him now. "We assumed having to deal with a more common variety of criminals. Or at least . . . Where's this coming from, Tim?"

"He can be well-off and have a serious position in life and still be a murdering psychopath, Jennifer. That sort of combination is not all that rare. I'm also thinking about some sort of conspiracy. You know, several people working together."

"People helping the murderer? On account of some obligation? Is that where we are going with this? Because this is a whole new turn this investigation is taking."

"Not necessarily. Until now, you knew nothing about him . . ."

Vassell shook her head. "We don't know anything about him now either, except we're looking for a black man driving a used van with an uncertain logo."

"Some obligations run deep, Jennifer," Tim said. "Other people might be involved without having blood on their hands. The blood, that will be his prerogative. And his alone. They might only be involved in the observations—or the kidnapping, whatever. As his sidekicks."

"And you're talking about someone who can organize this whole setup. He observes these girls and kidnaps them, with the help of at least one other conspirator. The main man might be high-up in society—what are you talking about? A senior civil servant, a judge, a financier? What sort of obligations would bind others to him?"

Tim shook his head. "It's a hypothesis, Jennifer, nothing more. Not at this point yet. But let's assume I'm more or less right. Such a conspiracy, to commit the most heinous crimes, would assume there's a demand and a supply. Of young girls, in this case. Now, in certain societies, there will be enough supply. And once these people are implicated and have blood on their hands, even symbolically, there's no turning back for them. They have sinned, if I may speak in religious terms."

"Is this where your imagination leads to? A group of people working together to terrorize, torture, and finally slaughter innocent young girls? A group of people who are all more or less hooked on this sort of thing or are bound by other commitments to one person, commitments so grave they cannot escape this conspiracy? Who would do that? I can relate to the lone psychopath. But a conspiracy . . ."

"Again, still a hypothesis," Tim said. "You should, however, include it in your collection of possible scenarios. By the way, there's something else . . ."

"More terrible things you need to share with me?"

"No, a down-to-earth comment. American studies—and also my personal experience—show that serial killers are never active across racial lines. Or at least very seldom."

"So you mean our man probably is black. We were aware of that. Or at least it's our assumption."

"If we are dealing with a lone psychopath, yes. But that might not be the case here. Not at all."

"A white criminal psychopath here in Kingston? Would surprise me."

"I'm just telling you . . ."

They fell silent. It was a bit too much for Vassell to take in. Tim's hypothesis might have been right, but then again, he was merely guessing. She was not going to the team with his idea. She wasn't going to share it yet, and certainly not with the Chief. Not for now, at least.

* * *

Anna was expected to be back at seven o'clock at the Harkaway residence for an extra bit of work. She had persuaded Terrence to take her and Lucy to her employer and that he would come and pick them up afterwards because Charlie wasn't around, and the bus was a problem at that time of the evening.

Harkaway House was completely illuminated. Happy lights everywhere, like it was Christmas. A reception was planned. She didn't know what the occasion was and didn't need to know.

A lot of people. All important people.

She and seven or eight other servants had been called in. It paid well. Just as Mr. Harkaway promised her.

She had her black dress on, the tight black dress. She would wear her little white apron once inside.

Lucy was allowed in a separate room with books, paper, crayons, soft drinks, and a TV set with cartoons. Enough to keep her busy for several hours. And with the strict reminder not to go anywhere else.

Anna got her instructions from Abraham, who for the occasion wore a tuxedo and a black bow tie over a white shirt. He looked less like a butler than a slightly overaged casino manager, as in a James Bond movie. James Bond, who was invented on this same island, or so Anna had heard from Abraham.

The first guests arrived around eight o'clock, all important men and women, in black evening clothes. Mr. Harkaway was clearly a popular man in certain higher circles. Meanwhile, the sultry heat of the day had subsided. A refreshing breeze came from over the ocean.

She served cold drinks, champagne, and chilled white wine, and if any of the guests had a special wish, she took care of that too, per Abraham's instructions. There were plenty of snacks on two tables against the wall of the salon.

Snacks like she had never seen before.

She had to ask Mr. Abraham the recipe for them. But they probably came from some expensive caterer in town. Or could one of the kitchen staff have prepared them?

The reception lasted an hour or so, and then Abraham officially came to ask if the group wanted to sit down at the table.

The party moved to the dining room, where the table was set. Anna had helped with that in the afternoon.

In the meantime, she picked up a few names. That one man was called Deveaux; the other was Vandermeer, and he looked like a retired soldier. A small and intense man named Cisco. Mr. Harkaway was the only white person in the group.

There also was a Doctor Smith present, which she, as a fan of *Dr. Who*, thought was funny. She was still catching names. Grace, Harrison. The top layer of Kingston had to be.

They might be the sort of people who could help her one day, here in Kingston, so she did her best to serve them as best she could. And made sure they noticed her.

The starter course was served. An extensive starter. Roasted lobster, oysters, a green salad, corn, strips of marinated chicken, dark red tomatoes, bread.

A white wine, chilled in large silver buckets full of ice.

Then soup that smelled of fish and garlic.

Good thing she had already eaten before coming here.

The conversation at the table was in English with occasional expressions in Patois, which amused the guests. The social divide was clear: only the queen's language was spoken in these circles.

The main course passed, accompanied by French red wine. Then came dessert, and finally coffee, served with cognac in the salon, behind a closed door. The servants weren't allowed in, unless Abraham said so. This was where serious conversations would take place.

Meanwhile, the servants tidied up the dining room.

Abraham leaned towards her. "Anna, would you go to the cellar and get us three bottles of Glenlivet in cupboard seven? You know where to find that?"

She knew where cupboard seven was.

She opened the cellar door. Someone had left the light on. That happened all too often. Some of the servants were not only afraid of the dark but also told her of ghosts who lived in these cellars. So they never turned off the lights, no matter how many times Abraham asked them to.

She walked downstairs.

Cupboard seven was in a room at the back of the cool and dry cellars.

Excellent place to keep alcohol. Not that she knew anything about storing alcohol. She got that from Mr. Abraham.

In the cupboard she found a few dozen bottles, carefully arranged in rows and by type. She counted six brands of whisky. All with unusual names: Glenallachie, Glenmorangie, and Laphroaig. And Glenlivet.

She took three bottles from the cupboard.

Careful with that stuff. Very expensive, Abraham told her. Mr. Harkway's treasury, although he wasn't a drinker himself.

But she was convinced the good things in life did not pass him by. Just look at this house. Just look at . . .

A sound made her look up.

The cellars were always quiet. When she was there on her own, she could hear the rushing of her own blood. She could almost hear her own thoughts.

Thick walls, heavy foundations, sturdy ceilings. No outside noise penetrated here.

But now she heard a sound.

She stood there, with those three bottles in her arms, and she suddenly felt vulnerable. The hairs on the back of her neck stood up.

Another sound. Like a sigh, as if silk was rubbed against silk. It wasn't a disturbing sound. It didn't seem alarming.

Perhaps Abraham had come after her to see if she had found the bottles. Yes, she thought, it's probably him.

She closed the cupboard and peeked into the hallway, expecting the man.

No one. But there was a persisting sound now—like people softly babbling, like people talking in the distance, like the whispering of ghosts.

Control yourself, she said. You're being stupid. You don't believe those stories, do you? Ghosts. Spirits. Returning dead. Voodoo.

It seemed to come from one of the other cellar rooms. She put her ear to a door. No, not this one. The other, further along. Yes. A murmur. A thick door. Thick as a wall. Impermeable. That soft sound again. Then sharp, short scratches. Something in need. A captured animal. Rats. Then nothing again. And again rustling, scraping.

She stepped back.

Keep it in hand, girl. There is vermin in the basement. Rats or whatever. You don't want to mess with rats.

She quickly climbed up and gave the bottles to another girl, who took them to the drawing room.

Abraham.

"I think, Mr. Abraham, there are rats in the cellar. I heard all kinds of noises. One of the locked cellars."

He seemed surprised. "Rats. That's unfortunate. They crawl through the smallest holes, those filthy animals. I will take action. Do not be afraid. They usually avoid people. Just leave it to me."

Later, when most of the guests had left, she found Lucy in the room she had been in all the time. Lucy, who was sleepy and bored.

Mr. Abraham ensured that the servants who did not have their own transport were personally brought home by him in the large Mercedes car that she had seen earlier in the garage.

"Don't think about those rats anymore," he told Anna. "They won't hurt you. I'll take care of them."

"It seems best not to walk too far," Vassell warned.

Tim thoughtfully tied his shoelaces. "Just a small stroll," he said. "This neighborhood isn't dangerous, is it? Would you live here otherwise?"

She had to explain to him the subtle difference between the latent danger on every street in Kingston and the in-your-face threat on some streets of East and South London. But then she decided not to mother him. She had only asked him for help because he was the best in his field. He was here for professional reasons.

But she knew she was not completely honest to herself. She paid for his plane ticket and then offered him the spare room in the flat. All this was not just about catching a serial killer. There was more to it, even if she would not readily admit it. This was mainly about trying to mend things that had gone wrong in the past.

"You're not coming?" he asked.

"I need to read some more reports."

She had read all the reports, and more than once. He knew that.

He got to his feet.

"Stay in the light," she advised. "Stay away from people."

She hadn't wanted to say that.

"No problem," he said.

Once outside, he quickly oriented himself. The street ran from east to west, with some night shops and bars. The side streets were mostly narrow and dark. Occasionally, a car would pass. This was not exactly a lively area. But he could live with that, since he wanted not to attract too much attention to his person.

But he would. Attract attention. A white male would be able to cross Brixton's streets these days, but this was not—as Jennifer had reminded him—Brixton. He would literally be the only white person around, and now he understood how Jennifer felt, day in and day out.

Heavy R&B music came from a bar with red and violet neon signs—a sultry female voice plaintively requesting love. A few boys and girls sitting at tables. Didn't seem threatening. There was laughter and flirting. He stepped inside.

A few glances were directed at him, but most of those present chose to ignore him.

Two young women behind the counter. Clear eyes, white teeth, discreet makeup. He asked for a beer and was served a moist bottle of almost half a liter, with the carelessness as if he came here every day.

The sultry voice came from a professional sound system, which had undoubtedly cost the owner of the business more than the worn-out furniture.

He tried to determine how old the boys and girls were.

Old enough to drink beer. Although he suspected that no strict rules would be enforced here.

The girls at the counter ignored him. One of them was talking to a tall, bald guy wearing a tight T-shirt over his muscular torso, and equally tight jeans.

The owner, probably. Or the bouncer.

As long as he kept to beer, Tim thought, nothing bad would happen.

Why was he here? In this bar? Had he just come in here because he was thirsty?

Did he want to see the underbelly of this society? Had he felt a need to go slumming in the presence of possible addicts, loan sharks, pimps and their girls, maybe pedophiles, and all kinds of human scum he could no longer meet in the United Kingdom since he went all academic?

But this place looked like any half-decent bar he had ever known, no worse than anything in Soho these days.

He drank the beer too quickly and walked out, leaving behind a ridiculously low amount in British pounds.

A bit more down the street, he found another but almost similar bar, with a couple of bald, sturdy men in jeans and thigh shirts standing outside, ogling him. He went in. The beer was more expensive, a spindly, nervous man tapping if it were poison. No bottles here.

Tim longed for an ice-cold Guinness, but that was not on offer. His beer was smooth enough, with a slightly bitter after-taste. Now that the heat was fading, he could appreciate the cold tingle of the brew. All the windows in the bar were open, letting in the evening air. In a country where people seemed to sweat for twenty-four hours, this was welcome, even if the air was heavy with city smells.

Groups of men and women sat spread at tables across the pub. They did their best to be oblivious to his presence. Perhaps they took him for a tourist, deviated from the straight and narrow pathway reserved for foreigners. Or a journalist, a travel writer, an adventurer—looking for local color.

One of the women came up to him.

That wasn't good.

He could do without that sort of attention. A woman who accosted him in a bar only could lead to problems.

The men would immediately drag him outside into an alley and beat him to a pulp for messing with one of their women.

"Seeing you here, Doctor Hesseltine," said the woman. "Not at all what I expected."

Only then did he recognize Sergeant Foote. Who wasn't in uniform, of course. Instead, she wore tight, light gray shorts and a low-cut top.

"You don't recognize me because of the clothes," she said. Smiling, teasing. "This is me, in my spare time."

"I couldn't imagine . . ."

"You drink beer? Why not rum?"

"I don't want to make it too late," said Tim.

"What is the connection between rum and late?" She spoke English with almost no accent. "You need to try the rum in a bar like this." She looked surprised. "O! You feel uncomfortable? It's impressive, so many black faces around you, isn't it. You're from London, right?"

He nodded.

"The Promised Land for many Jamaicans. Although they prefer the United States, as many do. But that destination has become less popular of late. All those stupid rednecks and conservative Christians and Republicans. Too much racism these days. Worse than it ever was."

She nodded at the bartender who placed a glass of rum in front of her. *Wand'rin Star*, by Lee Marvin, was playing on the sound system.

"It disinfects the body. It disinfects the mind. Give him one too, Rick."

Rick returned with a second glass with honey-colored rum. She toasted him, and he drank the glass in one go, as she did.

"There is already gossip about you," she said, rather pleasantly.

"There is?"

"About you and the Gov'. That she brought an old flame here. That'll be you, of course."

"I am not . . ."

"You don't lie well. Not that we mind. Old flames need to be fanned. This is Jamaica. We believe in second chances."

"There is nothing between us anymore."

"All in the past?"

"Yes, all in the past."

Foote smiled. She wasn't being fooled. "Not the way you look at her."

"How do I look at her?"

Foote glanced at Rick, who at once brought two more glasses of rum. "With awe," she said.

"Yes, I assume I do. I respect her. That has not changed."

"Respect. I did not mean that you should bother. The Gov' is not in need of respect. She says she left that in London—the need for respect, I mean. Maybe with you? Oh, it's none of my business, Mr. Hesseltine."

"It's not a big deal," he said.

"What's not a big deal?"

"The misunderstanding. I only come here in my technical capacity. As profiler. At her request."

"We know about her request. And she pays the costs?"

He downed the rum. It burned.

"It's none of my business," she said. "I should not ask."

"No, it isn't," he said.

"Except that I want to protect the Gov'."

"Does she need protection?"

"Not as far as you are concerned. But against . . . other people? Yes, she does."

"Against your bosses?" he asked. "Or against her own people?"

"Everyone."

"She's not that vulnerable, Foote," Tim said. "I think I know."

"Desy," she said. "With an *e*, not *ai*. No flower, although my mother had intended it that way."

She's avoiding my question, he thought. Who was this everyone Foote had—or wanted—to protect her commissioner from?

"Do you think she is out of her depth here?" he wanted to know.

Foote curled her mouth into a smile. "Here in Kingston? Who is not out of his depth here? Me, in this bar, where a lot of people don't want to talk to me because I'm a cop? Or you, for even more obvious reasons?"

He said nothing.

"Ah," said Foote, "what about the both of you there, in London? The boss doesn't want to say anything about London. Not even before you arrived. And we don't ask. What happened in London must stay there."

"One rarely leaves those things behind, Desy, without remorse," said Tim.

"I don't want to ask you what those things are, doctor. Nor do I need to know."

"No?"

"No. It doesn't take much imagination to guess what the Gov' left there. And why she came here."

"And what kind of things are those?"

"Matters of the heart. Where the heart is involved. She wanted to put that behind her. And then she comes here, where there is so much more passion than in cold England. I often think: the Gov' doesn't understand why people keep challenging life when . . . well, you know what I mean."

"No," said Tim. "No, I don't know what you mean. You're not

clear. People challenge life? In what sense? What does that even mean?"

"Guns, AIDS, poor health care, drugs, violence. All those challenges in the life of a police officer. A serial killer who can't be caught fits the bill too, don't you think? All the things our Gov' has to face here now."

"Why would that be a problem?"

She shrugged. "You could call it fatalism. We just call it life. Sounds pretty corny, doesn't it? Like in a movie."

"But people are still worried about a child murderer, I hope? They do care, I hope."

She looked thoughtfully at the empty glass in her hand. "What motivates us?" she asked. She looked up at Tim. "I mean: us, the police officers? What motivates us? It's the hunt. That I tell you. You have no personal business with the animal you hunt—he is not your enemy. He's just a dangerous animal that we have to take off the board. He's a disease we must eradicate. This animal must die, and others like him as well. There's our motivation."

"It has nothing to do with justice."

"Oh no! Nothing at all. It has to do with power. You are superior, and therefore the animal must die, because otherwise the animal wins. And we can't have that if we want this society to survive. That's why we have to catch that murderer."

"Isn't that exactly the sort of motivation that also drives him."

"What you say now?"

"Power," he said. "That's what I mean. He also wants power, in this case over these girls. He hunts as well, and his prey are these girls. He wants to affirm his power over them, and he will never stop because he will never be satisfied with what he has done. It will never be enough."

"Probably," Foote said. "And you? Why are you in this? Why did you come here?"

"Morality," Tim said. "He takes innocent lives, and I cannot allow it. I cannot heal all the world's wounds, can't even try, but if I can end this, if I can stop this man, I might feel . . . healed myself."

Foote nodded calmly, as if he had said something fundamentally decent. "Then we have a chance of finding him," she said. She put the glass on the counter with a few banknotes, nodded to Tim, and walked out.

Dogs barked at the rising sun, without any result. Glass surfaces sweated bulging drops of water. No night was cool, but certainly cooler than the day.

Vassell intently prepared her cup of specialty coffee; her indulgence, her personal addiction.

"In a city of, what, a million people," Tim said, "children and teenagers are disappearing every day."

She made him a cup of Blue Mountain as well. He drank it carefully, black, aware of the special favor. The conversation with Desy Foote was still on his mind. He wasn't going to tell Jennifer about their meeting.

"Sure, they are," she said. "But I don't have the numbers in my head. They can be found if you want them."

"How do you tell them apart?"

"How do we tell what apart?"

"How do you know that this particular killer hasn't kidnapped and killed other girls as well? Previously, I mean. Maybe he made more victims than you realize. Perhaps he is not always satisfied with each of his works of art and made bodies disappear forever. You may not be aware of all his victims."

"You may have a point there, one I already discussed with my team," she said. "But of the children and teenagers who go missing every day in this city, most reappear after a day or two. They pack clothes and toothpaste. They leave a note. The girlfriends knew. They tell people that they wanted to get away. They don't get killed. It is like London, where disturbing disappearances are rather exceptional. You know the standards used for that kind of occurrence."

He nodded over his omelet. "So you will only be informed if a disappearance is alarming—whatever that means in Kingston."

"And when the missing girl is in the right age category."

"Being?"

"Younger than eighteen."

"Unless . . ."

"I know, Tim," she admitted, already tired. After months of long days and feverish nights, she woke up tired in the morning from the day that had yet to come. "I know. But for us, there is a case every time we find a body with specific characteristics. Then it is one of his."

Tim nodded. This is how he would approach the problem as well.

And she had only one thing in mind: she didn't want to go back to Dr. Smith's dissection room for yet another body.

But suppose, she thought, Tim was right. That the murderer's earlier victims, the ones that hadn't been to his liking, the messy stuff, had never been found, and more teenage girls were involved than was generally assumed?

Suppose, at the end of this investigation, if there ever was a conclusion, dozens more victims would have to be added to his gruesome record.

Girls who were now only reported as missing. With family members still hoping they would one day return.

It was not an option she had been willing to consider, but perhaps she had to, now.

This was what she was thinking about while she cleaned up the kitchen and as she drove to the office with Tim. When she got there, she looked through her emails and read the reports from Ross and Thomson. The search for the van was still ongoing.

The famous logo remained meaningless for the time being.

Dead-ends, perhaps.

"How hot does it get here?" Tim asked. He was wearing beige cotton trousers and a thin shirt with the top two buttons open.

"It gets quite hot here. You'd better get used to it. And it's not even summer yet."

"Can I speak to the family members?"

That's how he was: carelessly jumping from one subject to another. "Do you mean the relatives of all the victims? Beginning with the first? I don't think those people want to be reminded of their daughter's fate. They are still trying to come to terms with their loss. I'm sure you, of all people, can understand.

"Denis, was she the most recent victim?"

"You think relatives know something they haven't told us yet?"

"They always know something," said Tim. "They don't always know that they know something important, but often they do."

"We really have done everything . . ."

"I'm convinced you did, Jen," he said. "Absolutely. I don't doubt at all that you wouldn't have done your job properly. But I have a mind as twisted as that murderer of yours. Twisted, but in a different way. You know that."

"And that makes you the most suitable person to approach the family members? I don't think so, Tim."

"Why exactly am I here? Would you mind reminding me?"

She sighed. It was already warm in her office. Maybe there was something wrong with the air conditioning. The air conditioner needed to be checked.

"Good," she said. "But I'm coming along."

"To limit the damage?"

"To learn from you," she said.

This time she drove. She wanted to sit behind the wheel of the Land Cruiser and feel the power of the heavy vehicle. She wanted to show Tim that she could master such a vehicle.

Why am I doing this? Well, why did she do this?

Did she want to prove something to him? Did she still, after all that time, need to prove anything?

No, she had nothing to prove to him. She had left all that behind her in London. They had both left that behind them.

Calm down, girl. That car has too much horsepower. And keep your eyes on the road.

She truly had no desire to reunite with the Denis family. The previous meeting had been very discouraging.

But after several dead girls, she had mostly shed her sensibilities and could handle the families' emotions better. If this goes on long enough, she thought, I will definitely become desensitized. That's what she was afraid of: losing all feelings for the victims. She would no longer be emotionally involved in the case. She would die inside. The search for the murderer would simply become a riddle to solve, one she would no longer be involved in emotionally.

The Denis residence was situated in a quiet neighborhood of small villas and bungalows, like those found on the outskirts of many American cities. In some ways, Kingston was American enough to be mistaken for the real thing. In other respects, it exhibited a mixture of influences from central and west African and Caribbean cultures. Some other parts of the city saw themselves as the true representation of Jamaica, or at least partly how that image was perceived abroad, with exciting rhythms, colorful drinks, and beautiful but potentially dangerous women. This neighborhood, however, told you it wanted to be nothing but middle-class. The people living here just wanted to be Jamaican, without the mostly artificial image the country wanted to project to foreign tourists.

Vassell introduced Tim to the girl's parents, like he merely was a new copper potentially investigating new leads. But he was white, as she was, and as such stood out as much as she did. She knew what father and mother Denis were thinking: two white people who are going to solve things. Who are going to run things here in Kingston, with their white methods and their white ideas.

Tim was not intimidated. He kept smiling, as if he were unaware of the impression he made.

That's how she knew him. He radiated respect. He radiated compassion. His words flowed from his mouth like liquid honey. He wove his net, his very thin but elaborate spider net. And he wove it around both parents. They, nor anything they said, would escape his attention.

Not ten minutes later, Mrs. Denis had made coffee and brought them cookies. Even Mr. Denis, intimidatingly menacing and large, had sat down in the armchair and suddenly seemed much smaller. She was curvy, and so was he, but in a more muscular way. He was also considerably older than her, a grandfather to Marcelline rather than a father.

"What kind of girl was she?" Tim asked. As had been asked often enough before. But the question sounded new and different, coming from him.

He knew what kind of answer he would get. Marcelline had been killed by a perverted murderer, by a monster, and that made her into a saint. No doubt she hadn't been saintly at all, just a teenage girl, but an averse discussion about her personality would be inappropriate.

"No, she didn't have a boyfriend," her mother said to the next question. "She's only fourteen. No, not a boyfriend."

"But she went out sometimes, I assume. A sports club? Some place or other with the rest of the kids?"

"Things other girls of that age do, sir. All at once, they're almost adults, and they think they are all grown up. There is a youth club further down here. Nothing special, a club organized by the municipality. With community workers keeping things tidy. Those kinds of people. Friendly people. Young people can go there in the early evenings and on Saturdays. Keeps them from hanging around in the streets. Nothing special or fancy. Sports, books, games, music, that kind of thing. Marcelline went there occasionally. Girls from her school too."

"And which club is that?" Vassell inquired.

"The Pembroke Club. Nice name, sounds very classy, not?"

"Absolutely." Tim looked at Vassell for a moment. "Did she ever mention who she met there and what they did?" he asked the mother. "The other girls, boys, employees?"

She shrugged. "Hardly. Girl things, sir. Stuff they don't want to share with their parents."

"Neither do my children," said Tim. Who had no children. Who had never been married.

"Aren't they all the same," said Mrs. Denis, who had found a common concern beyond the skin color.

"Only afternoons and weekends?"

"Sometimes there was a party in the evening. Always adults around to look after things. Kids, you know. Cannot always be trusted alone."

"Would there be people around that your daughter has not told you about?"

"Aww, who will say," Mrs. Denis said. "I mean, she might be in love with some older boy or what. Girls, at that age! But it doesn't mean anything. Usually they stay with their own."

"But there was no name she occasionally mentioned?"

"No. Nothing that stood out to me."

"Pictures? Letters perhaps?"

"No. No photos or letters. At her age." Mrs. Denis suddenly went quiet, with the realization her daughter would never grow older.

"Excellent coffee, ma'am," said Tim. He finished his cup. "Truly excellent coffee." It wasn't Blue Mountain, and he assumed these people would not buy such an expensive coffee.

All the while, Marcelline's father had not said a word. At most he nodded when his wife delivered an irrefutable truth.

Outside, near the sun-baked car, Vassell said, "My people have already visited that particular club, Tim. They didn't find anything out of the ordinary. They spoke to all who were present, the people who on occasion work there and such . . ."

"Let's go and look around anyway."

There we go, she thought. She had brought him along; she had no choice but to let him have his way. Maybe he would come up with some new ideas. He looked at things and people differently. And his mind was wired in a freakish way, which occasionally led to unusual conclusions.

The club was a concrete building with steel bars over the windows, a leveled gravel area around it for sports, an outside bar that only served coffee and soft drinks. It had its own generator. The roof had leaked—no exception in Kingston—and had been temporarily repaired with corrugated iron. At the side and back was a well-maintained lawn bordered by shrubs and some trees, providing shade.

"It's nice to have a bit of a garden," Tim commented.

Three young men in worn jeans and over-washed T-shirts hung around the outside bar, each drinking from a bottle of Ting with a straw. Vassell estimated two of them as eighteen, nineteen. The other was a bit older.

The eldest said, after she had identified herself, "What can I do for you, ma'am? The police have already been here. We don't have much to say, I'm afraid. Terrible what happened to Marcelline. We hope you lock that bastard up as soon as possible."

She hoped so too. "Are you the local community workers?"

"I am. These two occasionally work behind the bar."

"And in the garden, I assume," said Tim.

The man looked at him, surprised. "The garden is maintained by other people," he said. "It is specialist work."

"It shows," said Tim pleasantly. "Pretty well maintained, especially that lawn. Someone who comes around on a regular basis?"

Both boys chuckled, as if that were a joke, something between them. "Someone from some company. Does a good job."

Vassell said, "Have there been any problems with the young people? Between themselves? Or with others? From the neighborhood, for example?"

"Once again, something your colleague already wanted to know. Can't say there's never any problems. Boys getting jealous when someone eyes their girl or when someone shows up with a new bike. Better results at school, expensive clothing—all the small things without any significance really. Just what kids do."

"You see people around who clearly don't belong here?"

The young man made an all-encompassing gesture, including the building and the area around it. Down one side stood a row of buildings that were supposed to be used as workspaces, or so Vassell assumed, but now housed families. "This is a working-class neighborhood, and many people live here alongside each other. Who comes and goes? Nobody keeps track. I know quite a few people, but there are others I have no idea who they are. A stranger does not necessarily stand out here, no. But would Marcelline go somewhere with a stranger?"

"And that specific evening? Anything happened, out of the ordinary?"

"She was here that night. She had a drink, chatted with girls, maybe danced to some music."

"And then?"

"And then what?"

"What time did she leave?"

"Around ten, half past ten? We don't know for sure. Went home, we assume. Why would we know?"

"With a murderer who has already claimed several victims, no one pays attention to girls that age?"

"Should we stop breathing? Should we stop dancing? Should we stop eating?"

"No," said Vassell. "No, you should not."

"That answers your question plenty," said the man. "Life goes on. Nothing to do about it. May I offer you something to drink?"

"No," said Vassell, "thank you. We'll have to go."

"The man who takes care of your garden," said Tim, "is he an old man? Someone who still works after retirement?"

"A pensioner? No. I don't think he's that old."

"Can you give us a name and address?"

"I only know his name is Charlie. His boss does not send his bills to us but to the municipality. They owns this business. We are not concerned with anything like that."

"Charlie."

"Yes. He comes here most often. Drinks a lemonade, chats. We know him as Charlie."

"Thank you," said Tim.

They walked back to the Land Cruiser. "Why did you want to know about the gardener?"

"Because of the logo on that van. It might have something to do with plants. Plants grow in gardens. Gardeners work in gardens."

Which seemed logical enough. "Okay. So what? There are plenty of gardeners in this city."

"Gardeners don't stand out. They are there, and then they are not there. Nobody pays attention to them. They are like postmen. They see everything, they observe everything, and everyone takes their presence for granted."

"So we are looking for a gardener named Charlie who drives a van."

"That would be a good start," said Tim. "You would like to eliminate him from your investigation, if possible."

She called Porters. "Sergeant, find out which company the city billing department pays for the gardening around the Pembroke Club."

"I will, Gov," Porters said.


Division head Yalom had a lot of things on his mind concerning the state of affairs in Kingston. What it came down to was that he seriously doubted the professional seriousness of the three kidon.

After the most recent events, would he ever send them after an Iraqi spy or an Israeli who wanted to betray state secrets? Would he ever trust them with an execution?

No, he wouldn't. If they weren't even able to recover an item that was in the hands of an undoubtedly scared woman living without resources somewhere in Kingston. White, at that. Standing out like a rabbit in a barren field.

"We strongly assume we have her former husband under observation," Kerem said over the secure connection. "We traced her movements from Brussels to here; she disappeared, but we're almost certain we've found the right man. We don't know yet where the woman herself is, but this man Mason and the woman have a child together, so they'll probably meet up at some point."

"What is this? A romance novel? A weekend movie on television? This is fucking serious, Kerem. I just spoke to two ministers and three senior IDF officers, all in the Prime Minister's lounge. Yes, the Prime Minister himself. And they want that data card back, and they want it now. The information it contains . . . Well, you don't have to worry about the information. Get the bloody card."

"It won't be long, Sir," Kerem said.

"Even that's too long, Kerem. What are you actually waiting for? I want action right now. His daughter is involved? Have you seen her yet?"

"Not yet."

"When you see her, remember this: parents will do anything for the safety of their children."

"Yes, Sir."

"You have no children of your own, Kerem. So you don't understand those emotions. But I will tell you this: parents will do anything to keep their children safe."

"I understand."

"Good. I don't need to say more. Israel needs you. Under no circumstances may the information on the data card fall into the wrong hands. That is the bottom line of this affair."

"I'll keep that in mind all the time, Sir."

That was it. The phone went silent.

I hope, thought Kerem, that no one intercepts this message. Not the Americans, not some Arab group, not the Russians, not even the British or the French.

He walked to the back of the house from where Erez and Chayat were observing the street.

They had been here for some time now. They took turns. The one who was on a break went back to the hotel, the other two observed.

"Yalom is very impatient now," he said.

The other two did not look at him.

"Is he sending replacements?" Erez asked.

"He didn't talk about replacements."

"So we're still on the job."

"So it seems. Actually, he didn't say anything new. Only that ministers and generals are pushing him to the limit."

"A sight I wouldn't want to miss," said Erez. Who wasn't good friends with the division head.

"Oho!" Chayat said. Something seemed to be happening outside.

"What?"

"If that's Terrence Mason . . ."

The other two carefully looked through the holes and slits in the fence in front of the windows.

"Then that is. . . ?"

"That girl in uniform? His daughter?" Chayat concluded.

"Right on time," said Kerem.

"It's his daughter for sure."

"And what do we do now?"

"Now we follow them. And they will lead us straight to Anna Weiss."

<h1 style="text-align:center">6</h1>

"A real sight," Erez said as they left their shelter and followed Terrence and the girl.

Neither male kidon responded. They had other things on their minds than the sight of Terrence Mason and the girl who was most likely his daughter.

Kerem in particular was writing a number of possible strategies in his head. Kidnapping and an exchange for the card, or entering the flat where the mother lived. Everything was still possible for the time being. But not everything was equally safe or easy to implement.

The hardest part was going unnoticed on the street.

A little later they walked, separately and some distance apart, behind Terrence and the girl.

They inevitably got curious looks from local residents, even if they weren't the only whites or people of indeterminate race in the area.

But social control was probably strong here.

Luckily, they didn't have far to go.

Erez walked purposefully past the house where Terrence Mason and the girl entered. At the next street corner, she bought a newspaper and started reading, keeping an eye out on the house. Her position was not optimal, but under the circumstances she could not do better. On this street, it was even impossible to observe from inside a vehicle.

Kerem sat on a terrace and ordered a coffee, which turned out to be extra strong.

Chayat, who had the least experience in this sort of operation, leaned against a facade a bit more down the street and watched boys playing football, as if he were scouting for the next Barcelona star player.

All three were aware that their situation was far from optimal.

The house Terrence Mason and the girl had entered had three floors and apparently the same number of apartments. Not big, not exactly in good condition, not exactly a desirable piece of real estate.

But if Anna Weiss lived here, the kidon wouldn't care in what dump she had found shelter. They had located her. And probably the card too.

If she had lived in a rich neighborhood, on the other hand, observing the flat would be difficult. Because rich neighborhoods in countries like these—and in Israel as well—would be guarded by security officers with guns and dogs.

Kerem looked up from his coffee. A woman stood at the window on the first floor. He had the picture of Anna in mind.

Yes, this was Anna Weiss.

The woman they were looking for.

The woman who would presently hand them the data card.

If she still had it in her possession.

Suppose, he thought, she had thrown the damn thing away. Or sold it. Or . . .

No, she would not have sold it. Unless she had somehow magically come into contact with the Syrians. Or some other interested party.

His cell phone buzzed.

"Did you see her at the window?" Chayat inquired.

Kerem looked at the young officer from a distance. He played his part well, ostensibly having a chat with a girlfriend over the phone, smiling at something she said.

"It's her," said Kerem.

"And now? What's next?"

"We wait. At some point she will leave the flat."

"What do we do then?"

"I do not know yet."

Chayat rang off.

He was probably frustrated.

He wanted to take action.

Kerem fully understood. He wanted action too. They had been waiting for too long.

From the other corner, further away, Erez glanced in his direction. She didn't call. She knew nothing was going to happen right now.

She was a predator. She was a patient but dangerous predator. Kerem had heard about the operations she had participated in. He had heard the rumors. She had used a gun when needed but handled a knife with equal ease.

And he appreciated that about her. She wasn't picky, and she wasn't averse to killing and lacked remorse. He could rely on her, but the boy was a different story. He was the unknown factor.

He called Chayat.

"We're going back to our shelter," he said.

Then he looked in Erez's direction and beckoned her with a short movement of his head.

A little later, they found themselves back in the building opposite Terrence Mason's house and workshop.

"Let's review our options," he said.

"Oh," said Erez. "As if there's a lot to choose from."

"The main problem is that we are on potentially hostile ground."

"Oh, we clearly are," Erez said, stretching. "Did you see those washerwomen? Their asses are three times as big as mine. What you call dangerous ground."

"But you would run faster than them," said Chayat.

"Children," said Kerem. "Please pay attention. Next step? Do we search the apartment?"

"Suppose," said Erez, "that Weiss woman isn't even aware she has that data card in her possession."

"She fled Brussels with her daughter, and not because she herself was in danger. Or so I assume. The briefcase in which the data card was transported was left behind, empty. The terrorists don't have the card; otherwise, they would not go after her. Therefore, it must be in her possession. Maybe the Russian told her what the thing is worth."

"And she hides it somewhere in her flat," Chayat deduced.

"Seems logical. Unless she deposited it in a bank safe, but seen her social position, it seems unlikely she could get a safe."

"So the apartment it is."

"It's our main option. But we can't just walk in there, burglarize the place, whatever, since we would probably be spotted by the neighborhood. First, we must find out Weiss's habits. Does she have a job, and where? Or is she always in or around the flat?"

"All that will again take time . . ."

"It will," Kerem said. "We don't have much time, we can't afford to hang around here too long. Maybe we need to move faster."

"Let's kidnap her," Chayat proposed. "We force her to reveal the location of the card, possibly using the child as leverage, and then we proceed to escape." And he added, "And not a minute too soon."

"Mmm, that might be a suitable option," Kerem said.

"But that man Mason seems to hang around here a bit too much," Erez said. "He's a liability."

"Not really," Kerem said. "He's mostly in his workshop or he's away all day. Nevertheless, a kidnapping comes with considerable risks. She probably will resist, put up a fight, and we might lose control over the situation. I want to be sure we're in no way at a disadvantage."

"She has a daughter," Chayat said.

"And?"

"We kidnap her."

"The daughter?"

"Yes."

"And we exchange her for the data card?" Kerem asked.

"Of course."

"Dangerous, again," said Erez. "With all these girls disappearing and being murdered . . . Weiss might call in the police before we can convince her otherwise. And if we get caught, we might risk not only the police but the crowds as well. You heard about suspects getting lynched?"

"Weiss won't call the police if we get in touch with her before she even knows her daughter is kidnapped," Chayat said. "We keep full control over the operation. We can do it on the way to school, in the morning. How old is she? Twelve? Thirteen? We can more easily deal with a child than with an adult."

"What you think, Kerem?" Erez inquired.

"I am against," Kerem said. "We are Israeli, we are kidon. We fight terrorists and foreign agents, but we don't kidnap children. That's a bridge too far."

"But we . . ." Chayat objected.

"We continue our observation for the time being," Kerem said. "We wait for the right opportunity to act. Kidnapping children is out of the question."

* * *

"I want you," Vassell ordered her staff, "to go through all the conversations with family members, friends, school staff, people working in those clubs—and look for anybody mentioning a van, a gardener, a company that worked on the gardens of any place connected to all the missing girls, things like that."

"You have no idea . . ." Ross began.

"Yes, I actually do. I have a very good idea of what that means in terms of work."

"What do we do with the officers out there? Do we call them in?"

"Give them all a desk and a chair. And a pile of files. Get it done."

"Could we not," Thomson suggested, "approach all those relatives again and ask if they remember a gardener, or whatever? Would that not be more efficient?"

Vassell sighed. "You might be right. However, I'm unsure if it would be a wise decision. I don't want to stir things up, which will happen if we start making new visits."

Tim, standing in the corner of the incident room, made a face.

"What do you think, Dr. Hesseltine?" she inquired.

"Terribly bad idea indeed, in my opinion as well. Can ruin your reputation, as a force, I mean. You have already seen these people, extensively interrogated them, and now you're returning for what they would see as a minor detail?"

Thomson shook his head. "With all due respect, doctor, but my people prefer working in the field and not in an office. They prefer seeing victims and family and potential suspects eye to eye. Delving through stacks of files looking for words and phrases—nothing for them."

There you had it, Vassell thought. The old way of doing things they couldn't get rid of.

"But if you tour the relatives with specific questions, the press might pick it up, and your murderer might be warned you're on to him," Tim argued. "And that's a risk you can't take."

"Let that bastard worry," said one of the other detectives from the back of the room.

There was general agreement.

She couldn't compete with that. Or she didn't want to. It was a matter of choice and trust. She wanted to run the department the way she saw fit, but occasionally she simply had to trust the instincts of her detectives, even against her better judgement. And when these detectives were not inclined to give their all seated behind a desk and behind a stack of files, she would not get the best possible results out of them, period. That's what she had to deal with.

Tim, of course, would have another opinion, but then he was not the commanding officer in this case.

She was not going to win this argument, that's for sure.

"All right," she said. "Thomson, Ross, give your people the necessary instructions for these extra interviews. But proceed with discretion. I want a first report this evening."

Both team leaders took out their phones and started calling right away.

Porters handed Vassell a few sheets of paper. "List of all gardening businesses in the city," he said. "I don't have a list of employees per company yet. All of them probably are small businesses, so they'll work with just a few people, depending on the season."

"And probably few of them are officially employed," Vassell said.

"Most probably."

"Well, there we are, then."

"We only have a first name to go by," said the sergeant. "And the sign on the van, more or less. That's not really much."

"Better than nothing. Charlie. Or Charles. I wonder how many people in Kingston go by that name. Well, carry on."

Porters nodded.

In her office, a bit later, Vassell admitted to Tim: "This is not at all going as planned. And we are losing too much time. I said I didn't want a ninth victim, now it seems we're anticipating number ten and still are unable to do anything about it."

"At least now you may have a few clues," he said. "Some more than a few days ago."

That had been thanks to him, something she was willing to admit. But they should have discovered the gardener earlier on. But then again, a gardener? Who notices a gardener? And was he of any importance, or were they barking up the wrong tree?

The phone on her desk made an ominous sound.

Foote, whispering urgently. "Gov', the big boss is on his way to your office." She probably called from downstairs in the hall.

"Big boss?" Vassell asked.

"Chief Vandermeer himself. Like an approaching storm. Something very wrong."

"Okay, thanks, Foote."

She hung up the phone.

"More problems?" Tim asked.

"We'll see about that in a moment."

Chief Vandermeer barged in without knocking. Vassell hadn't expected anything else. He wasn't often around, but when he was, he always made his presence very noticeable.

"Commissioner Vassell," he began. Then he saw Tim. "And this is the man from London?" He made no move to shake Tim's hand.

Neither did Tim.

"Professor Hesseltine," said Vassell.

"I know who he is now," Vandermeer said.

He didn't sit down.

"What's with that gardener?" he asked.

No time for uplifting chats with the team. No time for an update. No time for encouragement. The Chief didn't believe in any of that. He needed results, which he was not getting.

"We may have a possible suspect," Vassell carefully said. And the way she said it implied: I don't want to talk about it yet. I'm not going to spout my damn theories here, knowing you'll shoot them down.

She had never given Vandermeer too many details about the investigation, and then only on a strict need-to-know basis. He knew that. He had kept his distance, seemingly trusting Vassell. But now here he stood, and he wanted to know. Why? She wondered what had set him into motion. Of course, a number of people wanted him and the whole team to show results. He was the man responsible for the investigation. The mayor, the minister of the interior, the director general of the police, and of course the press were hot on his tail, day in and day out, for months now.

So finally, he had enough, and here he was.

"Is there, as of this moment, a real chance of a breakthrough?" he asked. "Concerning the gardener?"

"Yes," she said. Simply because she had no other choice. Otherwise, he might very well have shut down the whole operation and have another team start all over again. That option had been in the works for a couple of weeks now.

"Do you have a name? Do you have a positive identification?"

"We have a name and some supporting elements, Chief," she said, more or less truthful. "My people are now looking for similarities in all murders. If we can link at least a few of them to the person we have in mind, then we will finally make some real progress. It then comes down to finding the man."

"Mmm," he said. "Pretty vague, it seems to me." He turned to Tim. "What do you think, professor? As a specialist? Doesn't this seem a bit vague to you?"

"I'm a psychiatrist," said Tim. "I don't deal with police procedures." Hell no, he thought. I'm not going to get involved in your infighting.

"Well, that's nice for you then," said Vandermeer. He didn't seem to be enjoying himself.

He turned back to Vassell. "And the name?"

"We know his name is Charlie."

"Charlie? A gardener named Charlie! Are you serious, commissioner?"

"He is the one single factor that may link the murders."

"So you're looking for some guy named Charlie."

"Yes, we are. We know where he works as a gardener. It will take us a while before we know more details and identify him, but we will get there."

"Mmm," said Vandermeer. He made a decision. "All right, Commissioner. Go ahead. But I am following you very closely on this. More than ever."

Without further ado, he turned around and stepped out of the office.

Tim looked at her.

Vassell picked up the phone and called Porters.

"Have you found out who the Pembroke Club invoices are paid to?"

"Just a moment, Gov," Porters said. "I just received an email. Ah. Yes, they have a name and an address."

"Send me that email."

"Coming."

She looked at the screen of her computer. The machine said *Bling*. Tim came to stand next to her. An invoice. From a gardening business that provided labor and supplied plants. The name of a company. Address. Phone number. Logo. A familiar logo.

"That's him," said Tim. "God damn it, we finally got him."

"No," said Tim. "That's not your killer."

She sighed. "Finally a good clue, Tim! This is our man!"

Tim shook his head. "A serial killer of this caliber who turns out to be a gardener? I do not think so."

"What's wrong with gardeners?"

"Nothing. Hardworking people. Specialists in their field. Not a bad word about them. But they are rarely, if ever, serial killers. Or at least successful serial killers."

"You don't know that, Tim. The most successful serial killers are never caught. So there might as well be gardeners among them."

"That's right. I mean, I gave you the profile of the killer. I don't think this man fits in with that profile."

She got up. "We are certainly going to visit that company. And I will bring armed assistance."

Lucy found all that math a mighty and fascinating maze. But still a maze. She hoped to find her way in it one day. The current combination at school was the problem: English and that mathematical maze. Numbers are numbers, but getting the explanation in a language you don't really speak well enough is an extra challenge.

Luckily for her, school was almost over.

Exams were coming. Which she would not pass.

The other students were excited about the exams. There was even some panic among them. More than ever, heads were bent over books and notes. More than ever, there were whispers about serious matters, such as conjugations, integrals, and the names of world capitals.

There was nothing wrong with her. She would only take the exams for form's sake, but she did not expect any positive results.

That wasn't the intention either. The headteacher of the school had discussed this with her mother. The woman had said we are preparing her for next year. By then she will have learned enough English.

Her mother was supposed to speak only English with her, even under the most everyday circumstances. And that's what Anna did. As best she could.

As such, school was not much of a concern with Lucy. She paid attention, made her homework, tried to learn her lessons, made fun with the other girls—but she was not under any pressure. She knew the others were a bit jealous, but on the other hand, she would not be in their class again next year. She would be with girls a year her junior. She would probably have less fun than with this lot.

Anyway, even with all these problems, school was more fun here in Kingston than it had ever been in Brussels. People in Brussels hadn't been able to enjoy themselves and generally took things too seriously.

She was eating a sandwich in the canteen now, during recess. She could eat local food from the kitchen, prepared by the school cook, but it was usually too spicy for her taste. She still had to get used to the temperamental Jamaican cuisine. But she would adapt. And secretly she hoped her mother would choose to stay here, never to return to Brussels.

In the afternoon, at about half past four, schooldays ended.

The older girls rarely went home straight away. Anna heard them talking about kidnappings and murders, but that only happened to other girls and would never happen to them, so they continued to go to the gym, the club, whatever, as they always did. Music, boys, the occasional cigarette, or maybe some ganja. Life was not too complicated.

The older girls didn't want her to tag along, considering her immature—and of course she was not yet one of them. You're too young for cigarettes and boys, they told her. She would follow them anyway. But not now.

Charlie was already waiting for her at the school gate with his van. He had been stowing away some of his stuff he had used for gardening. "Are you coming along, gyal?" he inquired. "Going home?" She wondered about his hands: clean, as if he had washed them after finishing his work. Of course he would. And he would wear gloves too.

She grinned. "The girls gossip about us. You and me."

"I'm too old for you," he said, also with a grin. His face black, his teeth white. "A grown-up man. Not your lover, gyal. I can be your grandfather." He smelled of fresh earth, mushrooms, grass, sun.

"I want to go for a walk this time," she proposed.

"Aww. It's very hot. Better that you stay out of the sun. You are too white. You better not walk too much in the sun. Not without suitable protection. You have nice skin, keep it that way. Boys will love your skin. Not much like that around here."

She had no hat, no cap. Her arms were bare.

"I'm not white," she said.

"No, you're coffee and milk," he smiled. "But still—the sun. If you are not protected by your dark skin, like the people here. . . ."

"Oh, okay," she said, and climbed into the van.

"I have to make yet a detour for an errand," he said, from behind the wheel. "But then I'll take you to your mother."

As long as she was out of the sun.

* * *

Terrence walked down the street leisurely. He did that deliberately. He wanted to know if the man was following him.

He didn't know who the man was. But he had seen him before. Once, maybe twice. The man who seemed interested in good old Terrence.

The man didn't belong in the neighborhood. He was clearly not a tourist either, he didn't do any shopping, didn't visit the clubs or bars, seemed to have no business at all in the vicinity. And that made him a suspect.

Terrence was sure the man was here because of him. Or Anna.

Was he one of those Arabs Anna had warned him for? He looked like an Arab, but it was difficult to tell. The man might be Middle Eastern, perhaps. So maybe he was one of them chasing Anna and the data card.

The man might actually be the solution to Anna's problems. She could approach him, hand him over the card, and that would be the end of it. It seemed even like the most logical thing to do.

Except Terrence didn't know what the man really wanted. If he and the organization he worked for did not want to leave any traces or witnesses, then Anna's life was in danger. And Lucy's. And his. And Tabita. Even if they returned the data card.

He didn't want to take that risk.

So he wouldn't advise Anna to just give the thing from the locket to the suspicious man.

Then what?

The man was young. Thirty, Terrence guessed. Neatly dressed in beige slacks and a dark blue polo shirt, an expensive jacket, and leather shoes. Neat shoes, bought in a decent store. Another reason why he was out of place in this neighborhood.

Anyway, there he was, that man. He was just walking around, as if he had every right to do.

I can handle that man, Terrence thought.

But the man would not be alone. Terrence was sure the man would have company. So he had to be careful.

Meanwhile, Anna's hiding place was known to these people, whomever they were. Nothing could be done about that. He could find her another place to stay, but that would only temporarily solve the problem. He himself could not go into hiding. And he wasn't planning to.

He also assumed these people by now would know where Anna worked. And perhaps where Lucy went to school. Both could not leave work and school behind and hide somewhere else. Anna was at work, Lucy at school. He couldn't protect them both at the same time. That bothered him.

If they knew all that, why weren't these people attempting anything? They could probably break into Anna's house with ease, maybe kill her, and take the card. What stopped them? What hadn't happened yet could happen at any moment. So Terrence understood he had to act at once.

He walked in on Kearns, a man who lived down the street. He too had a workshop, where he repaired household appliances. The man did good business in this neighborhood. On occasion, he also sold illegal stuff.

"Jimmie," Terrence said, when he saw Kearns behind a damaged washing machine that would become an intact and functional washing machine again within hours. "I need a gun."

"Well," said Kearns, a rugged man in his forties with a pointy beard. "You surely don't beat around the bush. Fi wa? I thought you had a gun at home? Do you need another gun?"

"I have a rifle. But I can't take that with me on the street."

"Ah, see what you mean. You want to solve problems on the street."

"Hopefully not. But you never know. Be prepared and all that."

"Mmm," said Kearns. "Do you want small? Do you want semi-auto?"

"Must fit under my clothes. Semi-auto would do. But not one of those lady things."

"Then I have something for you," said Kearns. "Come in the back . . ."

"And some ammo . . . Come, mon! Mi deh pon has'e."

"Anything good old Kearns can provide and you can afford, Terrence," the man said, smiling.

Kearns grabbed a key from his belt and opened a steel locker in the back of his shop. He took out two cardboard boxes. Inside were several weapons, each neatly wrapped in oily cloth.

"You don't want a revolver," he said. "Believe me. Here, a little Glock. Nothing better than Glock. Always buy European. Those Americans can't make good pistols. Buy German or Austrian. Those Krauts know how to make weapons. Our boys found out during the war."

"Our boys?"

"The Americans, Terrence. The Americans. The good guys."

"There's some problems in your head, my man."

"Are you buying a gun or what?"

"This one. How much?"

"Three hundred. The real stuff, hardly used. Good money worth. A bargain for that price. Untraceable too. Look, number filed off. And a box of cartridges included. Yu waan some? You can defend yourself with that, dude. No one screws around with you in this town anymore."

"Except Tabita."

"Ahaha, except Tabita. Where's your money? In your stocking? Well, man. First place they look. You have to put your money in your underpants. Men don't like looking there. Ahaha."

"Three hundred?"

"Yup."

Terrence walked back to Anna's apartment. He was expecting her shortly.

She had left early that morning, so she would be back on time.

Tabita. He should have an explanation for Tabita concerning the gun. Anna being threatened—she wouldn't accept that, Tabita, but she would have no choice.

You should be with me, Terrence, Tabita would say. I am also threatened. Every day. By men in the hospital. Visitors. Doctors. Salespeople. Cleaners. And then you're not there. These foul-mouthed men wanting me for my body.

The man who followed him earlier was no longer around. Had like vanished.

He looked at his watch.

Was Anna really late? Was she later than usual?

God, he would never forgive himself if something happened to Anna.

And Lucy? He was responsible for her too.

Tabita would say: They came here voluntarily, Terrence. Out of their own free will. It's not your fault something happening to them. Not you responsible. You have nothing to do with their stuff. Doan come sheg rohn mi, my man! You're not fooling me! You have to take care of Tabita, and Tabita alone. And for the child. Good, the child too. But the white woman? She can take care of her meager batty herself. Yes, her skinny ass! God damn sure. Do you love her? Eh? Nuh lie! Don't tell me lies!

But he wasn't thinking of Tabita.

He was thinking about Lucy.

And Anna's skinny ass.

Vassell should have worn her uniform, she suddenly realized, because having a white woman as commanding officer for an armed intervention team was still somehow unusual for the police officers involved, all the more since they were not members of her own team. The eight men in bulletproof vests and kevlar helmets, armed with submachine guns and a few shotguns, were led by a lieutenant, but the operation itself was her responsibility.

She had no need for so many armed men, not even when raiding the place where a dangerous murderer could be found. She had six detectives with her, each armed with a pistol, and in her opinion this would have been enough.

But somehow sergeant Foote had found it necessary to find a complete SWAT unit, now ready for action. They had come in two black vans, like in some American movie.

They stood opposite a flat concrete building with a black roof and wide windows. On the right, five vans and a larger truck, all green with the now familiar logo: a circle, a stem, a leaf. A high steel fence surrounded the compound.

The gate in the fence was open.

No one was present on the premises.

Damn, she thought. It's just way too quiet here.

"We're going in," she said.

The detectives, equipped with radios, guarded the back and side streets. She, Ross, and Porters entered the site through the gate, followed by five of the armed officers.

Just like in a movie. With a real show of power. Boots and city shoes crunching on gravel. Rattling of metal equipment. Smell of oil in the hot air.

They entered the building.

The receptionist, a young woman in a colorful T-shirt and denim skirt, was shocked by this sudden invasion.

Vassell displayed her badge. "There's a gardener named Charlie who works here," she said.

The young woman didn't know what to do. She couldn't get a word out.

"Calm down," said Vassell, who felt anything but calm herself. "We just need to see this Charlie. Where is he?"

"He's not back yet," stammered the young woman. "Would you like to talk to the manager? I can get you the manager . . ."

Vassell, who at once understood what was happening, ordered the troops to withdraw and leave the immediate vicinity of the building.

Damn it, she thought, we've done something stupid. We went in too early. We should have waited till we had spotted him. Now Charlie would see them first. And he'd do a runner.

"He's not here yet," Ross said on the radio. "Everyone falls back to the previous position."

At once the troops disappeared from the hall and from the compound. Only Vassell and Porters remained in the entrance hall.

"Can you reach him?" Porters asked the young woman. "Does he have a radio in his van?"

"No, we don't use . . ."

A fat man, around sixty, came out of an office, sweating despite the air conditioning. The yellow palm tree motif on his tie cheerfully contrasted with his green shirt. "Melissa! What the hell is going on here? And who are you?"

Vassell again showed her badge. "We are looking for one of your employees, sir. His name is Charlie . . ."

"What has he done? There's nothing wrong with Charlie, is there?"

"We just want to ask him some questions, that's all."

"Ah!" the man said. "With those goons from your SWAT team outside? No, me not believe you, lady. Don't know what you're up to, but Charlie he not the man you looking for, whatever it is. Nothing going with him . . ."

"We want to speak with him in the context of an ongoing investigation," Vassell said. She knew she was going to lose her patience with this man.

"It must be quite some big reason you want to speak to him, you are. What he suspected of, eh?"

"I am not at liberty to discuss this matter with you, sir. I must ask you to share any information concerning Charlie with us . . . Like: when does he come in from his job?"

"Whenever he feels like it. My people work hard, lady. There's no way I'm going to chase their butts to check on them. As long as the work is done . . ."

"Yes, sir, I understand. And we have a job to do as well. We will be waiting for Charlie right here."

"This is bad for our reputation. . . !"

"That cannot be helped," Vassell said, without any remorse.

The man wanted to go back to his office.

"Porters," Vassell ordered.

"Gov'?"

"Stay with that gentleman and make sure he doesn't call anyone."

The owner seemed ready to explode, looked at Porters, and then walked back into his office, leaving the door open.

I need Tim, Vassell thought.

But taking him along for a raid was something she hadn't wanted to risk.

He was and remained a citizen after all.

Her first concern now was Charlie.

She hoped it would show up right away.

* * *

Charlie said into the phone, "Understood, sir," and finished the call.

Even Lucy knew you weren't supposed to drive and talk on the phone at the same time. But here in Kingston, no one seemed to care.

Hence the many accidents, her mother said. People were careless when driving. Careless with their own lives, but with those of others as well.

Terrence, for his part, had no problem with this sort of lax attitude. You didn't use your two hands while phoning, did you? Well? What difference did it make? Everyone did it, driving and phoning. All those stupid rules imported from the States or Europe, only to make life difficult! People did need none of those in Jamaica.

Charlie slowed down.

Lucy noticed he was making quite a bit of a detour. And he hadn't stopped anywhere yet.

But he had promised to take her home. And because he was Dad's friend, she believed him.

He was a nice man. All teeth and smiles. He was just *Charlie*.

He seemed a little out of sorts because of the call he just received. Maybe bad news. Someone in the family who was ill. Someone died. Sir, he had said. He had spoken with respect, in English. Different from the Charlie she knew. Well, she didn't really know Charlie, but he hadn't spoken Patois.

Charlie suddenly seemed a little different than before.

Because of that phone call.

"It's still a bit of a drive, girl," he said. Focus on the road.

"Where to?"

"Oh, you'll see, you'll see."

"Aren't you taking me home?"

"Yes, yes, but I told you—just a quick detour to arrange something. No problem."

With some difficulty, the van climbed a hill. Charlie was hunched against the steering wheel, tense. It seemed to Lucy he was going somewhere he'd rather not go.

Why the detour, she thought. He could also have dropped me off at home first.

At home.

That's how she thought about the apartment now. The new home, perhaps indefinitely.

However, they weren't going there now.

"Charlie?"

"Yes?"

"Have you known my daddy long?"

"For a while."

His hands were firmly on the steering wheel.

"Has he known Tabita long?"

"For a while now," said Charlie, his mind seemingly elsewhere.

"Oh," said Lucy.

He looked at her for a moment. "He's with Tabita now, girl. They are a couple. You and your mother will have to make do with that."

Behind a bend loomed a park with a villa.

"He's not coming," Porters said, angrily. "He knows something is wrong." He was upset, as if it were all Vassell's fault, and he had predicted this would go wrong. As it currently did. "He's seen us, or someone warned him."

"We have his home address," said Ross. "I'll send some people there right away."

"Signal the van," said Vassell.

"I already did," said Porters.

The armed intervention team had withdrawn and was now waiting for further instructions. The detectives smoked a cigarette and drank a can of Coke or Ting. They seemed relaxed. They weren't. They just didn't show it. After all, they were the elite of the JCF. And thus the best of the best in Kingston when it came to crime fighting.

A car drove up where Vassell and some investigators were standing. It was Foote with one of the Land Rovers. She had Tim with her. Foote frowned from behind the wheel. Not her idea—bringing this passenger.

"He didn't want to stay in the office," she said. She probably wanted to say: he's your problem, Gov', and I don't want to intervene in whatever relationship you're having.

"You've not arrested him," Tim concluded.

Vassell shook her head. "We haven't. Yet. We are looking everywhere for him. He doesn't get far."

"In this town . . ." said Ross. But he left it at that. They all knew that a black man in this town could disappear instantly and never be found again. But that might put an end to Charlie's criminal activities.

Maybe.

Or he went somewhere else and started all over.

"Break down the door to his apartment," Vassell said into the radio. "Turn everything upside down. I want to know where he is going with the victims. I want to know about his hideouts." She had no authorization to do so, but Charlie would be in no position to make a fuss about something like police brutality or an unlawful search. Unless he got himself a good lawyer.

"We still don't know it's him," Foote warned her.

"He's part of this, at the very least," Ross said.

A detective questioned Charlie's few co-workers who were present, especially the boss. Who still made a nuisance of himself.

"They know Charlie as an unremarkable employee," the detective said. "They have nothing bad to say about him. But in the end, they don't know anything much about him either."

"The van," said Tim, "was he the only one using it?"

"Yes, they all have their own vehicle in which they store their tools. Sometimes they also use them privately."

"A perfect cover," said Ross. He put a piece of gum in his mouth.

"Nobody pays attention to the gardener," said Tim. "Still, I just don't think it's him."

"You told us so before. But why?"

"I have another scenario for you. Let us assume Charlie only takes care of the kidnappings and the transportation. . . ."

"All right, let's assume . . ."

"We have so far assumed that the kidnapper and the murderer are one and the same person."

Vassell said nothing.

"Because it is common knowledge that serial killers are loners. Their inflated egos prevent them from having a partner in crime."

"But not in this case?"

"No," Tim said. "Here we have a kidnapper—your gardener, Charlie—who is in charge of supplying the children. He chooses them to certain specifications, kidnaps them, and delivers them to an agreed location. And then, afterwards, he arranges for the bodies to be left somewhere in the city."

Vassell said nothing.

"Which means he is in the service of the real murderer. Not that he's innocent—far from. He kidnaps children, knowing they will be tortured and killed. The question we have to ask ourselves is: how does the man deal with that? And why does he do it?"

"Because he too a monster?"

"Maybe he is. Yes, he is a monster in some way. However, it's worse than that: he is in the service of someone who is even more of a monster than he is. He is not just a slave to his own passions. He is also the slave to the passions of another monster."

"That's your hypothesis."

"It is merely a hypothesis, at least for now. This is the best idea I have. And it is provisional, of course. I might still be proven wrong."

"Oh," said Vassell, "to me it sounds like a plausible enough scenario. But there's this: we now are looking for two people, one of them being Charlie. Who's the other?"

Anna came to Terrence's door, looking worried. "Have you seen Lucy this afternoon?"

Terrence shook his head. "Not recently. Why? Isn't she home yet?"

"No, of course not; otherwise, I wouldn't be here."

"When are you expecting her?"

Anna took a deep breath. "Half an hour ago."

"Well," said Terrence, "half an hour doesn't mean anything. She might have gone off with some of the girls. Nothing to worry about."

"She never does that. She would let me know if she'd be late."

"Well, that's kids for you. Suddenly, they do something out of the blue."

"She would not. Not in this city."

Tabita joined them.

"It doesn't feel right, Terrence," Anna continued. "I know it's only half an hour, but we should go look for her."

"School isn't far," Tabita said, glancing at Terrence, implying that he should go look for her, because Anna deemed it important.

"You stay near the apartment," Terrence suggested to Anna. "If Lucy comes back, call us." He understood Tabita was now on Anna's side, and he should not go against both of them.

"Shouldn't we call the police?" Anna wanted to know.

"They can't be bothered with a teenager who is half an hour late," he said. "Even not with what's been going on. Teenagers are always late. Half an hour means nothing."

"Just a minute," he said, and walked inside. Coming out again, he had tucked his new gun under his waistband, where Anna would not see it. Then they walked towards the school.

"Lots of rubbish in that flat of him," Ross said after listening to the radio. "No women ever been there to clean up; that's what they tell me. Do you want to see it for yourself?"

"I do," said Vassell. She looked at Tim. "Yeah, I'd like to see the place."

"I'm coming as well," Tim said. It wasn't far: the flat was situated in the infamous Trench Town suburb.

Foote drove, with Ross in the passenger seat and Vassell and Tim at the back. Foote had switched the sirens on. Why not? Charlie probably knew by now that he was wanted by the police and that his apartment was no longer safe for him.

One of the detectives had called in forensics: three of their people dressed in white bunny suits searched the apartment and took samples of everything that looked like human residuals. Charlie's place was not large: two dusky rooms and a bathroom, with sanitary facilities that could kindly be described as Victorian. An odor of spices hung everywhere, unsuccessfully trying to cover up the smell of unwashed clothes.

"It will take some time before we can start working with the DNA here, seen as this place is dirty," said the man in charge of the trio, "so don't expect results right away, Chief."

"No preliminary conclusions?" Vassell asked.

She looked around and thought, I don't want to end up in a dump like that. London would be better in any respect. Even the worst of London.

"It doesn't look like anyone was murdered here," the man said. "The flat is cluttered with his things and is not exactly clean, but we have not found any blood yet. Maybe he's very cautious. But torturing people, with those thin walls? No way."

"The torturing and killing do not happen here," said Tim. "Not in the place where he has to eat and sleep. He doesn't want to contaminate his own private space. If he does the killing at all."

"He probably has some other space, better suited for his grisly work," Vassell said. She looked at Foote. "See if you can find something like a rental contract for a warehouse, a workshop, or a garage if necessary. Proof of payments. Anything like that."

"Will do, Gov," Foote said. She consulted with one of the forensics, who showed her a stack of documents.

"Is the neighborhood being monitored?" Vassell asked. "Do we have teams in place?"

"He's not coming back here," Ross said. "He's not that crazy."

"No, but maybe he's watching us. Maybe he's just passing by to see what we're doing."

"Yes," said Ross, "he must be that crazy."

Lucy didn't quite understand how she had suddenly ended up in this basement, after having been driven in Charlie's van. And where was she anyway? What kind of place was this?

They had driven up to that large and imposing villa.

She remembered the villa. Hadn't seen a villa like this anywhere in Kingston so far. Only rich people could live in such a place.

Charlie had gotten out. A man had come out of the villa. A big, burly, black man. Older than Charlie and dressed in a smart suit but without a tie. A distinguished man. And that man had told her: come in, girl, and have a lemonade. This will only take a moment. Then Charlie will drive you home. He and I, we have something to discuss.

And now she was in the basement, seated on a chair and feeling dizzy. Her hands were tied to the armrests of the chair. Her ankles were tied to the legs of the chair. All with nasty and strong adhesive tape. Silver-gray adhesive tape. Why had they tied her up?

She had gone inside. She had left her books in the van. Leave those books in the van, said the other man. It's only for a little while. Nobody will take them. A lemonade? Maybe a cookie? Come into the drawing room, where you'll be cozy. Yes, this way.

The lemonade had been tasty. Very sweet. Everything was very sweet in this country. The cookies were dry but soft at the same time. She tasted ginger in them. She had learned to eat ginger, mostly in cookies. Candied ginger.

And then she had waited in the drawing room. She heard voices. From Charlie and from the man. They weren't arguing, but they apparently disagreed about something. She had been waiting. In the drawing room. The drawing room exuded distinction and was notably serene.

And now she was tied to a chair in a basement. Probably the basement of the villa. Deep underground. Where it was cool but humid. In a basement with only that chair. Nothing else. No window. No door. Maybe behind her, but she couldn't see it. She couldn't turn her head that far. That hurt.

She could not figure out how she got from the drawing room to the cellar.

A small cellar. Kind of like her bedroom in mom's apartment. No bigger.

Tied up.

She wanted to get out of here.

She shouted.

There was no answer.

She shouted again.

A door opened behind her.

Terrence and Anna had walked all the way to the school, had asked about Lucy, but were assured by the last remaining teacher that everyone had already gone home. They walked back to the flat, again interrogating people along the way. No one could remember a mixed-race girl in a school uniform. There were plenty of girls in school uniforms around. But none like her, no.

Terrence caught a glimpse of the man he had seen earlier in the street. The man who followed him. He felt for his gun, but the man had already vanished.

Did that man have anything to do with Lucy's disappearance? The man from the Middle East. Or a Greek? A Turk?

Had that man kidnapped her? Was he a terrorist? Was he the one who wanted Anna's locket with the data card? Was he an agent of some foreign power, like in a movie? A spy?

But the man was nowhere to be seen.

If he had kidnapped Lucy, Terrence would not hesitate to confront him with the truth.

He wasn't going to share his thoughts with Anna. Anna was having a hard enough time as it was. "She's just someplace with one of the other girls from her class," he assured her. "They are sitting in front of a TV eating chips. They laugh at a cartoon," he said.

"She never does that sort of thing," said Anna. "She knows I would be worried, and she would phone me."

"I don't know anything about girls that age," Terrence admitted, "But I know how I was back then. Without a worry in the world, and I didn't share any of my little secrets with my parents. I assume girls that age are as unpredictable as I was."

But Lucy hadn't returned to the flat, where Tabita was waiting for them. Nor was she around Terrence's place either.

"I'll ask around some more," said Terrence.

Tabita put her hand on Anna's shoulder. "I'll make us some tea in the meantime," she said.

"I want to wait for her here," said Anna.

Two big black men. Both in dark suits, white shirts, no ties. Big, burly men. Civilized men, Lucy would assume, if she saw them under different circumstances. Spoke English, but with that particular Jamaican accent. Charlie wasn't around anymore.

Charlie, who had betrayed her. Because that's what he had done: betrayed her. Delivered her into the hands of these people. He didn't take her home as he promised. He hadn't planned to do that from the start.

Lucy couldn't do anything. She was tied up. She wanted to leave; she wanted her mother. She wanted Terrence. Terrence would come and get her. Terrence would save her and return her to her mother.

"She's fine as far as I'm concerned," said one of the men. "Although she is not really black."

"It doesn't matter," said the other. "You don't want to be picky all of a sudden, do you?"

Lucy looked at them both. "Please," she said, in her best English, "let me go. I won't say anything."

"Shut up, child," said one man. "You're not the first, and by God, you won't be the last. Accept your fate with patience and humility."

"Oh," said the other, "let her do whatever she wants. Let her scream her little heart out. Who will hear her?"

"My nerves can't stand all that screaming," said the first man.

"Then what are you doing here?"

"It's my fate. I too bear my fate with modesty."

One leaned over to Lucy. "You're extremely beautiful, you know? A particularly beautiful pikney. We have had beautiful children here, but you are the most beautiful."

The other, who had complained about his fate, snorted loudly. Outraged. "She's not your daughter," he said. "You don't have to pet her. Not your fucking daughter."

"She is. Look at her eyes. Wouldn't you want a daughter like that? A lovely half-blood girl? Look at those calves and knees. Look at what's hidden under that blouse already."

"I think she's a bitch. And that she must be punished."

"You think all women are bitches," the first man grumbled.

"They are. And they already are bitches at a very young age. This one is a bitch, for sure. Untie her, and she will bite you."

"Well, maybe that's a new sort of experience. Shall we untie her?" the first man suggested.

"No way," said the other. "Remember a previous occasion, and how that went south? I'll tell you again: you trust them too much. Once they are here and know what will happen to them, they become monsters."

Then they said nothing more and just looked at her.

Until that one said, "Where did you leave the knife?"

And the other: "In the car."

"Why is it in the car? Go get it!"

Vassell and Tim had driven back to the office. There was nothing left they could do in Charlie's apartment or at the company where he worked. They had left some people in the vicinity, in case—very unlikely—he returned. But they didn't count on it.

Foote was on the phone. "Forensics says they have found nothing in his papers about a contract with an employer, someone for whom he did jobs, certainly not aside from the company's customers. We're looking at those customers now. There aren't that many, but they're all schools and clubs and stuff. No private persons."

"It is all too clear how he found those girls, being around schools, keeping an eye out for them."

"What else do we know about him?"

"Almost nothing. He's from Trench Town. Not married. No children. Has been working for that company for ten years. A bank account with some savings. A rental apartment. No car. Nothing really. An unremarkable man."

"Neighborhood survey?"

"Not until tomorrow, I'm afraid. When we can call some more people."

"Tomorrow is too late. He'll be gone by then."

"My guess, Gov', is that no one knows who he really is. They see him around in the neighborhood, but everyone is minding their own business."

"My only question is: where is he now."

"We are looking," Foote said.

During all that time, Tim had nothing to say. Foote left them alone in Vassell's office. They both knew finding Charlie would be all about needles and haystacks. But he had to be found, or the whole investigation would still not be near its conclusion. Even if Tim was right, and Charlie was only a middleman, they needed to have him confess. They needed him to name names.

Vassell was now convinced Tim had been right. In that case, Charlie would be in danger himself. Someone was not going to like the loose tread he represented. Someone was not going to like the idea that Charlie would talk to the investigators. Charlie's life was in danger.

"Do we have any precedents for this sort of cooperation, where different people play separate roles while murdering people? Except for what crime syndicates do?" she inquired.

"Well," Tim said, "Britain used to have the infamous case of Ian Brady and Myra Hindley, working together, abducting and torturing children to death. There have been others. Like-minded souls who found each other in the executions of the most cruel crimes. Perverse, inhuman souls. You have them everywhere. Sometimes they form an alliance. I can't logically explain their motivations."

"You said something about obligations and people with power."

"Yes. Sometimes that power is purely psychological. One person who has moral power over the other, a truly dominant figure who forces the other to do things that he or she does not actually want to do. Your Charlie fits that pattern. Like the reluctant slave—I have no better word for it—who is able to push his feelings aside."

"As long as he takes us to the real killer . . ."

"But you still have no real proof of Charlie's guilt."

"No, but he is the first real lead since the case started."

They sat together for a moment, without talking.

Then Vassell asked, "Tim?"

"Yes?"

"Is that what you're doing over there, in London, teaching this stuff?"

He envisioned himself in his familiar lecture hall. He looked at the faces of young people, boys and girls, who had probably never seen a dead body, let alone a mutilated one. And who might never see a dead victim. Because victims of serial murder would never end up in their consulting room. The perpetrators would not. Those twisted minds they might have to deal with, not in their private chambers but somewhere in a prison, where they would be trying to analyze the most devious minds and help the justice system to decide if the possessor of that mind would have to be incarcerated forever or walk free again.

But would they be able to recognize psychopaths? Would they recognize the monster as someone who walked into their cabinet one day, perfectly innocent, telling them about their feverish dreams and their terrible urges. Would they see these people for what they were going to become? No, he suspected they would not. As he himself had not been able to recognize certain potential monsters, all through his career.

He had come face to face with the ultimate Evil, which only humanity can produce, and he had not recognized it. At least not always. And probably not often enough.

"What else is there besides teaching?" he asked her. "Can't go back to the Met, or any other police service, can I? I've had enough of that."

"Really? And yet you came here as soon as I called you."

"Not right away."

"No. But you didn't need much convincing either."

"Well, maybe I've come here for the climate and the beaches and the rum. Although I haven't gotten much out of these last two yet. So you seriously owe me. May I also remind you that you did not even mention a fair financial compensation for my services."

"I'll take you to a beach and to a decent bar when this is over."

"It's far from over, Jen."

* * *

Terrence looked at his watch. Lucy was two hours late now. No, almost three hours. Anna was in complete disarray. They had walked to the school again, all the way, and then back, to Anna's flat, where Tabita had made them very sweet tea. Tabita was worried about Lucy as well. Whatever her feelings for Anna, Lucy was Terrence's daughter.

Terrence almost felt at home in Anna's flat, even though he didn't recognize any of the stuff she had. Yet the flat was everything like Anna—the way she organized the kitchen, the way she hung her clothes, the choice of rugs on the floor and the old, worn sofa against the wall, and the curtains.

The flat was completely Anna.

"We have to get the police involved," Anna said. "We can't wait any longer."

Terrence rose to his feet. He had a strange feeling. Lucy hadn't just disappeared. There was more to this. He feared the worst: she might be in the hands of the child murderer. The thought filled him with a deep dread. Lucy would become the murderer's tenth victim, and there was nothing he could do about it.

"Yes," he said, "let's call the police."

He stood by the window, curtains partially closed against the sun. The young man he had seen earlier was hanging around in the street, as before. Was he involved in Lucy's disappearance? Was he in collusion with the murderer? Was he part of some cruel, frightening plot?

Was he himself a child molester?

And then, something inside Terrence snapped.

He didn't know exactly what it was. Suddenly a suppressed anger within him was unleashed, something he could no longer control.

He hurried outside—down the stairs and into the street.

The young man only saw him when he was close by.

Terrence had drawn his gun.

He aimed it at the young man.

"Where's Lucy?" he shouted. He was absolutely convinced the young man was involved in her disappearance. Maybe not as an accomplice to the murderer, but as a part in the plot to steal the medallion, the data card. This man might be a terrorist or whatever. Anyway, to Terrence, at that moment, he was the only one who would have something to reveal about Lucy.

The young man held out his hands, palms forward, toward Terrence. A calming gesture. A gesture that said: I am not armed.

But he probably was.

"We don't have Lucy!" the young man shouted. "We don't have her!"

"Where is she?" Terrence couldn't even control his voice anymore. Around them: people scattering, people taking cover, because of the gun. Guns were not uncommon in this neighborhood. But you always avoided a man with a gun.

"No, no, I'm telling the truth! We don't have her. Has she disappeared? We will help!"

Terrence pointed the gun over the man's head and pulled the trigger. The bang reverberated off the facades.

The young man cowered. His right hand disappeared under his jacket.

Another man stepped into the street.

Terrence only saw him out of the corner of his eye.

He turned to the newcomer, who had his own gun pointed at Terrence. "Put the gun down, Mr. Mason," the second man said.

English, both with the same accent.

Arabs. Or whatever.

They would shoot him without further ado. But they didn't.

"Put the gun down, Mr. Mason. Then we'll talk about this. If Lucy is gone, we have nothing to do with it. We will help you find her."

Terrence pointed his gun at one man and then at the other.

Both had now drawn their weapons.

A siren. In the distance.

Police, here in Trench Town?

Police, immediately responding to a shot? That was truly exceptional. But there were more police on the streets these days. Because of the child murderer.

The two men looked at each other.

"We don't have much time," said one. "The police will be here shortly. And then things are out of our hands."

They're not terrorists, Terrence thought.

They would have shot him immediately if that were.

"Who are you?"

"Mossad," said the eldest of the men. "Israel secret service. We are Mossad agents, and we want back the item your lady friend brought from Brussels. It is property of the Israeli government."

The other man looked at his companion but said nothing.

"I want Lucy back," Terrence said.

The siren was nearby.

Both men lowered their weapons.

They stepped back, their eyes on Terrence.

He also lowered his weapon.

Then both men disappeared.


"Kidnapped?" Foote said. On the phone. "Where? In Trench Town?"

Vassell looked up.

Foote listened carefully to what the phone had to tell her.

"Okay," she finally said. "I'll tell the boss."

"What?" Vassell asked.

"Trench Town. A local resident with a gun threatens two men in the street, also armed. But no gangs involved, no local crime. He is looking for his daughter, who didn't come home from school. Local school's uniform. But she's a mixed race. His wife—ex-wife—recently arrived in Kingston, a white woman from Europe."

"Wait a minute," said Vassell. She looked at Tim. "The man's daughter is missing, and he starts a gunfight in the street with. . . ."

"He shot once, without hitting anyone."

"Take us there, Foote. Right now."

Tim followed them. In the car, Vassell called Ross. "Is your intervention team still ready?"

"Still is, Gov'. In two groups. At the company and at Charlie's apartment."

"Good. Keep them ready. We may have another lead to follow."

"The father of a possible victim shooting people on the street?" Tim said.

"Yes, it seems bizarre. But I want to see this up close."


Lucy was alone in the basement again. The two men had left, perhaps looking for a knife. She was cold. In hot, sometimes even sweltering Kingston, she felt cold. Because of the moisture in the basement. And because she was afraid.

She wanted to go home. But first she had to get out of this basement. First, her arms and legs had to be freed. That would be difficult. The tape was strong and tight.

A sound, behind her. Probably from the hallway behind the door.

As if a piece of furniture had been moved.

Then she heard steps. Clear enough. Maybe the men again.

She waited. Until they came back in.

But nothing more happened.

She was cold.

She wanted her mother.

She cried.

Her heart clenched.

Then her stomach.

She would die. She had heard about the man who took girls from the street and killed them. Her mother made sure she didn't read it in the newspaper, but she heard what the girls said about it. About what that murderer did to his victims.

Let it be quick, she thought.


Commissioner Vassell and Tim Hesseltine sat close to each other on the sofa. Sergeant Foote stood by the window and pretended to take notes. The white woman, Anna Weiss, sat in the armchair, tearful and anxious. The black man and the woman were standing near the kitchen. The flat was too small for this many people.

"Your daughter has been missing for how long?" Vassell asked.

"Since four o'clock this afternoon. That's the time she normally comes home from school."

Vassell noticed Foote looking at her watch to note the current hour.

It was now eight o'clock. Four hours. Far too long. Much could have happened in four hours.

"You didn't call the police right away?"

"We weren't thinking about the kidnappings, ma'am," said the man at the kitchen, Terrence, who identified himself as Lucy's father. "We assumed she'd be with friends. But not this long, no."

"And the men in the street?" Vassell asked. She wondered if

Terrence was telling the truth. These days, any child not coming home on time would cause instant panic in most households. There was something else at play here.

She continued: "The two armed men you confronted? Who were they?"

Anna Weiss looked up at Terrence.

They will come up with a lie, both of them, Vassell knew. To cover up the real story. Whatever that is.

"Mrs. Weiss," she said, "I think it would be a very good idea if you told me the truth. This is about your daughter. If you don't get straight with us, we might not be able to find her. I hope you understand."

"We fled from Brussels, me and Lucy," said Anna, "because my partner was murdered there. He was involved in . . . something . . ."

"Something? Something . . . what exactly?"

Anna told her all about the robbery in the Brussels airport, the locket Alexei gave to Lucy, the data card inside, the murder of Alexei and the other dead man in her flat in Brussels, and about her flight to Jamaica in search for Terrence.

"And now you assume the same people who robbed the plane in Brussels are after you and the data card. Have you heard from them? Did they contact you?"

Anna shook her head.

"And you, Mr. Terrence . . ."

"Yes?"

"Those two men in the street."

"I thought: those are the men who want the card back. I saw one of them here before. I was being watched. Anna too. I thought: they know more about Lucy. They may have kidnapped Lucy . . ."

"But they said they hadn't."

"They are from Israel, they said. Mossad. Isn't that their secret service?"

Tim leaned forward. "If they are Lucy's kidnappers, Mr. Mason," he said, "it would be logical to me that they would have approached you to propose an exchange. They didn't. So they don't know anything about Lucy."

"By the way, where is that data card now?" Vassell asked.

Terrence opened a drawer. "Anna had hidden it in the wall. We're eager enough to trade the card for Lucy. But who do we talk to about doing this?" He handed the data card to Vassell.

"It's not about an exchange. We can assume now that Lucy was taken by the man who . . ." Vassell glanced at Anna. "Who previously kidnapped nine girls."

Anna moaned. The black woman kneeled down next to her and put her arm over her shoulders. Vassell wondered about those two. Both involved or previously involved with Terrence?

"You can help us," Vassell said. "Lucy disappeared between the school and this flat. That is a distance of barely a few kilometers. Did she always walk that distance alone?"

"Not for the first few days. Now she does. She already knows her way around here. It's straightforward enough," Terrence said.

"During the first few days, you or your wife took her to the school? And they picked her up too?"

"Yes," Terrence said. "Most of the time."

"Charlie also dropped her off or picked her up a few times," said the black woman, still squatting next to Anna Weiss.

The three detectives looked at her.

"Who?" Vassell asked.

"Charlie," Terrence repeated.

They looked at him.

"Charlie? Who is Charlie?"

"A buddy of mine, from around here," he said. "He sometimes comes to my garage if his car breaks down. Which happens all the time."

"He doesn't have a car," Foote said to Vassell. "Not that Charlie."

Terrence looked at her. "The Charlie we're talking about owns an old Toyota Land Cruiser. Well, it's not his. It's registered to some sports club, actually, but because he often works there, he drives their car. He pays for the gas and repairs out of his own pocket. He was recently here for . . ."

"Charlie?" Vassell asked. She saw that Foote had taken out her phone. "What's Charlie's name again?"

"Um . . . I don't actually know. He's not the kind of customer you . . . Well, you know."

Vassell knew. Terrence Mason did not write invoices for Charlie, who did not officially own a car.

"Does Charlie work for a landscaping company?"

"Yes, he does."

"And does he also drive a van? An old van? With a logo. A circle with a stylized leaf."

"Yes. How do you know that?"

"Mr. Mason. Please listen carefully. It's crucial that you tell me everything about Charlie. We want to know where he is now. Do you know where he works, outside schools and clubs, in the service of his employer?"

"Does Charlie have anything to do with . . ." said Anna.

"He also works for private individuals," Terrence said. "In their garden. He gave me some work for a few days at. . . ."

"Where, Mr. Mason? With whom?"

"With Mr. Harkaway. You know . . ."

"I know who Mr. Harkaway is," Vassell said.

Terrence said to Vassell: "Anna told me she had heard noises in the cellars of the Harkaway residence, when one day recently she worked there late. Could not explain . . . Oh, God!"

"What?" She turned to Anna. "What exactly did you hear?"

Anna looked scared. "I don't know . . . It might have been . . ."

"Let's not jump to conclusions too soon, Mr. Mason, Anna," Vassell quickly said. "And now, please, I'd like to talk to Dr. Hesseltine alone."

She took Tim aside, out of earshot of the others.

"Harkaway?" Tim inquired.

"Sort of a big shot here in Kingston. He does shipping and trading and owns a large and isolated property. If there's a place Charlie might go and hide his victims, or whatever he does, that might be the place. And if Anna heard something . . ."

"Aren't you leaping to conclusions a bit too fast, Jen? If the man is important, why would he be involved with this case? Why should someone like that . . ."

"I'm not assuming he's involved, Tim. But Charlie is not hiding these girls in his own place, and you said he's not a murderer, but he might work for one. Can I follow this hunch, and can we at least have a look in that house, which he seems familiar with?"

"If you're wrong and you go barging in the house of an important citizen, you may well end your career today, Jen," Tim said. "On the other end, you might be onto something."

"Would you not agree that rich people, with money and power, might be psychopaths as well? But they'd be able to hide their crimes better than anyone else, might they not?"

"Well, yes, there's always the chance . . ."

"There we are," Vassell said. "We will pay Mr. Harkaway a visit. But we'll take the team along, just in case."

* * *

Kerem and Chayat had retreated to their shelter, the building opposite Terrence's apartment, after the incident with the man himself. Kerem had convinced Erez to have a look in the street with Anna's flat, but Erez had been back soon after. Police vehicles, she said, blocking the street, and plainclothes officers all around.

"Damn," Chayat said to Kerem. "Should I have shot him?"

"No, that would have served no purpose at all. It wouldn't have gotten us the card back. He's not our enemy." Kerem realized they had blown their cover as far as their targets mattered, but they had not yet drawn the attention of the authorities. He wanted to keep it that way.

"This way we won't ever get the card back," Erez complained.

"It still may be in possession of Anna or Terrence," Kerem said. "Let's not despair. And you know what Yalom said: by all means."

"But I'm sure he will not appreciate a diplomatic incident, us confronting the police or whatever."

"Shitty job," Chayat said. He was angry with himself because he had drawn his gun out there in the street.

"We are kidon," said Kerem. "Every assignment sucks. But not necessarily for us."

The two men had re-entered the basement. They now stood at Lucy's side, pulling away the tape. That hurt.

"Oh, go on and cry," said one. "There will be a lot more pain in what remains of your life."

The other pulled Lucy to her feet after having cut her ties. Roughly. He made no effort to be careful.

His hands were big.

He smelled of deodorant and of sweat.

"I hope we have a little more time," said the second man. "Not like the last one. I don't like to be rushed. I paid good money for this and want it to last."

"Oh," said the first, "there is always plenty of time. At least until early tomorrow morning."

The other man grinned.

"Turn around, little girl."

"How old do you think she is?"

"Doesn't matter," said the man with the wicked grin on his face. "Today we are once again doing the world a service."

"One less bitch, you mean."

"That's it. She will never get the chance to fuck up the world."

"The Bible itself warns against women," said the first man. "Did you know that, girl? That the Bible itself damns your kind? You haven't read the Bible yet, I assume, at least not thoroughly. What do they teach those kids at school these days?"

"Nothing good. Drugs and booze and sex, before they can read books."

"Enough. We'll have her ready as soon as. I have other things to do today."

Suddenly both men looked up.

Even that deep, hidden behind thick walls, certain sounds from outside could be heard in the cellar.

"I want to come with you," Anna said.

Vassell knew she wasn't going to stop this determined woman, unless she used violence, and she wasn't going to. She knew she could not stop a mother from looking for her child. But she knew what Anna was thinking: that she might have heard her daughter in the Harkaway residence. And she could not possibly live with that. But had Lucy already been abducted at that time, or had she heard another girl?

On the other hand, she had to comply with certain rules. No civilians involved in police operations.

Although there was Tim. Adding Tim to her team had been

a logical move, but one she might pay dearly for. Involving him had been a violation of certain written and unwritten rules in the Jamaican police force. But in Londen, Tim had already been a civilian member of the Met team, and he knew the stakes. He also knew how to conduct himself professionally.

"I'll allow it," she told Anna, "but you will have to stay in the car at all times." By way of compromise. "Either that, or nothing at all."

The convoy of four marked and unmarked police vehicles had stopped a couple of streets from the Harkaway residence. She wanted them out of sight until she had confirmation of her search warrant, which Foote was arranging for her. The sky was already darkening.

"I know the house better than any of you," Anna pleaded. "I work there, I've seen the cellars. Lucy must be in one of those cellars."

"We will certainly look inside those cellars, Anna," Vassell promised.

"The judge says you need tangible proof if you want a search warrant," Foote said.

"Call Deveaux," Vassell said to Foote. And to Ross, she said, "Send your teams closer to the Harkaway residence. Even without a search warrant, they can monitor the perimeter of his property. If Charlie shows up, they must arrest him at once." Then she shouted, "Porters!"

The sergeant showed up. "Gov'?"

"Call Chief Vandermeer. I want to speak to him right now." Involving him in this operation, she thought, might get her a search warrant, even with the judge having doubts.

"Right away, Gov'."

Vassell looked at Foote, who was sitting in the backseat with Tim. With the phone to her ear.

"Deveaux is not at his desk," the sergeant said. "He is at a conference in Portmore. They can't reach him now. Without him, no search warrant."

Unless we can convince the judge willingly, Vassell thought. But that would take too much time. "And the Chief?"

"He will come to the phone as soon as possible."

"Right now," said Vassell. "All vehicles: drive up to the house, but don't enter the property yet.

Porters, behind the wheel, steered the car through two streets and then slowed down. He finally stopped just next to the closed entrance gate. The other three cars had followed them.

Vassell got out. Tim followed her. They looked at the villa, which was partially hidden behind trees and shrubs.

"That garden seems well maintained," said Tim. "The house, too. Damn, what a house. Someone lives here who has quite a bit of money to spend."

"You won't find anything better, bigger, or more expensive in Kingston," said Vassell.

Ross and a uniformed officer got out of the second car. Anna sat in the back seat, with Terrence next to her. The two other cars brought part of the intervention team.

"We look damn stupid if we make a mistake," said Porters to Vassell. He wiped sweat from his forehead.

Yeah, we do, Vassell thought. But looking stupid was the least of her concerns. She was betting high and just on a hunch.

Foote examined the villa through binoculars. "I don't see a van," she said. "But I don't see any vehicles at all. There's a large garage door. Vehicles will be inside, is my guess."

The phone in Porter's hand vibrated. He accepted the call.

"The Chief?" Vassell asked.

He nodded and handed her his phone.

"Commissioner Vassell?" Chief Vandermeer's voice sounded

muffled and gritty, but with a different tone than she was used to from him. However, he sounded authoritarian and self-righteous, as always. That's how she knew him. But at the same time, he seemed nervous. "What are you actually up to?"

"I need a search warrant," she said. Straight to the point.

"In connection with the murders?"

"Yes. We have a strong lead but need to search a property."

"What property?" He sounded a bit out of breath.

"Harkaway's house."

There was silence on the other side. For a moment she feared she had lost the connection. But then she heard the Chief again. "Harkaway is one of the pillars of our community here in Kingston, Commissioner Vassell. You should know that by now. A search of that man's house? Have you gone completely mad?"

"I believe that a girl who was kidnapped this afternoon is in that house."

"Do you have any witnesses who confirm Harkaway kidnapped the girl?"

"No, Chief. And I'm sure he didn't. Not personally."

"Are there clear, irrefutable indications that Harkaway is directly involved in that kidnapping?"

"Not at the moment, Chief. But the man we are looking for, whom we know as Charlie, works for Mr. Harkaway as a gardener. He is familiar with the girl. He sometimes takes her to and from school. He knows her parents. He is missing. If he kidnapped her, there's a good chance . . ."

"I can't see the connection with Harkaway . . ."

Ross, standing diagonally in front of her, gestured with his head. She turned around and saw the rest of the intervention team arriving, with two Land Rovers. They parked on the other side of the street. The officers, in their black uniforms, remained in the vehicles. Ready for the action.

She turned her attention back to the phone. "Mr. Hesseltine, the criminal psychologist who advises my team . . ."

"The man from London."

"Indeed. He believes that the kidnapper does not kill the children himself but works on behalf of another man, a man who has power over him. That man is the one who tortures and kills the girls."

"That again seems far-fetched to me, Commissioner. It seems all the more far-fetched that that killer could be Harkaway. Good God, Commissioner! Where do you get those ideas from?"

"Chief . . ."

The Chief's voice sounded angry now. "You're desperate, Vassell. Otherwise, you wouldn't have come up with such an idea. Forget the whole thing. You are not investigating Harkaway!"

She knew she had to decide at once. She couldn't enter the house without that court order. She needed an order. Otherwise, anything found in the house could not be used in a lawsuit.

Unless, of course, they found a victim. Unless they found Lucy Mason. Unless they had a compelling reason to enter the house without a warrant.

"Chief Vandermeer!" she said, suddenly excited. "We hear something in the house. Someone calls for help. A girl. We have to . . ."

She pressed the red button on the cell phone.

"We're going in," she said to Ross.

He signaled the intervention team.

The Land Rovers immediately drove to the gate of the villa, followed by the police cars.

**7**

Lucy sat next to her mother on the purple bench that took up too much space in the small apartment. To Vassell, the bench was a horrible piece of crap, but that was not the point right now. Dr. Smith examined the girl, finding only superficial wounds on her wrists and ankles from the tape and some bruising on her upper arms.

He declared himself not competent to deal with the psychological damage. But children are very resilient, he said. "She will be frightened, dislike being alone, and distrust strangers for a while. But over time—months perhaps—that will wear off."

Vassell had thanked him. The doctor had found no strange marks on the girl's body.

Strange marks. Vassell knew very well what he meant by that euphemism.

They first took her to headquarters, where an artist tried to turn her memories of the two men who had threatened her in the basement into usable portraits.

That attempt was not successful. The girl remembered two large, heavy, bald black men, not young but not very old either. An entire legion of locals looked like each of those two portraits. A legion of men who could not be questioned about their alibi.

"How did they get away?" Vassell wanted to know.

Porters reluctantly came up with the answer. There was a track that led from the back of the house to the hills, and from there to freedom. Yes, he had overlooked that exit. He was sorry. He would personally look for witnesses, but unfortunately there were no houses in that area, and it was highly unlikely that there had been anybody passing through there at that time.

The house was fully explored. Forensics had come down with the entire team. The place had been deserted, except for Lucy. The men and women in the white suits discovered certain items in two of the locked cellars, photographed them, and cataloged them. These photos and descriptions would form a central part of the upcoming trial.

Trial against whom? This was Vassell's main problem.

She contacted a judge at his home, apologized for the very late hour, and obtained an arrest warrant for Mr. Harkaway.

They found the body of the man they knew as Charlie—and whom Terrence Mason identified—in the garden, behind a row of shrubs. Someone had carefully slit his throat from behind. Which, some investigators felt, was an appropriate death for him.

But Vassell was now short of an important witness.

Harkaway remained untraceable, even two hours later, when they were sitting together in Anna Weiss's small apartment, she and Tim and Foote, with Anna, Lucy, and Terrence. It was close to midnight now, but nobody wanted to go to sleep, not even Lucy. Certainly not Lucy.

Chief Vandermeer had called her fifteen minutes earlier, from his office. He was still in his office at this hour. Of course he was, considering the breakthrough in the case. And probably because Harkaway's name had been confirmed as at least a person of interest. Because a real kill room had been found in his house, with enough traces to keep forensics busy for a few weeks. It wasn't yet clear whose prints and DNA were present in and around the kill room.

The conversation between the Chief and Vassell had been brief: congratulations on the outcome achieved, yet dissatisfaction that she had acted on her own initiative and potentially jeopardized the ongoing investigation and possible lawsuit. Own initiative: of course he was angry because she had entered the Harkaway's residence. Without a warrant. And despite his warning not to do so.

But now, in front of Anna and her daughter, she knew she had done the right thing. Lucy might not be alive anymore without her initiative. The raid had sent the two men fleeing, without the opportunity to kill Lucy.

"Did they have an accent?" Vassell asked.

She had already asked most of the relevant questions.

Lucy knew little about the men. She could not really recognize accents. Everybody talked weird in this city.

Vassell knew she had to repeat the questions over and over again, if possible. Tim had insisted she did. Rarely do the most hidden memories surface immediately after such traumatic experiences. This process could take weeks and even months.

Vassell, however, didn't have weeks or months to spare. They were after Harkaway and these two unidentified men. Problem was these might already have fled Jamaica.

Their descriptions were on the computers of the various police services and emigration, but it could already be too late. And the descriptions were vague, certainly in the case of the two men.

"They didn't use names? They didn't address each other by their names?" she wanted to know.

"One was talking about his fate," said Lucy. She didn't know if that was important. A man, a murderer probably, who spoke about his fate. She had remembered clearly.

"Like he felt compelled to act as he did? Not out of his free will?"

Lucy shrugged.

"They're not coming back, Lucy," said Foote in her most convincing voice. "You're safe from them. And you really should get some sleep."

"They called you a half-breed?" Tim intervened while having remained discreet until then. But nothing seemed to have escaped him.

"Yes, that's what one of them said. He said . . . something about half-breeds and about, I don't know, as if they wanted to rid the world of women."

"Did they use difficult words?" Vassell asked.

Lucy shrugged again.

"She doesn't know much English yet," Terrence said.

"Were they talking about Mr. Harkaway? Did they use his name?"

Lucy shook her head.

As far as Vassell was concerned, the hunt was now all about Harkaway. It was his house, where these gruesome discoveries had been made. Had he been innocent, he would have turned up by now. But he seemed to have disappeared.

She rose to her feet.

"We'll talk later again, Lucy," she said. "You have to go to bed. Everyone has to go to bed. We are all tired."

Although Lucy probably wouldn't sleep.

Terrence followed them to the door. "What happens with those other men. . . ?"

"A few police officers will be around in the street and in front of Anna's door. Also at your apartment, Terrence. For a few days anyway. Then we evaluate the situation again."

He nodded. He had handed over his illegal gun. Vassell had not made a point of the weapon. She had other things on her mind.

She first drove with Tim to the head office, where there were only three officers on night duty. The whole team had gone home. Rightly so, she thought.

"And what about us?" Tim wanted to know.

She looked at him. "We deserve a glass of wine," she said.

"I need some food," he said. "Or I'll keel over."

"Do you know how late it is?"

"I assumed Kingston never sleeps? Your place, then? You'll have wine and crackers or something, would you not?"

She had.

The next day, Harkaway presented himself to the police, accompanied by a lawyer. The lawyer, Desai, had an expensive reputation. He was forty-ish and graying, wore a gold Rolex and gold cufflinks with his monogram, that kind of lawyer. He would not get out of bed, so to speak, for something like car theft. Unless the thief acted compulsively and was wealthy and there existed the prospect of a smooth and positive outcome of the case.

"He doesn't want to go to jail," said Thomson, who was sitting in Vassell's office with Ross and Tim. For the time being, Harkaway waited in one of the interrogation rooms, accompanied by said lawyer. "He thinks he's too rich for jail. And he's pleading innocence." But he had been officially charged with murder, conspiracy to commit murder, and a number of other crimes.

"What have we got against him?" Ross asked. "Do we have something substantial against him? What can we really charge him with?" He realized that a watertight case might not be in the works. Too much circumstantial evidence.

"I want to hear his explanation," Vassell said. "About how those men ended up in his house and in his cellar, and how they managed to smuggle Lucy in. Was that with his permission? Does he know who they are? And what does he have to say about the other stuff in the cellars? Let him answer that first, and then we'll see what to do."

She looked at Tim, as if inviting him to make suggestions.

"He has had time to discuss his position with the lawyer," said Tim. "They have their story ready, make no mistake. They'll probably fall over each other's feet to prove his innocence."

Vassell rose to her feet. "Let's listen to what they have to say." The others followed her out of the office. "Me, Tim, and Ross. Thomson and Sergeant Foote behind the mirror. Sound and video, in case this does end up before a judge. As I sincerely hope it does."

A moment later she entered the interrogation room.

"Gentlemen," she said, without shaking hands with either man. She never did when she questioned someone. You are not on confidential terms with suspects, was her principle.

"I'm Commissioner Vassell, and Mr. Harkaway is here because he can help us with details concerning the child murders."

"Mr. Harkaway," said the lawyer, "first wants. . . ."

"Just a moment," said Vassell, holding her right hand up, palm forward. "I want to discuss the course of events with you. And I mean what will be happening here, in this room, for the next hours and days. In this little kingdom of mine. Where I set the rules."

Desai looked hostile. "My customer has a statement that he . . ."

Vassell knew she was not going to leave the lawyer the chance to get his foot in.

"He only is allowed to make a statement, sir, when I ask him to," she said. "He is not here because he is a friend of the police, despite his social standing. He is here because there are very concerning allegations against him, allegations that can only be dismissed when we become convinced, in the course of this interview or of later ones, that he does not play or has not played any significant role in this case. But for now, sir, things don't look great for him."

But Desai was not going to be defeated that easily. "You have made up your mind about my client in advance! That is unacceptable."

"I am not a judge. I'm not a jury. I don't have to judge your client at all, as you know very well. I am leading an inquiry into very serious crimes, and he's suspected of having committed these crimes, for which we may hold proof and evidence. I am here to determine if your client can be charged with these crimes. Is that at all clear, Mr. Desai?"

"The public prosecutor is the one to set charges, madam," said the lawyer.

"Not at this stage, as you are well aware," said Vassell. "I want to point out that Mr. Harkaway is helping us with this investigation, but as a suspect, not a witness."

"But he can walk out when he pleases? He's not formally charged?"

"That's correct. He can walk out. But if he does, I will arrest him immediately. The choice is yours."

"On the basis of what?"

"On the basis of assistance in a criminal activity and harboring wanted criminals. There's at least that. And then I'll think of a few more things. Like actually murdering children."

Desai looked at Harkaway, who gave an almost invisible nod. "Okay, Commissioner, we will listen to what you have to say."

"Mr. Harkaway," said Vassell, "our investigators have found material and traces in two of your basements, which were locked at the time, that point to the child murderer who has already claimed nine victims. We also found a room where we assume one or more people have been killed, more specifically the girls concerned. We have found a girl, held against her will. We have also drawn up a list of what sort of objects were found in these rooms on your premises." She pushed a sheet of paper forward. "Do you recognize any of these objects described herein?"

Harkaway took a quick glance at the sheet. "I don't know anything about that," he said. "No, I have no idea where those things come from. They are not mine."

"Children were tortured and eventually murdered in those cellars. Do you know about that?"

"No," he said. "No, I don't. And I don't believe that happened."

Desai twisted his mouth but said nothing. Harkaway continued to look intently at Vassell.

*He knows we don't have much to make a case against him,* she thought. *Not without his DNA on the tools and in the rooms. Which they hadn't found yet.*

"Have you ever noticed anything suspicious in and around your house? Never heard anything to that effect?"

"No," he said.

"The man you know as Charlie is an accomplice in the kidnappings and the murders of nine young girls. You know him?"

"He occasionally works for me in the garden. Worked. I hear he's dead."

"That's right."

"I spoke to him a few times. I am not involved professionally with the people who work in or around the house. That's what Abraham, my butler, does."

"Abraham is missing, Mr. Harkaway. We can't question him for now. We remain, of course, looking for him."

"People like Charlie were hired in a completely legal manner. The intention was to help people who need work and money to get ahead in life."

"Your social involvement is all too well known," Vassell said. "Can you explain how the aforementioned crimes could have taken place in your home without you noticing?"

"I'm not often at home, Commissioner," Harkaway said. "I'm usually in my office in the city or somewhere abroad. I also often sleep elsewhere. You can imagine that I have wondered several times why I am keeping the house."

"You have a small army of servants. They didn't notice anything either? They didn't mention anything to you?"

"You have to ask them," said Desai.

"Let's do that. As we will at a convenient time. But now I ask your client: was there no one who spoke to you about unusual things happening? People coming and going in the house, unusual noises they heard?"

"No one spoke to me about any of that."

"All your servants are people you brought from the slums of Kingston and employed in your house. We can assume they are very loyal to you."

"You assume whatever you want," Harkaway said.

"In light of the current developments, they may lose some of that loyalty," Vassell said. "They may be inclined to keep a certain distance from a man who may be associated with these heinous crimes."

"Are you threatening my client?" Desai asked.

"I'm just expressing my opinion on the future evolution of this case, sir," said Vassell.

She saw Tim looking at her approvingly.

A point for you, his look said.

"Who has access to your property and your home?"

"I do not know. Abraham keeps himself occupied with the daily management of the place. I leave that to him."

"But access to your house was controlled, right? Not just anyone could walk in and out there?"

"Indeed," said Harkaway.

"So?"

Harkaway sighed. "I have to repeat myself. These are matters that you should discuss with Abraham. I run a business empire, Commissioner. I really don't have time to worry about that house. I receive guests there, I walk in and out. It's like a hotel. Everything is arranged for me, so I don't have to care about daily, er, stuff."

"Arranged for by Abraham. Whom we haven't been able to find yet. Not in your house. Where he lives, by the way. He has his own studio on the premises."

"That's correct."

"There are no surveillance cameras in or around your home."

"Is that a question?"

"No," she said. "It is an observation. Strange, isn't it? A house like yours. And no surveillance cameras. I wonder why that is."

Harkaway said nothing.

"Charlie kidnapped the girls and brought them to your house. There they were held for a while, then tortured and finally killed. And you say you know nothing."

"You continue to repeat yourself, Commissioner," said Desai. "Where do you want to go? My client already told you he knows nothing about these . . . activities. And he doesn't associate with criminals, especially not of this kind."

"What you have to ask yourself, Mr. Desai," said Vassell, "is whether a judge and a jury believe that too."

"We are very far from an actual court case," Desai said. "My client isn't even arrested."

I can change that in an instant, Vassell thought. But for that, she needed Deveaux. She had sent him a text message on his phone and asked Porters to keep calling the man until he showed up.

The question, however, was whether Deveaux would be willing to charge Harkaway based on the current evidence. There still was a problem with proof of involvement.

And evidence for what? Conspiracy? Murder? Even that was debatable.

The Chief wasn't supportive of her either. He had made a statement to the press, praising Vassell and her team. That had just been window dressing. The message to the press and public was clear: the case is as good as solved, but the details of the investigation will not be released for the time being. And no names had been named.

However, the newspapers and TV channels were speculating. They knew that Harkaway's mansion had been raided and that the man himself could not be reached.

Tim leaned forward, as he often did when joining a conversation. "Mr. Harkaway, what is your position on this case? It must be very annoying for you to be named in a multiple murder case involving children."

Desai looked at Tim. "Commissioner Vassell," he said, "I cannot prevent you from involving Dr. Hesseltine in this investigation, but he is not a police officer and therefore has no right to ask questions."

Tim sat up again and frowned in Vassell's direction.

Desai knows who Tim is, she thought. How does he know him?

He knows because someone told him.

And he knows that he cannot give Tim the opportunity to interfere with his client.

He knows a lot about Tim because someone from the police force told him.

That much was clear.

"Doctor Hesseltine is assisting us," she said, "and I will ask his questions for him. Mr. Harkaway? Would you like me to repeat the question?"

"No need, Chief," Harkaway said. "I regret the deaths of these children. Especially because I have always been concerned about the less fortunate on this island. Hence my work for and with many social organizations. I hope that you catch those responsible for these crimes as soon as possible and that they be brought to justice. I also think that the police has not done a good job these recent months because there have been too many victims. I have no explanation for the things that were found in my house and the role some who work for me may have played. I have no knowledge of any criminal activities that may have taken place under my roof. That's all I have to say about that, and I will repeat that publicly."

Yes, you bastard, she thought, you will definitely do that.

She was suddenly convinced of his guilt.

She was suddenly absolutely certain that he was a murderer. A cold and cruel man, a psychopath, a monster. With absolutely no regard for the suffering of others.

Only she couldn't prove it.

Charlie dead. Abraham perhaps too.

No witnesses.

Except Lucy. Who, however, had seen two black men, not white. Which was a problem, because now Vassell could not directly link Harkaway to the murders.

She got up. "Thank you, gentlemen," she said. "I'm done with you for now. Please do not leave Jamaica while the investigation is ongoing, Mr. Harkaway."

He wanted to say something, but Desai put his hand on his arm.

"Forensics cannot find any of Harkaway's DNA in the basements," Foote announced, clearly against her will.

Sandwiches had been delivered and strong coffee had been made, but no one was in the mood.

"We have identified the killer," said Thomson. "Why look further?"

Vassell knew he was talking about Charlie. The consensus among some if not most of the investigators was that Charlie should be responsible for the murders. He was most suited for the role, and nobody would have to be bothered about him anymore, him being dead.

She didn't want to go that way, because it would allow the true guilty parties to go free.

And those were, for now, the two men Lucy had seen in the basement.

Neither of those two men was Charlie.

And that's what she told the others.

"But Lucy cannot give a clear description of the men," Thomson complained.

"Why don't we make a deal with Harkaway?" Foote suggested.

"Because the man knows well enough not to open his mouth," said Tim. "He will admit to nothing. And certainly not to being involved in this affair. You heard him. And he has good reasons to keep his mouth shut. Why would he make a deal, and about what anyway?"

Vassell looked at him. "You assume he is under pressure from others not to talk? Others with blood on their hands?"

Tim slowly nodded. "Yes, I think so. Maybe he doesn't have blood on his hands himself. That explains why no traces of him were found in those rooms. But from . . . from how many others?"

"Too many," said Foote. "Forensics still has to figure it all out. There will be traces from some of the victims, maybe even all of them. And then from some strangers. Two, three, maybe more. It's a bit of a mess."

One of the officers looked into the office. "Commissioner, I have someone on the line who would like to speak to you, confidentially."

"Can it wait?"

"He was very insistent. In connection with your investigation, he said. Didn't want to give his name."

"Transfer him," Vassell said.

The others left her alone. Foote closed the door behind him. Vassell answered the call.

"Commissioner," said the civilized voice in plain English, but with an accent, on the other end. "You cannot trace this call, so don't bother. I would like to present you with a proposal.

"Who are you? I don't like talking to nameless people."

"I'm not willing to go into details through your landline. Go outside. Take your cell phone with you."

"But why . . ."

"Just do it, Commissioner. This is very important."

There was something . . . compelling about the voice. Moreover, he had taken the trouble to find her number. And that of her cell phone.

She got up, hung up the phone, grabbed her cell phone, and

walked out of the building. She was standing in the parking lot when the cell phone vibrated.

"Excellent. Please be patient. Walk to the corner of the parking lot, towards the gate."

She did that. There were a few cars parked in the area, but no one around. The asphalt was full of cracks. Dirt accumulated between concrete barriers. Further on, she saw the silhouettes of two tower blocks.

"Step up to the garbage can."

She saw a rusty thing tied to a post.

"Look inside."

She looked. A black telephone lay on top of a wad of paper.

"Pick up the phone and end this call on your own phone."

She turned off her phone. Immediately the other one buzzed. It was the same man.

"I'm the Mossad agent who stood in front of Terrence Mason, with a gun drawn," he said. "I apologize for that. That was unacceptable behavior. By the way, Mr. Mason is not our enemy."

"You must have more than enough enemies."

"We can handle them. I'll keep it short. Ms. Anna Weiss has in her possession an item that belongs to the Israeli government. I assume you have confiscated that item in the meantime."

"That's right," said Vassell.

"We want it back."

"That's clear enough. But why should I give it to you?"

"It is not part of your investigation into the murders."

"Maybe it is, maybe it isn't."

"No, it is not. My government is very concerned about the information contained on that item. It is very sensitive information. You may not be able to read this information, but there are enemies of our nation who can. The object must not fall into their hands."

"That will not happen. The item is in my safe."

"Which is a reassurance," said the man. "On the other hand, my government also needs that information. There is some urgency involved. I suggest you get us the item."

"Then I would have to steal confiscated material from a police safe."

"Has it actually been confiscated? I just heard you say that the item is in your safe."

"The safe in my office."

"But it hasn't been officially confiscated, has it not?"

"Maybe not."

"In that respect, you are not committing an offense if you give us the item that currently has no clearly defined owner."

"Just like that?"

A short break. "No," the man finally said. "Not just like that."

"What then?"

"I can do something for you, as a favor, in return, so to speak."

"Such as?"

"We are a special kind of agents," the man said. "We are kidon. There's help we can provide that you cannot otherwise get, not officially at least. You currently have a problem with your case."

Kidon. She knew that term. From her time in London. "Yes? Do I?"

"You do. And that problem concerns a man who just left your building, accompanied by his lawyer. You want to accuse him of killing children, but you can't. You don't have enough evidence. But you are certain he did it."

Nice, she thought. He can read minds. Or he was a police officer himself. Very clever of him. And he's keeping an eye on our building.

Mossad?

That made him a formidable opponent.

Or an ally. Rather an ally. She'd rather have him—they—as an ally. Unofficially.

She therefore decided to come clean.

"The man in question knows who the real killer is," she said. "Or murderers, plural. He doesn't want to share that information with us, however. We have no way to make him talk. He is not untouchable, but that doesn't make much difference."

"But he knows."

"I'm convinced he does."

"You are personally convinced of this?"

"Yes," she said. God, she thought, make sure no one overhears this conversation.

"So that man can give you the names of the real murderers."

"I am sure he can, yes."

"But he doesn't want to do that. And you can't force him."

"Exactly."

"You get me the item in your possession, Commissioner," said the man on the other end of the line, "and I'll get you the names of the murderers."

"What did he mean?" Tim asked.

He was the only person Vassell had informed about the Mossad agent's proposal, mostly because he was an outsider and she could absolutely trust him.

"It doesn't take much imagination," she said.

"He is going to get us the names of the murderers. Plural."

"That's what he said."

"But what then? What are you going to do once you have those names? Will you disclose the names to the press? Because in your capacity, you're in no position to talk to these men on the record. Are you going to arrest them? Surely not based on what an unknown man, pretending to be a Mossad agent, tells you?"

"No," she said. "No to both."

"Actually, let's face it, you have no idea what you're going to do."

"No, Tim, I have no idea. I don't know what to do with these names. For the safety of Anna and Lucy, I will do what I have to do, which is: hand the data card over to this Mossad agent. And hope he is who he claims to be."

"And hope that no other parties intervene, like those Syrians."

"Those Syrians are dead. We can easily divine who's behind that. But that's not our concern right now. I hope, once we hand over the card, Anna and Lucy will be left in peace, since they no longer have anything to offer."

"Good. But these names . . ."

She was getting impatient. "What about them, Tim?"

"He'll give you names of people he believes—and want you to believe—are involved in nine killings. Will you concentrate your investigation on these men, assuming his information is correct? They might be people like Harkaway: important and powerful and not the sort you want to be messing with, certainly not if you don't get the support of other important and powerful people. I don't have to draw it out for you, Jen. You've seen this in London. It will be no different here."

"Get off my back, Tim. I want those names first, and then I'll decide what I'll do."

"And how reliable do you think this man is?"

"I don't know," she almost shouted. "I have no idea what I'm getting myself into. But he knows about the data card and about Anna, and so, yes, I'm strongly inclined to accept his story."

They had retreated into her office again, the door closed, the other members of the team in the incident room. There would be some speculation about what the Chief had to discuss with Tim. But she couldn't care less.

"Suppose that one of the names is that of a senior police officer. Or a judge."

"I'll then have to start an internal investigation. We don't have a department for those kinds of cases here in Kingston. Yes, I know what you're going to say next: a white, British, female commissioner starting an internal investigation into the connection between some senior officer—or several—and a ring of child murderers. Yes, I'm aware of how bad this sounds."

"Your team might not be inclined to support you," Tim said.

"I can only hope none of their names pop up."

They remained silent for a while, each with their own thoughts.

Then Tim said: "I want to do it."

"Do what?"

"Hand over the data card to the Mossad agent."

"And why would you?"

"Because I'm not officially part of this investigation and of your team. If problems arise, you know nothing. Never heard about the data card, never seen it. Never any contact with a Mossad agent. I will maintain that it was me he contacted, and you knew nothing."

She wanted to protest, but realized this was the only sensible action. Tim was right. She could not be involved in this Mossad thing. Not officially, at least. And she would have to keep the identity of her source, concerning the names, a secret. That would be the hardest part.

Later that day, in the evening, Tim was drinking a Red Stripe at the Liguanea Club across from the Jamaica Pegasus Hotel on Knutsford Boulevard. He was a bit surprised by the British colonial style of the club and the well-maintained tennis courts behind the clubhouse and realized that this was where the upper class spent their time. Why the Mossad agent had chosen this exact spot was clear to him as he sat at the bar. It was full. They wouldn't stand out, even as white people. Perhaps all the other guests were diplomats, because he saw different ethnicities and heard different languages. But he wasn't the only white face around.

He had a copy of the Times with him, as agreed. Not unique here, but it certainly made it easier for the young man who approached him.

"Doctor?" he asked. They were not going to use names. "You have a data card for me, I assume."

"Is that what it is?" Tim asked.

A thirty-something, he assumed, who had seen more than his share of the world and conflicts. Mossad. The elite of the intelligence community. He wasn't going to play around with people like these.

"Yes, really, that's what it is, but what does it matter to you?"

Tim handed the man the newspaper inside which the card was hidden. "Have a look at the financial reports on page five," he said.

"Excellent," said the young man. "If we are satisfied with the item, I will contact you again, or your colleague, and I will provide you with the information you requested."

"Why?" Tim asked.

"Why what?"

"Why is this card so important?" he insisted.

"This conversation ends here," the young man said kindly but firmly, and disappeared among those present.

Tim didn't follow him.

He knew Mossad's reputation.

If they could find Harkaway in his current hideout, then they were worth their reputation.

"That's why they urgently need to move," Terrence said.

Tabita did not object. As long as the two men Lucy had seen in the basement were at large, the girl was in danger. She understood very well what the problem was. For the time being, Anna and Lucy stayed with Terrence and her again. Terrence didn't leave them alone for one minute. He hadn't been in his shop anymore. Neither had Tabita gone to her job in the hospital.

"This situation is untenable," he said. "So they have to go somewhere else. Where they can't be found."

"Those men find her everywhere," Tabita argued. "You'll see. People like us are pyaa-pyaa—meaningless. They are big men, they do whatever they want. How else did they get into that big white house, eh? They are bakra."

That was a term Terrence hadn't heard often. Slave master. Like in colonial times.

"Lucy says: I didn't get a good look at the men. Was also in the newspaper. They shouldn't be afraid of Lucy—those men. Why would they do anything? A lot of risk for them."

"They are looking for someone to do it in their place, gyal."

"And you're going to stop them, big man? With your gun, big man? Where is your gun now?"

"I'll get another gun from Kearns."

"He's already giving you the cold shoulder. He doesn't want to know you anymore. Because you let yourself be captured with that first gun. By the police. He's afraid they'll find out where you bought it, once they start an investigation."

"They don't make a big deal out of it. Have other problems now."

"No? Not yet. But then? What then? You have the gun. That man is coming. During the night. What are you doing? Tek them out?"

"Geez," said Terrence. "I will—yeah, I will. I'll blow his head off. For messing with Anna and Lucy."

"Big man! He shoots first. That man, he better than you. My poor Terrence. Always a hero. But he doesn't know the dangers."

He wanted to be angry, but Tabita was right. If someone came to kill Lucy, there was little he could do. The police were now at the door, much to the consternation of the neighborhood, but they would not stay about forever.

He thought about that commissioner. The white commissioner.

He had to call her with this problem.

She would have a solution.

Erez was quite happy with the situation and the way things had developed, something which Kerem fully understood. The assignment had been rather frustrating so far, but now at least they had achieved their goal. The data card was in their hands. Everything else was no longer a concern for them. Nevertheless, Kerem wanted to fulfill his promise to Vassell. Erez was less happy with that, but she understood. This did not concern the Mossad, but it concerned them.

They had found Harkaway quite easily, and were wondering why he didn't bother hiding. The press might also have easily found him had they gone through the trouble. His lawyer had gotten him out on bail, since the police didn't seem to have anything serious on him, and had found him a flat. Chayat had worked his charms on some young assistant in the lawyers office, and had gotten the address. It helped if you looked like an Italian, smooth-talking your way into very badly kept secrets.

Kerem had expected Chayat to be the one discussing his

orders, but the young man didn't. Somehow he went along with his leader, although they all knew their objective had been attained. Chayat might be the one who later got in trouble, certainly when the young lady in the lawyers office would recognize him on photos the police would show her. That would probably happen as a result of what was going to happen with Harkaway.

That same evening, the three of them surprised Harkaway in his flat. There was no security, no bodyguard, no alarm. Harkaway didn't feel threatened by anyone, that much was clear. The man must have been delusional, Kerem assumed, with all that had happened. But the police had let him go—why would he worry?

Persuading to give them the names they wanted didn't prove to be much of a problem. Kerem let Erez do what she was good at, while he and Chayat stood guard outside the flat. Erez had gagged the man, he made no sound. That would probably make things worse for him.

It took Erez twenty minutes to convince Harkaway that giving up the names of the men in the basement was in his best interest, and would be best to avoid further physical arm. Harkaway understood he needed to make a positive contribution to the police investigation. And he gave Erez two names. Eventually.

Kerem left him on the bloody floor of the bathroom with some good advice concerning the sort of friends he seriously needed to avoid. He knew that this man was as responsible as anybody for the deaths of nine children, but it was not up to him to carry out the punishment.

That was up to others.

Although the police and the judiciary here in this city would not take the necessary steps, he suspected, not in the way that would satisfy Kerem.

The three kidon left the apartment in a hurry and drove their rented Ford Taurus to the edge of a park.

There, Kerem called the number Commissioner Vassell had given him. Undoubtedly a burner phone. Because the commissioner wouldn't be crazy enough to have this conversation on her own telephone.

Vassell looked at the screen of the telephone. It was a cheap and simple device that she had bought for cash in a shop far away from her neighborhood. She had subsequently acquired the phone card anonymously elsewhere.

Now she was sitting in a bar overlooking one of the city's busier intersections, even at this hour. It had rained a bit, for which she was grateful. This city needed a downpour now and then. But the next day, the dust would be there all over again.

The bar was almost empty.

She didn't give her name. There was only one person who could call her on this number.

She recognized the voice of the man on the other end.

He only said four words.

Two names.

She ended the call at once. She would throw away the phone. She sat in the bar for a long time.

The next morning Vassell got a call from Terrence Mason at her office.

She had just finished an early meeting with Ross and Thomson about the further division of work now that the search for the child murderers had to be redirected.

As far as Ross and Thomas and the rest of the crew were concerned, two anonymous men were missing, both suspected perpetrators of the kidnappings and murders, while Charlie was listed as an accomplice. As much as Harkaway was. The missing men, however, were very good at remaining missing, mostly due to the fact that they still officially had no names.

The newspapers, TV channels, and social media made a big splash with the whole story, which would grace their headlines for days to come. As long as the true monsters roamed free, no one could rest. The police had only half done their job. The government had to urgently reform the corps.

And so on.

Vassell knew both names now. Or at least she knew names that Harkaway had wanted to share with the Israeli. She wondered if they had tortured him. She had no news from or about Harkaway, so for the time being, he was not her concern.

And now Terrence called. To tell her, Anna and Lucy still felt in danger. "More than ever, Commissioner," he said. "They consider going back to Brussels."

"That bad, eh," Vassell said. She had arranged for patrols outside of both their flats, but this could not go on indefinitely. She had to find these two men. But to do that, she would have to share their names with the other officers.

She understood Terrence's fear. He didn't know about who was behind this affair, but he could make guesses. They'd be very dangerous enemies, who would not want to leave witnesses. But he could not lock Lucy and Anna up, could he?

Vassell realized she now had to resolve this thing as soon as possible. But she had no proof of the involvement of the two men whose names she had been given. Who could she confide in? Tim? Probably the only one.

He knew she had the killers' names, but he hadn't asked anything yet.

She could trust him. But at the same time, he would have little sympathy for the decisions she was forced to make. In fact, he wouldn't sympathize with the fact that she couldn't make a sensible decision. Because she had no evidence against the men. She couldn't open an investigation against them. That was out of the question.

Terrence expected trouble at night. He knew men with guns always came at night. He had his rifle under his bed, loaded, as usual. He thought about buying another gun, a pistol again, but he suspected the police would not treat him so mercifully for a second offense. So he kept to the rifle. And at night he slept superficially. The slightest sound woke him.

During the day he worked on cars in his garage. Tabita was home and kept an eye on things from the kitchen. Anna and Lucy lived in their own flat. But now they were here, in the garden. Terrence did the shopping for both households when necessary.

He made up scenarios for later. He thought about Anna and Lucy's future. And his and Tabita's.

The current situation was a waste of time. Normal life would resume later, hopefully within a short time.

A gray Nissan passed in the street with a man at the wheel.

Terrence had already seen that man that same morning. In that same car.

He didn't know the man, but after four years he knew everyone who lived in this neighborhood.

A man in a car passing his house twice in one morning. And casting a quick glance in his direction. Maybe he was a future customer. Maybe not.

The man had certainly seen the police car ten meters away, with two uniformed officers in it.

Two bored cops.

However, Terrence expected the problems to happen at night. When these officers would be asleep.

Not much by the way of protection. But he knew what to expect from the cops.

He quickly wiped his hands on a cloth and closed the hood of the car he had been working on. He stepped outside. Looked in the direction the gray Nissan had disappeared.

He no longer saw the car. Probably turned down a side street.

A neighbor passed by with a basket full of vegetables. She greeted Terrence warmly. No one said anything about the police and the shooting. People just acted as if nothing had happened.

But he knew better. Terrence was now a special man in the neighborhood. Not just an invisible member of this community. He now had a reputation. Good. Or bad. That depended on who would be talking about him.

He wondered if the man with the Nissan had come alone.

If he had come alone, it meant a lack of respect for him, Terrence. Sending a man alone doesn't give your target much credit. Just what he expected from the kind of men who kidnapped and murdered children.

He stepped back inside.

He opened the hood of the car again and loosened the air filter.

Maybe he should buy a pistol again. He could not count on those cops in their car. They would be late if anything happened, and they wouldn't risk their lives for him or his family.

When it came to protection, he had to do it all himself.

He stood in the workshop and listened.

Kingston, and especially this neighborhood, was always loud. Music from radios or TV, vehicle engines, voices, children, arguments between husbands and wives. Not a moment of calm.

And yet something was missing.

Sounds he had heard just moments earlier.

Lucy, in the garden behind the building. And Anna's voice, talking to her.

He straightened up and listened attentively.

Then he stepped out of the workshop and went to listen at the door that led to the flat.

He opened the door.

The room behind it was empty.

He stepped into the hallway and climbed the stairs to his own apartment. He listened there too.

No sounds from the kitchen. Where was Tabita? She wasn't in the bedroom either.

He reached under the bed for the rifle. As quietly as possible, he loaded a cartridge into the chamber. He immediately stood back in the hallway and continued to listen.

The rifle was heavy in his hands. He should have had a pistol. Indoors, a pistol is much more effective than a rifle.

Maybe they went out for a walk, the three of them. But then they would have told him.

He peeked through a window into the garden. It was deserted.

Then he moved back. Toward the kitchen and dining room.

He stopped behind the wall. He tried to breathe calmly.

He quickly looked around the corner.

The kitchen was deserted, as was the dining room. Where were they then? Was he worried about nothing? Were they at the neighbors' house, just for a little while?

No.

Something was wrong.

He slid along the wall through the dining room to the double doors that separated the dining room from the drawing room. That door was ajar. Usually she was completely open.

He realized he couldn't afford to hesitate. Nor did he have time to walk to the police officers outside and raise the alarm.

He pushed the door all the way open with his foot.

There was a muffled sound from inside.

He stepped over the threshold, weapon raised, finger on the trigger.

Tabita, Anna, and Lucy were sitting on the sofa. A man stood opposite them. The man from the Nissan. He was holding a pistol, a large and ugly weapon. He kept it aimed at Terrence.

The weapon had no silencer.

Terrence had expected a silencer.

The man wasn't even professional enough to bring a silencer.

The man's weapon was pointed at Terrence's head.

"If you shoot," Terrence said, "those officers will be here immediately." He kept his rifle aimed at the man.

"They won't even notice," said the man.

"Neither will you. Because you already be dead. I don't even have to aim with this rifle at this distance."

The man hatefully looked at him. He knew Terrence was right.

"Killing a little girl," Terrence said, "that's different from having an armed man in front of you. Is it not?"

The man said nothing. He calculated his chances. He'd had a chance to kill Lucy earlier, but he probably wanted to get Terrence out of the way first. Because of his reputation. He shouldn't have done that. He should have shot Lucy and Anna straight away and then run off.

But he hadn't done that. For which Terrence was grateful— but not to the man.

"What do you want?" Terrence asked.

The man said nothing. He didn't seem to know how to get out of this situation. Maybe he wasn't paid enough for this job. Because Terrence had no doubt that this man had been hired. A few thousand dollars to shoot a girl. In Kingston, you found plenty of candidates for such a job. Even for less money. But then you'd get an amateur. Like this man.

"I'll give you a chance," Terrence said. "You leave the gun here, and you go free. And alive."

The man said nothing.

"Is your life worth a few thousand dollars?"

The man said nothing.

"Money that your family won't get when you're dead."

Terrence saw it in the man's eyes. He saw that he had made a decision. He would deal with Terrence first and then finish his job with the women. Then he would run away. And take his chances.

Before the man could carry out his decision, Terrence pulled the trigger.

In the afternoon, Vassell took one of the service vehicles and drove to the port, where she found a secluded spot among sheds, containers, and stacks of boxes and where she would not be disturbed.

She called the Mossad agent's number on her burner phone. The one she was not even supposed to have.

"We shouldn't speak to each other anymore," he said at once. "Didn't we agree to that? We have nothing more to say to each other." They would not be using each other's names. Not during this conversation.

"I am looking for a solution to a specific problem."

The man on the other end said nothing. He waited. He was careful.

He expects me to take the initiative, she thought. And he may have been listening to the radio, listening to the news, watching TV. She asked, "What does a kidon team do?"

He didn't hesitate. "We solve problems for Israel."

"What problems?"

"Anything. But mostly what you could call extreme problems. Problems nobody else would want to touch."

She already knew that much. She knew what kidon did. Hitmen. No, that wasn't entirely correct. They were professional agents permanently employed by Mossad and therefore by the Israeli state. The point of the dagger that defended the Israeli people. Murder would be a necessary byproduct of their employ.

"You provide extreme solutions?" she asked. "To your country?"

"Correct."

"How long will you be here?"

"Tomorrow evening we fly to Athens. Then to Tel Aviv."

She didn't hesitate. She knew exactly what she wanted to ask the man. "I now have those two names. On the other hand, there's a terrified little girl and an equally terrified mother. And it has just become clear that they are right to be afraid. I can't do anything about the two men. I have no proof against them. Maybe I'll have proof in a few weeks, but the girl and her mom can't wait that long."

"You asked names. Now you have been given names."

"Names alone don't solve anything."

"No, we know that. That's the whole point of our existence. As kidon, I mean."

Of course you know that, she thought. But you don't want to be more involved than is already the case. Not here, in Kingston. "That's exactly why Israel is sending kidon like you. To look for solutions," she said. "And to apply them."

"What exactly do you want?" His voice remained neutral.

"I need you to solve my problem."

"Why would we do that?"

"To help a terrified mother and child. Isn't that what you do? Ensure that mothers and children do not have to fear monsters?"

"Israeli mothers and children," he said.

"Yes. But there are other mothers and children. Who are as scared as yours. And who have the same rights to protection."

Short break. Then he said, "So you want us to solve your problem."

"I do."

"In a most definite fashion."

"Yes."

As far as she was concerned, this was a definitive step. She couldn't go back now.

"What if we don't? Will you then close the border? Will you let us be arrested?"

"No. I do not do that. You helped me."

"Yes. There was an exchange, that too. For which we remain grateful."

"And now I ask you again for help. Not for myself."

"No: a mother and her daughter. You play this game very skillfully."

"Thank you. Are you doing it?"

The man said nothing.

"This afternoon a hitman tried to kill the girl, and he would probably have killed the mother as well. Terrence, the girl's father, intervened. But those people, those behind this hitman, are at their wits' end. They will send somebody else. Hitmen come cheap in Kingston. I want to make sure that this does end right now."

A short break. Then: "Get me more information about those men."

Afterwards, she sat in the car for a while. She had opened the door because it was damn hot. It would again be a hot day in Kingston. She was thirsty. She would drive back to the office in a moment. She would ask Tim to meet with the Israelis again. This time with a sealed envelope.

Of course he would want to know what was in the envelope.

But she wouldn't tell him.

She would keep the names of the two men to herself.


Public prosecutor Deveaux hurriedly walked out of his office and looked at his watch. He was late as always. He had to hurry as always.

He was expected in court. The judge would not be kind if he did not show up at the agreed time.

Balancing on the edge of the sidewalk, he looked out for a taxi. There were always taxis around in Kingston's business district, but they never seemed to be there when you really needed one.

He just had a quick lunch with the assistant public defender, who assured him that three suspects in a child pornography case would not immediately see the light of day again. They would have to wait another six months for their trial, but at government expense.

Not that the government spent a lot of money on people in prisons.

Ah, a taxi.

The vehicle, a black Japanese SUV, stopped right in front of him.

He opened the back door, snarled, "Main Court," assuming every cab driver in town knew where it was, and then sat back in the seat.

Only then did he realize that the taxi already had a passenger.

That was highly irregular. There were laws against this.

The other passenger was sitting in the front seat, next to the driver.

The car accelerated quickly, crossed the road, and made a sharp turn onto a side street.

This was certainly not the route to court. And why was the driver so rude?

The man in the passenger seat turned to Deveaux.

He pointed a gun at the prosecutor. A gun with a silencer.

Devaux's first thought was: organized crime. I put the wrong people behind bars.

But no, that would never have happened, because he knew very well how to settle matters with organized crime. He knew very well who was untouchable, and he steered free of these people.

"Who sends you?" he asked. He felt he had a right to know. He would settle things with these men or with their employers.

"A woman and her daughter," said the man with the gun.

He had an accent, although he took care to enunciate his English clearly.

"A little girl who doesn't want to die because of your perversions," the man added.

Deveaux realized that this was not an organized crime case.

After that, he didn't realize anything anymore because his brain and part of the back of his skull ended up against the back window of the car.

An hour and a half later, two visitors announced themselves at the office of police chief Vandermeer. The man and woman identified themselves as diplomats from the Canadian embassy. They wanted to talk to the police chief about the safety of a group of Canadian sportsmen and surfers who wanted to come to Jamaica for a winter internship, sometime in December.

"And that's what they want to talk to me about?" Vandermeer asked his secretary. "Where are they now?"

"They said they got your name through the State Department, sir," the secretary said. "They're waiting in the hallway."

"Foreigners," said Vandermeer. He looked at his watch. He

actually wanted to go to his favorite club and then, when it got a bit cooler, play golf. He had people to see at golf.

But now: Canadian diplomats. About safety.

"Well, let's see them then," said Vandermeer. "Let them in." Here was perhaps a chance to earn a bit of cash. Canadian dollars, why not.

He lifted his bulky body from his large leather chair. The man and the woman who entered were still young, in their thirties, he guessed. They didn't look like he imagined Canadians to look. But hey, it was an immigrant country, like the US. He shook their hands and sat down again.

"Madam, sir," he said, "what can I do?"

"Chief Vandermeer," the woman said in precise English. "We come here because of a woman and her daughter."

He sank back into his chair. "Not related to surfers?"

Had his secretary misunderstood?

"You already know the daughter," said the woman. "You kept her tied up in the basement of Harkaway's house."

Vandermeer froze.

For a moment.

Then he opened the drawer of his desk.

Where he kept his gun.

However, the woman already had her gun in hand.

The last thing he saw was the thick, matte black silencer on the weapon.

After a few moments, the man and woman stepped out of the office.

The man turned and said, "Thank you for your cooperation, Chief," and closed the door. Then he smiled at the secretary.

They both quietly stepped out of the building into a waiting car.

* * *

With the storm in the press somewhat subsided, two days later, Vassell had accompanied Tim to the airport. They had coffee in a bar in the departure lounge. She wanted to offer him his last Blue Mountain coffee, but the bar did not sell such an expensive brew. Too expensive for the average airport user. She would send him a package over the mail.

She had come to wave him out. Least she could do. She owed him that. Even more so because she had done her best to avoid him for the past two days.

Because he probably had some pertinent questions, which she was not going to answer. But she was sure he would not force her to. If he wanted, he could have locked both of them in her office or taken her to a bar, where he would have confronted her with what he assumed had happened. He would have figured it out.

But he had done nothing. Their last conversations had kept to the surface of the whole case.

Anyway: he would not be able to prove her involvement, even if he wanted. The murderers of the two high-ranking officials had long since returned to Israel. They would never be found. Apart from two bullets, they had left no traces.

But Tim knew about the agreement with Mossad regarding the data card.

He also knew that Lucy and Anna would have no peace until the true murderers were caught.

He had heard that Harkaway had suddenly and hastily left the country, despite the ongoing investigation, and that he was the object of an international police search. He would hide, maybe successfully, maybe not.

Vassell could not care less. As far as she was concerned, Harkaway could rot somewhere in a faraway country. He would never return. He would assume another identity and disappear altogether, minus a significant portion of his fortune. He knew that Vassell knew about his involvement in the murders, even though he may not have had any blood on his hands. He read the news. He read about the murders of Deveaux and Vandermeer. He might as well connect the dots.

She and Tim had very little to talk about for the last two days of his stay. More important was what they didn't share. They were now bound by a mutual silence and by the hope that the whole conspiracy, which had caused the death of at least nine girls, was eliminated. What they did not know was this: had anyone else been involved in the kidnappings and murders besides Charlie, Harkaway, Deveaux, and Chief Vandermeer?

They didn't know the answer.

Vassell realized she would probably never know the answer.

The murders of two prominent citizens of Kingston had not been linked to the case of the murdered children. The reputation of these men remained intact. Vassell regretted that. No one knew what sort of monsters they had been.

Still, she assumed Lucy and Anna would now be safe. She told Terrence that much, but in confidence. He hadn't asked her to explain. Maybe he too knew how to connect the dots.

# ABOUT THE AUTHOR

Guido Eekhaut has published crime books, thrillers, and speculative fiction in both Dutch and English. His novel *Absint* (*Absinthe*) won the Hercule Poirot Award, and he has been nominated twice for the Golden Noose Award, as well as the Diamond Bullet. In addition to his Noir series, Eekhaut also writes detective novels under the name Nellie Mandel. He divides his time between Belgium and Spain.

# GUIDO EEKHAUT

## FROM OPEN ROAD MEDIA

OPEN ROAD
INTEGRATED MEDIA

# EARLY BIRD BOOKS

### FRESH DEALS, DELIVERED DAILY

## Love to read?
## Love great sales?

Get fantastic deals on bestselling ebooks delivered to your inbox every day!

Sign up today at
**earlybirdbooks.com/book**